I0591014

DEATH NEAR KENTMORE ABBEY

A STAR O'BRIEN MYSTERY

MARTHA GEANEY

TURLOUGH, NOLAN PUBLISHING

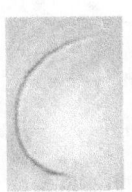

This is a work of fiction. All of the characters, organizations, and events portrayed in this novel are either products of the author's imagination or are used fictitiously.

DEATH NEAR KENTMORE ABBEY

Copyright © 2022 by Martha Geaney

All rights reserved.

Library of Congress Cataloging- in-Publication Data (TK)

Produced in the United States of America

10 9 8 7 6 5 4 3 2 1

First Edition

ISBN: 978-0-9600567-7-4 (print)

For requests and information, contact:

Turlough, Nolan Publishing

PO Box 193

850 Teague Trail

Lady Lake, FL 32159

Email: *mgeaneyauthor@gmail.com*

Website: *www.marthageaney.com*

Facebook, Instagram: mgeaneyauthor

ACKNOWLEDGMENTS

Many thanks and shout outs to family and friends who support my career as an Indie writer.

In Ireland, there are "the cousins" who always amaze me with their abundance of love and support.

My cousin, Anne Hughes Kenny who serves as my "reading detective". Anne scours my manuscript for any errors regarding Ireland and County Mayo that I may have made.

In the United States, special thanks, again, to Nick Johns, fellow Indie author, who provides the first read and edit of my manuscripts. My writing is stronger because of tough feedback. At times, I think he knows Star as well as I do.

I also want to thank the editors at Formatting Fairies. I am grateful and confident that when my book gets into the hands of readers, the manuscript is as good as it can be.

Robin Vuchnich, founder of New Media Art studio, for the beautiful covers adorning the four-book series.

This book is dedicated to George W. Reichert, Jr. (my Bill). Bill passed away on November 28, 2022. He was my forever love who always believed in me. I know he would be proud of me and I was oh so proud of him. Until we meet again, my love, this one is for you. Always and ever.

CHAPTER 1

Connemara Region, Ireland
Summer, 2009
Wednesday, 2:10 pm

In a clearing laced with wildflowers and herbs, a male figure crouched over a prone body. Semi-crusted blood caked the left side of the corpse's face, creating a rivulet like the tears painted on a clown's face. A tote bag, the initials JQ embroidered on the front, lay close to the body's right hand. The stooped figure rose, keeping his feet in place lest he further disturb the scene. He scanned the area and memorized the tableau. Satisfied that whatever weapon had created this cruel mess was not at the crime scene, he lifted the tote bag, noted its emptiness, and slung it over his shoulder. Next, he glanced down at the meadow grass. Thankfully, the recent dry spell meant his shoe tread wasn't visible. Again, he surveyed the surroundings, listening for signs of human life. Instead, birds' twitter and the sound of the nearby lake's pristine aquamarine water gently lapping against the grassy field's boundary filled the air. Assured he was alone, he furtively retraced his steps, reached the dark sedan parked in the off-road hideaway, and drove, frequently checking the rear-view mirror.

CHAPTER 2

I stood as if transfixed outside Evelyn Cosgrove's home at Number One Abbey Street in Cong, County Mayo. Just past her cottage, the pavement fed into a winding driveway toward Ashford Castle. The memory of my last visit to Cong flashed through my mind. Draped in ivy, the residence's stone walls still looked as ancient as the Augustinian abbey ruins situated across from the house. The white lace-trimmed curtains, which previously covered the street-facing windows, were tied back to allow whatever sunlight existed to peek in. A red riot of ivy geraniums cascaded from baskets posed on the exterior window ledges. Multi-colored petunias trailed over their containers along the short cement walk from the gate to the traditionally painted green front door.

I breathed deeply and rang the bell. In my hands, I grasped the official paperwork. When Evelyn appeared in the doorway, I was again reminded how much her hazel eyes and freckled pale skin mirrored mine.

Her smile lit her face, and she beckoned me inside. The first thing that struck me was how cozy the interior felt despite the tabletops being cluttered with books, papers, and photographs. I couldn't help but stare at the framed images representing various stages of Evelyn's life. Some were of a younger Evelyn with a man and woman standing behind her. In another, Evelyn wore a scarlet-colored academic gown edged with myrtle green stripes on the sleeves. I recognized Trinity College in the background, recalling Evelyn's Doctorate of Science degree. Then I noticed a wedding picture. Evelyn wore a short white dress and held a bouquet of baby's breath. A young man stood next to her, grinning from ear to ear. His blond hair created a stark contrast to Evelyn's ebony tresses. According to the background research I'd conducted into Evelyn, Donal Cosgrove was an investigative journalist who'd vanished in London two years prior. His disappearance remained an open case.

"I'm famished." Evelyn's words interrupted my thoughts. "How about you, Star? You must be exhausted from the trip back over the Atlantic."

"I'll be fine. It was important to me to have this discussion in person."

"So, let's sit in the kitchen then. I've been writing a journal article about the Charterhouse Square dig in London. I'm at the point where I need to make recommendations based on the statistical results. I could use a good strong cuppa."

I nodded and followed her along a narrow, short hallway to the kitchen. Standing at the room's triple window unit, I watched the River Cong flow past a stone wall that buttressed the cottage's side yard. In the distance, I glimpsed the top of St. Mary of the Rosary's church spire.

"Please, sit down." Evelyn pointed to a dinette table with two chairs.

I sat while she boiled the kettle and set two giant mugs in front of us. "I'm not very formal," Evelyn said, placing a saucer filled with tea bags she'd wrenched from a red and green carton onto the table. Then she pulled a milk container out of the refrigerator and plunked the carton next to the saucer. "I'm sorry. I hope you like Lyons' Irish tea. I don't have peppermint on hand."

"This will do," I replied, placing a tea bag into one of the cups she filled with the scalding water.

"So," Evelyn began, settling into the other chair, "you have paperwork for me."

"Yes." I unrolled the document, placing the page squarely in the middle of the table, and repositioned the milk carton to hold the sheet in place. "Our relationship is official. We're half-sisters," I said, pointing to our names, *Star O'Brien* and *Evelyn Cosgrove*, spelled out on the document's first page.

Evelyn's face beamed with a smile as she perused the notarized letterhead. But when she raised her eyes and saw mine, she pursed her lips. "You don't look very happy about the news, Star. I thought you'd be pleased to scientifically confirm my identity."

"Discovering a blood-related sibling is bittersweet." My hand clenched the phone holstered to my jeans. "I've dedicated my life to searching for my mother." I stopped, considering how to communicate my feelings. "I'm working hard to accept where my quest has taken me, but I don't understand why my father, our father, didn't look for me."

Evelyn nodded. "I never knew I had a sister. Not until our da was dying," she said, emphasizing the word our, which sounded utterly foreign to my ears. Evelyn continued, "So, on the one hand, I understand your shock. But I won't pretend I can even imagine the depth of your pain." She shook her head and said, "The last time I saw him, he directed me to a drawer at the bottom of his armoire. I found a large brown envelope with the name Maggie written across the front. When I opened the clasp and looked inside, I found a page with Maggie's first name and a notation of a baby girl. The paper was thin and opaque, like something torn from a Bible." Evelyn stopped. Her eyes glistened with tears. "Before you ask, the paper didn't indicate the child's name or place of birth." Evelyn tapped the DNA document that lay on the table between us. "At first, I didn't understand. But my father gripped my hands and wouldn't let go until I agreed to find this Maggie and her daughter. 'My daughter' were the last words he uttered before he lost the energy to speak." Evelyn's voice broke, and she stopped talking long enough to wipe away her tears. "That's all he said. He never woke again from the morphine. After he passed, I wrote the query on the online message board—the one your office identified, and then, well, you know what happened and why I couldn't respond to your calls."

I nodded, remembering the numerous times I'd dialed the phone number provided in Evelyn's post. Finally, in desperation, I'd flown to Ireland for a second time in 2008 to locate the woman named Evelyn Cosgrove, who'd posted looking for anyone knowing the whereabouts of a Maggie O'Malley. I hadn't found Evelyn on my first visit to her cottage. Instead, I'd stumbled over a female body at the Obelisk on the walking trail near Ashford Castle. Suddenly, I was immersed in the search for a murderer—whether I wanted to be or not— which led to the identity of the stalker who'd caused Evelyn to fear for her life and go into hiding.

"Did your biological mother know about me?" I asked.

"I don't think so. Mam and Da met at university. My mam was a secondary school teacher. She loved children. She would've attempted to find his daughter if she knew."

"What was his name?" I couldn't believe I was asking this question. I didn't even know my father's given name.

"Michael, Michael O'Malley."

I sat back in my chair. The wave of sadness threatened to wash me away.

"Wait here a moment." When she returned, Evelyn handed over a snapshot. The two people in the photo looked like teenagers. I may have been six years old when my mother disappeared, but I recognized her dark, wavy hair and brown eyes immediately. "That's my da in the picture. Is that your mother?" Evelyn asked.

I nodded and whispered her name, "Maggie."

"I found the picture in the envelope with the torn page. He must have looked at the image quite a bit because it's well wrinkled."

I thought of my mother's picture, which I'd carried with me since the day she disappeared. Like my father, I'd spent years gazing at her face. My hand reached for the tiny, dented, heart-shaped gold locket I wore around my neck. Evelyn had thrust the children's locket into my hands when she'd approached me near the Charterhouse Square dig in London. When I'd placed my thumbnail into the worn notch, I'd found what I'd expected —two pictures. One was me, and the other was my mother— two smiling faces regarding each other.

Evelyn inclined her head toward the pendant, saying, "The jewelry was in the drawer along with a letter"—she paused before continuing—"from your mother."

"Where's the letter?" I demanded, launching my butt from the chair.

Evelyn's face froze at the sound of my voice. "I'm sorry. The letter was in worse condition than the photograph. The writing in the creases was faded... I suppose from folding and unfolding." Evelyn's face looked pained as she tried to explain. "I wanted to be sure it was protected and intact if or whenever I found his Maggie. I put the letter into a plastic pocket protector and placed the packet into a filing cabinet."

"Great. Let me read what she wrote."

"No, that's not what I mean. The letter isn't physically in the cottage. The cabinet is in a storage unit along with my father's other belongings." Evelyn paused before continuing, "I'll get the letter for you."

I sank onto the kitchen chair, still holding the photo of the two teenagers. "When?" I asked. I understood Evelyn wanting to protect her father's stuff, but as far as I was concerned, that letter belonged to me.

Evelyn reached forward and touched my hand. "I have a meeting with Dr. O'Dowd in Dublin. I'll be away for a few days, but I'll ring as soon as I return. We'll meet at the storage unit, and you can peruse our father's belongings. Honestly, I haven't had the heart to go through his papers. Perhaps with some company, I'll keep my emotions in check."

I didn't know how to react to the news that I'd have to wait to see the letter. I wanted to forge a connection with Evelyn, but at the same time, the search for my mother had consumed my life. A dark feeling struck me. Frustration, resentment, and grief ripped through my body like a tsunami. But I didn't have the luxury of wallowing in the flush of sensations threatening to overwhelm me. I shook the emotional reaction off and focused on forward action.

"I don't want to wait. Why can't I go myself? Give me the address and the key. Besides, you have a habit of disappearing, and Dr. O'Dowd wasn't very forthcoming the last time I tried to locate you. Why should I trust you?" I asked, remembering when I'd met the tiny Dr. O'Dowd with her wrinkled, tanned face and sparkling blue eyes.

Evelyn reported to her in the National Museum of Ireland's Archeology Department. I'd gone to Dublin, searching for Evelyn, only to have my efforts stymied by her boss. O'Dowd had also informed me that my efforts related to my mother were as futile as the search for the Holy Grail.

Evelyn nodded. "I don't blame you, but you know why I had to remain in hiding. Thanks to you, that part of my life is all done and dusted," she replied, twirling her tea mug. "Sitting here, talking to a grown woman who's my half-sister, is a very strange feeling. Growing up, I used to wish my parents had had more children. I've been a solo act for a long time."

I didn't say how lonely spending my early years in foster homes had been for me. But then the O'Briens had adopted me, and later, I'd met Dylan Hill, the man who'd rescued me from my loneliness. I'd experienced belonging to a family for what seemed like the blink of an eye.

"I guess we'll have to see how this goes," I replied and reached my hand forward, intending to return the photograph of my parents.

"No, please keep that. It belongs to you."

"Do you know where the picture was taken?" I asked, gazing at the two young people in the photograph.

"I assume somewhere on Achill Island. That's where our da was from. But I can't tell from the photo where on Achill they were."

"When were they photographed?" I asked, surmising they were possibly in their early teens from the long-legged, gawkiness of the man who was my father.

"I don't know, Star. Da met my mother in university. They may have been teenagers, but I'm not sure."

"Do you know anything about how they met?" I asked, taking a desperate shot in the dark for some clue to my mother's disappearance. I raised my eyes to Evelyn's and waited for an answer, which didn't come.

Evelyn sighed. "I don't know any more than I've told you." She rose and stepped forward as if to hug me, but when I moved away, she turned and led the way to the front door.

Outside, I glanced at the walking path that wended through the woods and ended in the castle courtyard. The last time I'd walked along the path, a black and white border collie had bounded out of the woods and tagged along. He'd alerted me to Jane Doherty's body near the Obelisk. When no one came forward to claim him, I'd dubbed him Ashford and taken him to French Hill Cottage with me. He wasn't chipped, but eventually, the owner, who'd been in the hospital when the dog went missing, returned home and contacted the local vet, who in turn contacted Lorcan. I'd had to relinquish my adopted pet after Lorcan explained how critical and valuable the collie breed was to a farmer's livelihood.

I waved goodbye to Evelyn and walked toward my car. Changing my mind halfway across the street, I strode into St. Mary's. I lit a candle and sat in a pew at the back of the empty church. My adoptive parents, the O'Briens, and I regularly attended Mass, but I stopped once they were gone. It was not that I didn't believe in God—I just didn't think we found him in churches. I preferred to believe he was in the people and the angels we met along our journey.

That day, my prayer became a conversation with God. *Why do I always come so close to knowing what happened to my mother, but then something or someone throws up an obstacle?* After a few minutes of letting the dark silence comfort me, I emerged into the sunshine, climbed into my car, and drove toward Castlebar.

I STOPPED AT THE GOLDEN THREAD, AUNT GEORGINA'S SHOP ON Main Street, when I reached Castlebar. Ever since she'd been kidnapped and almost killed by a serial maniac, I worried about her. But she'd bounced back as if nothing had ever happened. I reminded myself daily that Georgina didn't let anything or anyone slow her down.

"Good afternoon, Star. How did the meeting with Evelyn go?" she asked, ushering me into the shop. She pointed to one of the chairs positioned near the window that looked out onto Main Street. "Take a seat. I'll brew a cup of tea, and we'll chat."

I held up my hand. "No tea for me. I have Consulting Detective business to do. I plan to call Ellie and Phillie this afternoon. They should be in the office by two p.m. Irish time."

"What did Evelyn say? Any information regarding your mother?"

I pulled the snapshot of the two teenagers from my wallet and handed it to Georgina.

She stared at the two faces. "They looked so innocent and happy."

I nodded, reached for the photo, and returned it to my wallet. "Evelyn says she has a letter that my mother wrote to my father. Perhaps her words will provide a way to move forward."

"Don't give up, Star. The truth about your mother's disappearance will come out eventually."

"I'm not giving up."

"But you look discouraged, agra. You might find an address or an insight into what your mother was doing when she disappeared. At the very least, you'll confirm your mother didn't abandon you as the New York police told you."

"The police were wrong. My mother didn't abandon me. But at this point, the clues are slim, and if the letter doesn't provide an explanation, I don't know where I'll turn or what else I can do—other than hope for the rest of my life." I stood up and stared out at Main Street. "I'll talk to you later."

"Star, wait." Georgina disappeared into the shop's tiny design area and reemerged with a loaf of homemade brown bread in her hand. "Here, take this with you. I can't stop by this evening, but at least you'll have one of your favorite baked goods while making your calls."

"Thank you, Georgina," I replied, hugging her, and then wiped my tears away before they made a soggy mess of the loaf.

CHAPTER 3

At 2:00 p.m., I dialed my office in Ridgewood, New Jersey. "Ellie Pizzolato, the Consulting Detective."

I noticed a hint of tiredness in my executive assistant's usually upbeat voice. "Hi, Ellie, how was your weekend?" When she didn't answer immediately, I knew something was wrong. An uncomfortable feeling tingled in my stomach. Had something happened to Phillie Spring, our technical guru? "What's going on? Is everything okay?"

"No. I hate to bring my private life into the office, but Ralph's investment firm laid him off."

"Ellie, I'm sorry." Two years in, the United States was still reeling from the great recession due to a mortgage-backed security insurance fiasco. "Ralph has an amazing resumé. He'll bounce back better than before." I paused, searching for the words to lift Ellie's spirits. I imagined she was feeling pretty unsure of the future—"maybe even find something closer to home with less of a commute."

"But...." Ellie hesitated.

"What is it? Something more is going on. I can tell by your voice."

"I'm worried about you and the Consulting Detective

business. Yesterday, I received several emails from clients expressing concern about only interacting with you via phone calls or email."

"What? Which client has gotten that idea? I've only been out of the country three times before this trip."

"But it is your fourth time since last year, Star. You know how much our clients love working with you. They get antsy when they can't meet with you on demand."

She was right, this being my fourth visit to Ireland since June 2008. I'd never forgive myself if I had to lay off Ellie or Phillie because of my relentless search for my mother. Dylan hadn't told me about the cottage for this very reason. According to Lorcan, Dylan worried about how broken I'd be if I never found my mother.

"Don't worry, Ellie. I have plenty of assets in the Consulting Detective's reserve account. We can weather a business storm. Nevertheless, I promise to resolve the issues. Send me those emails and each client's phone number. I'll address their concerns."

Ellie's voice sounded stronger when she replied, "Will do."

We said goodbye, and the call ended.

I gazed out the window and replayed the discussion with Ellie. My company, the Consulting Detective, primarily researched lost birth certificates and marriage licenses. More than that, I sometimes found missing financial accounts or property so a will or estate could be finalized. Most of the time, my work was accomplished by scouring through public records, microfiche, or obscure online databases.

I started my business in my junior year in college when I started trying to find my mother. After paying a private investigator, who delivered little more than her name and the address we'd lived at in the Bronx before she'd disappeared, I founded an information brokerage company so I could help people like me.

Having access to data unintentionally placed me at the heart of a mystery more times than I like to count. Most of the time, the mystery involved finding proof of divorce, adoption, and missing heirs. Sometimes, a family wanted to make discreet inquiries—not wanting the particular relative to know the family had initiated a search about the status of a long-lost relative. Nevertheless, I'd gotten involved in several murders the last three times I'd visited Ireland.

But it was a mistake to label me a private investigator. While occasionally my research pointed the way to murder, I was most definitely no Miss Marple!

~

I SLIPPED OFF MY ROCKET DOG BALLET FLATS, DONNED MY sneakers, and headed outside for a long walk. I needed to think about Ireland, this cottage, the people I'd come to love on this island, my business back in New Jersey, and my responsibility to Ellie and Phillie. I'd put off selling the cottage I'd inherited from Dylan, but if my being there placed the Consulting Detective in jeopardy, I'd have to relinquish French Hill, whether or not I ever found my mother.

A while later, just as I returned to the cottage gate, a dark sedan pulled up, and Detective Thomas O'Shea emerged. I looked around for his Hardy-boy detective twin, James Keenan, but for once, O'Shea's partner was absent.

"What can I do for you, Detective? I didn't think you frequented rural roads—unless you're planning to arrest me for something. Don't you have enough mysteries to solve?"

The scar that streaked across part of O'Shea's cheek deepened at my words. "I need to talk to you, Miss O'Brien—hopefully alone." He glanced around the cottage grounds.

"I'm busy with work matters but can spare a few minutes. Come on in." I was intrigued. O'Shea's clothes didn't look as pressed as usual. I imagined the matter must be serious if he wanted to speak with me.

"Has something happened to Georgina?" I asked, suddenly alarmed.

"This call has nothing to do with her."

I exhaled a long breath through pursed lips and walked O'Shea to the cottage's side door. Once inside, he looked around the kitchen, taking in the small space. Most of our previous meetings had occurred in the living room when he and his partner had interrogated me in the Clare Island case and other investigations since then.

I pressed the button on the electric kettle and invited O'Shea to sit down. Surprisingly, he did. I pulled a couple of mugs from the cabinet.

"Do you take sugar?" I asked.

"No." He smiled. "Just black tea is fine for me."

"Okay," I replied, pulling out a box of peppermint tea bags for myself. I sliced a bit of Georgina's bread and put Kerrygold butter on the table. I didn't know what O'Shea wanted to discuss, but I needed some fortification. If the past were a prologue, this conversation would end badly.

"I won't waste your time, Miss O'Brien. I need your help."

"Go ahead," I said. O'Shea seeking my advice? I definitely wanted to hear what he had to say.

He loosened his tie and put his elbows on the table. After pushing his cup away, he began. "I have a friend; her name is Julia Quinn. She's in trouble."

"What's the difficulty?"

O'Shea blew out a breath. "The incident will probably be all over the news this evening. Her husband was found dead in the Connemara region. Julia's been implicated."

"Why reach out to me? You're the detective."

"The murder site isn't in my jurisdiction. My active involvement is out of the question."

"I guess the shoe is on the other foot, as the saying goes. You're beginning to understand my frustration when you tried to keep me out of an investigation. I felt as if I weren't a real person, ignored, and my observations discounted."

O'Shea didn't respond to my retort. But I saw pain and pleading in his blue eyes. "Julia and I have been friends all our lives. She's innocent of anything that may have happened to Alex Quinn. But the local detectives are all over her. They haven't arrested her yet, but they've searched her home." O'Shea held his head between his hands. "If Séamus Riley, the detective in charge, agrees, I may participate on the periphery of the case. We've worked together before. But for the time being, I have to keep my distance."

I wondered about the motivation for O'Shea's deference to the investigating team. The O'Shea I knew wasn't usually the epitome of humility. "Why not jump right in? Or, at the very least, find an experienced lawyer for your friend?"

"Julia's husband was a human resources lawyer. From what I've heard, all legal counsel in the area has closed ranks. No one wants to get involved until they see how the proverbial wind is blowing."

I didn't trust O'Shea. Yes, he'd come to the rescue or had come around to my thinking on several cases I'd been involved in since the first time I'd visited County Mayo. Still, I remained leery of cozying up to the police. My history with law enforcement was forever tainted since the age of six, when my mother disappeared, and they hadn't lifted a finger to find her.

I shook my head. "No, I can't help you. The lawyer's murder has nothing to do with finding answers to my mother's disappearance. Besides, the police haven't charged your friend yet, have they? I think something more is going on. What haven't you told me, O'Shea?"

O'Shea glanced around the kitchen as if searching for an answer to my questions. When he spoke, the words came in a torrent. "But Julia is like you, Miss O'Brien. She's independent, an entrepreneur, and...." His eyes glistened with fear. "She's in danger of being accused of a murder she didn't commit." O'Shea paused. "You claim to be a voice for the dead, the missing, and the lost. Isn't that your mantra, Miss O'Brien?"

"But Julia Quinn isn't dead, missing, or lost, and according to you, she hasn't been officially accused of a crime." I paused. "Unless you have additional information...."

"I've spoken with her. She happened upon her husband's body. She rang me immediately. When the guards learn she discovered her husband, there'll be no disavowing them of her innocence. And...." O'Shea hesitated.

"Yes, and?"

"She and her husband were in the middle of a messy separation. He was doing his best to keep Julia from claiming her half of their assets."

"Okay, I understand why the police consider a messy marital situation as motivation for murder. But why me? Why or what can I add to solving this crime?"

"You, Miss O'Brien, have a nose for details and solving murders." O'Shea's laugh sounded ironic. "I've come to appreciate your knack for getting results."

O'Shea's words surprised me. In the past, he'd accused me of being an American who didn't belong, poking her nose into Irish garda business. But I still wasn't convinced I wanted to become embroiled in a murder scene in the Connemara area. The Consulting Detective clients needed my attention. The business also funded my trips to Ireland and access to information databases, allowing me to continue searching for my mother.

"No, I'm sorry," I said, sitting back in my chair. "I'm not a private detective for hire."

O'Shea's shoulders slumped. He pushed back from the table and stood. "I understand. You and I have a history complicated by an unfortunate bias against law enforcement. I won't bother you again, Miss O'Brien. Good day." He swung the kitchen door open and walked toward his car. As he drove away, I heard the engine roar.

I put the tea mugs into the sink and gazed out the kitchen window onto the green field that rose above the cottage grounds. A few horses, their tails swishing, dotted the grassy area. I reflected upon what I'd done. I hoped I wouldn't regret my decision. O'Shea was right about one thing—I prided myself on being a voice for the voiceless. Glancing at my phone display, I realized I could fit in another walk to settle my unease before showering and dressing for dinner with Lorcan.

CHAPTER 4

He knocked on the kitchen door at 7:00 p.m. I hadn't seen him since the fateful day he'd escorted Evelyn into Rooster's Café at the Turlough Museum.

"Lorcan," I said, inviting him into the cottage.

He was dressed casually. His thick blond hair grazed the top of the navy button-down shirt he wore under a time-worn leather jacket.

"I'm just about ready. Give me a minute to get my wrap. Where are we going?" I asked, unable to refrain from looking up into the blue eyes—behind his John Lennon-style glasses—that drew me to him.

"I thought we'd take a drive along Pontoon Road toward Healy's Restaurant," Lorcan replied, stretching his long legs in front of him as he rested his body against the kitchen counter.

"I'd like that." My walk hadn't eliminated the uncomfortable feeling I'd had since refusing O'Shea's plea for assistance. Maybe a long drive would help.

~

LORCAN HELD OPEN THE PASSENGER-SIDE DOOR TO HIS TOYOTA Crown sedan. The last time I'd ridden in this car was when we'd attended a funeral, and I'd become embroiled in proving Aunt Georgina wasn't a murderer.

Midwest Radio's evening show of country, folk, and Irish music wafted through the car's speakers, and we listened in comfortable silence. The landscape became stark once we were out of the Castlebar town area onto Pontoon Road. I relaxed back into the passenger seat and enjoyed the view of the Nephin Mountains, the craggy rocks, and the bits of heather peeking out from the white limestone that bordered the narrow, winding road.

"You're quieter than usual," Lorcan remarked when he'd parked the car and escorted me toward the restaurant door.

"Oh. I enjoyed the ride and the scenery." I smiled up at him, glancing around at the hotel's exterior.

Ivy covered the facade of the 19th-century Healy's Hotel and Fishing Lodge. Baskets brimming with petunias and geraniums decorated the stone wall, which separated the hotel from the road. Lough Cullin's shoreline bordered the opposite side of the road.

The dinner at Healy's was the first time Lorcan and I had been on what I considered an actual date. I looked forward to sitting across the table from him and sharing the discussion I'd had with Evelyn. I wanted his practical, thoughtful advice. Still, butterflies danced in my stomach, reminding me of my attraction to Lorcan, which I didn't want to face.

The hostess, Mary, seated us in a quiet corner of the main dining area and said, "I'll be back in a moment."

My eyes scanned the room, which accommodated seating at no more than a dozen tables. White linen cloths, wine, and water glasses graced each table. A gas fire glowed inside a black cast iron fireplace framed by an elaborate mantelpiece that extended to the ceiling. The few other patrons in the room spoke in hushed tones.

Mary returned and placed a bottle of sparkling Ballygowan water on the table. She offered the custom wine list to Lorcan, who turned his gaze to me. "Would you like a wine, Star?"

"Not for me," I said.

Lorcan smiled. "We'll stick with the water, Mary. Thank you."

"Sure enough, Lorcan."

I raised an eyebrow. "I guess you've eaten in this restaurant before."

"Oh, yes. Healey's used to be a favorite place for my mother when my father was alive. We often celebrated a pre-holiday dinner here."

"How do you celebrate a pre-holiday dinner?" I asked.

Lorcan laughed and said, "My mother enjoyed making holiday dinners, so my da and I used to come here to give her a break from the baking and cooking duties before holidays like Christmas."

I nodded, remembering when Dylan and I enjoyed quiet holiday dinners at Macaluso's in New Jersey.

Mary returned with the menus, and we spent a few more minutes perusing the entrée list before placing our orders. Lorcan decided on a prime sirloin steak, and I chose the fresh-caught trout.

"How is your wind turbine project getting along?" I asked while we were waiting for our dinner to arrive.

"There've been some problems with the rotors, and I've had to do more handholding than expected. But the team has been doing a good job of following up with my instructions."

"Do you think you'll have to go back?"

"I'm not planning on it anytime soon," Lorcan replied, pouring some Ballygowan water into our glasses. "Summer in Ireland involves pest management to protect the crops and sheep shearing, so I want to be available to our land manager should there be any problems."

"I suppose you're always on call, so to speak, with the amount of property you own."

"I do my best to manage things for my mother," he said before asking, "How did your meeting with Evelyn go?"

"The DNA results prove we're related."

Lorcan's blue eyes held mine from across the table. "I'm happy for you. You haven't been part of a family unit since Dylan's death."

Dylan and I had dated for five years before we'd agreed to live together. Our happy life ended when a widow-maker's heart attack claimed his life.

I nodded. "Yes. But knowing I have a sibling doesn't replace finding out what happened to my mother. I can't move on until I know whether she's dead or alive."

When the server arrived with our dinner, interrupting the conversation, we focused on enjoying the meal. My dish, plated on a bed of kale with a drizzle of honey mustard cream sauce, looked elegant, served on an Irish pattern china piece. Lorcan's steak looked just as yummy, flanked by steak potato fries and flat field mushrooms.

Finally, Lorcan pushed his empty dish away and said, "With Evelyn's help, you should be able to unearth more information about your mam."

"I certainly hope so," I replied. Resting my silverware on my plate, I remarked. "Funny, I never thought about my father much."

"Why is that?"

"My mother never spoke of him." I paused, debating whether to tell Lorcan about the many times my mother and I had attended Our Lady of Angels Church in the Bronx. In the end, I decided to share the memory. "Whenever my mother and I were in a church, she always lit three candles. I asked her once about the three candles. She smiled and said, 'It's a light for the one who's not with us.' I didn't know what she meant by that. I've held what she said in my mind for a long time, imagining and believing that the light was for my father—that we were separated for good reasons." I shook my head. "But since my meeting with Evelyn, I've been wondering why he didn't work harder to find us."

"Did he even know about you?" Lorcan asked. "In those days, women in Ireland hid their pregnancy if they weren't married. I imagine your mam might have left for the States once she knew she carried a new life, especially if the father wasn't going to marry her."

"He must have loved her. Or, at the very least, he regretted what he did or didn't do. He kept the locket and the page from the Bible that noted my birth, and according to Evelyn, he had a letter from my mom."

"He may not have known your mam was pregnant until he received the bible notation. Where and when was the envelope postmarked? That might help."

"There's no envelope, so I'll never know."

"What does the letter say?"

"I haven't seen it yet."

Lorcan raised his eyes as if wondering why not. "Really?"

"Yeah, Evelyn placed the letter in a storage facility for safe keeping along with the remainder of our father's belongings, some outfit called Extra Space Storage in the village of Bohola. She thinks I might want a few mementos from his life."

"Do you think the letter will provide answers to your mother's disappearance?" Lorcan asked.

I smiled. "I don't know, but I feel hopeful. Maybe she wrote something that will provide me with a thread to follow."

"From what you've shared, your mam sounds like she was caring, warm, and responsible. She must have been just a girl herself when she had you. She wouldn't have wanted to abandon you."

I leaned toward Lorcan and said, "I really appreciate you believing in her that way and me, for that matter."

I couldn't help but remember when Lorcan had revealed why Dylan kept French Hill and his connections in Ireland a secret from me. In his efforts to protect me from disappointment and hurt, Dylan had kept a part of his life from me—a decision he'd discussed with Lorcan. As a result, they'd had a falling out. I believed Dylan would be happy to know his childhood friend, Lorcan, was my friend too.

The server arrived with the desserts we'd ordered, along with a pot of an herbal brew for me and Irish black tea for Lorcan. While we enjoyed the sweet chocolate, pear, and whiskey tart, I couldn't help but notice how often we fell into a companionable silence.

Then Lorcan said, "Tom O'Shea came to see me. He told me about your conversation."

I nodded and took a sip of the hot tea.

"He needs your help, Star," Lorcan stated. "At a minimum, you owe him the courtesy of asking a few questions."

"What?" I sat back in my chair. "I don't owe him anything. I'm focused on my mother and my consulting firm."

Lorcan stirred the tea in his cup and looked down at his empty plate. When he raised his blue eyes to me, I thought they'd turned icy. "Right. I understand about the search for your mother. But why can't you put a little time into talking to some of the people who knew Alex Quinn? Tom doesn't believe Julia is guilty. The way he described the situation to me, I imagined you'd want to help an unjustly accused innocent."

Although I didn't like that O'Shea had gone to Lorcan, I wasn't surprised. They were pals from their school days and had played football on rival teams.

"My clients in New Jersey are getting antsy. They want to see me in person, not via email. Besides, what's to keep O'Shea from coming along at some point and telling me to butt out? You have to admit, he's done just that several times in the past."

"Star, Julia Quinn is a friend of Tom's, and Letterbrack is out of his jurisdiction. The investigative team must request his participation, which may or may not happen." Lorcan paused. "What are we talking about in terms of commitment? A day or two of your time? Surely, you can spare some effort to at least give your insights to Tom." Lorcan's voice quieted.

"I'm sorry. I'm not getting involved. I made a spur-of-the-moment decision to return to Ireland to share the DNA results with Evelyn. My plans include meeting with Evelyn, inspecting the contents of the storage cabinets, and booking a flight back to the Consulting Detective," I replied, meeting Lorcan's eyes in a steady glare.

When he responded, his words were measured. "I am sorry, Star. I thought you'd grown as a person—especially since Georgina's recent brush with death and finally meeting your half-sister. But I can see how mistaken I've been. Ever since I met you, I've supported your fiery, independent streak. My heart has ached for your sadness and losses, but you need to stop being so self-centered. Can't you respond to the anguish of others?"

Lorcan tossed his napkin onto the table.

I'd never seen him lose his cool before. I felt a zap in the pit of my stomach. But I'd refused to assist O'Shea. I couldn't reverse my decision. "Lorcan, I just...."

Lorcan didn't wait to listen. He nodded to the server standing near the kitchen door. When he arrived, Lorcan requested the check. Within minutes, Lorcan settled the bill, stood up, and moved around the table, placing his hand on the back of my chair, and then he said, "Let's go, Star."

Unlike earlier, an uneasy disquiet punctuated the walk from the restaurant to the car. When Lorcan opened the passenger door, I gathered my wrap around me to combat the evening's coolness. The sun was sinking into the horizon as we drove west. Several times, I wanted to remark on the beautiful landscape, but the silence between us weighed heavily upon me.

When we arrived at French Hill Cottage's gate, Lorcan bolted from the car, opened the passenger door, and escorted me to the kitchen door. After he made sure I'd stepped inside, he turned on his heel and headed toward his car—without one word.

I ran to the cottage's front windows and watched him drive away. At that moment, the cottage's silence, usually a comforting balm, seemed more like an admonishment. I paced the living room floor, replaying our conversation over and over. When I couldn't stomach analyzing the evening anymore, I sat at my computer and made the client calls I'd promised Ellie to make. The one to the Warrens was the most difficult. Kathy Warren answered the phone on the first ring.

"Kathy, it's Star O'Brien. How are you?"

"I'm glad you called. I'll feel better if I hear you have good news for me," she replied.

I winced at Kathy's words. When she came to the Consulting Detective, she'd already invested money with a detective friend, which netted negative results. The Consulting Detective was a last straw effort to find her sister, Cynthia, who'd been missing for five decades.

"I'm afraid I don't, Kathy. We've searched Social Security's Master Death file as well as Rhode Island's state death index with no results. We've also gone through the regional newspapers from the 1950s. Our next step is to look at marriage records from that time period, but I'm not optimistic."

"I guess I'll never know." Kathy's sigh sounded thunderous in my ear.

"It's not your fault your parents didn't look for your sister.

You were just a kid," I said, trying to soften the blow that her sister probably wouldn't ever be found. Too much time had gone by without anyone looking for Cynthia.

We ended the call with a promise from me to call again soon. Another hour passed while I called two other clients whose cases regarding searches for missing family members had produced positive results thus far. Afterward, my thoughts turned to my search for my mother, who'd been missing for more than two decades. I told myself it wasn't too late, but I also knew from my Consulting Detective experiences that I may have to face an unpleasant truth at some point.

Finally, I climbed into bed and pulled the covers over my head. Counting sheep accomplished nothing to help me drift off. The image of Lorcan's piercing blue eyes never left my head.

CHAPTER 5

The following morning, Georgina's knock on the kitchen door sounded more like a hammer pounding on a nail to my throbbing head. I hadn't slept a wink, and a quick power walk along Cottage Road hadn't done anything to alleviate the cloud my mind seemed immersed in.

When I opened the door, she breezed in. Her signature style, an ultra-long scarf tied in a knot at her neck, billowed behind her five-foot-four frame. The scarf's leopard print pattern complemented her light-beige wrap dress. The warm colors highlighted her dark olive skin and brown eyes. I wondered, though, why the change from her usual style of taupe-tinged nylons and flats to black leggings and ankle boots?

"Good morning, Georgina."

She put up her hand and said, "We need to talk. I'll put the kettle on. Go get cleaned up. I'll be here when you're ready."

After showering, I donned a pair of capris and a pink button-up sweater. I ran a comb through my pixie-cut black hair, ignoring the cowlicks at the crown. Finally, I glossed on a light pink lipstick in an effort to brighten my sleep-deprived appearance.

When I returned to the kitchen, I found Georgina had set two cups on the table along with a jug of milk, a bar of Kerrygold butter, and a few slices of her homemade brown bread. I slid into my seat, eager to feast on the contents of the breadbasket.

"I'm surprised to see you in leggings," I noted, reaching for a slice of the dense, slightly tangy-tasting bread. "Special plans? Or are you revamping the store's offerings?"

Aunt Georgina's dress shop catered to most of the women in the county, whether for business, galas, or bridal parties. Her designs and the other Irish designers she offered, like Brown Thomas, attracted clients of all ages.

"I'm meeting Deirdre for lunch at Rooster's. I thought I'd switch things up a bit. The poor girl needs a role model—show her that change is good."

"I shudder whenever I think of how she kept the years of abuse hidden from everyone. I'm glad you're helping her break out of her shell," I said, reaching for a second slice of bread.

"She'll be fine. The counseling is helping. Bright colors are seeping into her wardrobe, and she's been experimenting with Thai-style recipes on the café's menu. Before long, the memory of what was done to her will fade."

"What about you? Do you have any reservations about befriending the sister of a serial killer?"

"No, I'm not one to hold grudges or spend my time on what-ifs, Star."

"I'd say you have a right to hold more than a grudge. You were seconds away from being murdered." I gave her a grave look.

"I'm older than you. When I'm in the autumn of my life, I don't want to regret that I didn't live each moment to the fullest, which brings me to this morning's discussion."

Since I had an intuition about what Georgina planned to

say, I tried a delaying tactic. "Let me heat up your tea," I said, rising to reach for the kettle.

"Sit back down. Marcella rang last night. Lorcan is a grown man. But anger at you and sadness for her son overcame her reticence about being labeled an interfering mother."

A twinge of guilt washed over me. When I'd first arrived in Ireland and heard Marcella referred to with the title "Lady," I'd pictured her passing her days in the mansion where she and Lorcan resided, reading and having tea with friends. Boy, had I been wrong!

After finally meeting her at a benefit she'd hosted, I revised my mental image. The tall, willowy, blonde Lady Marcella had hugged me as if we'd known each other all our lives, saying, "Georgina has been singing your praises since she learned you were coming to County Mayo. We're so happy you're here. The west of Ireland needs independent women like you."

Just when I thought I knew what someone was like and how they might behave, I learned something that caused me to reassess my initial observation. Since that first meeting, I'd come to like and respect Marcella. She'd been a strong ally when her best friend, Georgina, was accused of murder and went missing.

I didn't reply to Georgina. Instead, I waited for her to continue.

"Lorcan asked for your help, and you refused. What were you thinking?"

"I explained my position," I replied. "I have several urgent projects at the moment."

"What's more important than supporting Lorcan's request?"

"Lots of things," I replied, ticking the issues off on my hand. "There's the letter from my mother in a storage unit. Ellie is worried about the Consulting Detective. Some of the clients are unhappy because we haven't had face-to-face time. I can't drop everything just because Lorcan wants me to. Besides, why should I jump at O'Shea's command? He hasn't been shy about telling me to mind my own business in the past."

Georgina sighed. "Lorcan's been nothing but supportive of you since the day you arrived in County Mayo."

"I didn't expect him to get in a huff with me, Georgina."

"Oh, my goodness, Star O'Brien." Georgina's voice sounded angry. "How many times have I reminded you that your life, the good life you have, requires you to do the right thing? I'd hoped your fear of relationships might have lessened. Not only were you blessed to have been adopted by the O'Briens, but since you've been in Ireland, who has done the most to help you find your mother?"

"I know, but...."

"No buts, Star. Who used his relationships to open up the archives in Dublin? Who rescued you from the priest's hole? Who made sure you and Evelyn were reunited?" Georgina's right hand tapped the table as she listed out the ways in which Lorcan had made a difference in my life. "What is your excuse for not giving more in return for all the good you've received?"

In my heart, I knew Georgina was right. I'd begun to allow my feelings for Lorcan to blossom. I'd started to believe that perhaps love was part of my story again. But when he petitioned for O'Shea, my baked-in stubbornness and suspicion of the police raised its ugly head. I bent my neck and stared at the table to hide the tears that threatened to spill.

"I know you're right," I admitted. "Why do I push people away?"

Georgina's tone softened when she replied, "Because, you poor bairn, your mother's disappearance left a hole in your heart. But, Star, you are loved. By Marcella. By me. And I'm sure by Lorcan. I've seen the way that man looks at you." Georgina spoke her next words softly. "You can still mend your unfortunate falling out with the lad."

"What should I do?"

"Have lunch with Julia, for a start. Listen to her side of the story before you make up your mind. Make your decision based on whether you believe her, not because of O'Shea."

"Do you know anything about her?" I asked, realizing the rhetorical nature of the question. Georgina is on a first-name basis with just about everyone in the county and surrounding countryside. Partly because of her business but mainly because Dylan's family, the Hills, have had roots in County Mayo since literally the beginning of time.

"I've worked with her on several wedding occasions. She's a talented textile artist. I carry many of her designs and fabrics in the Golden Thread."

"What are the police saying?" I asked.

"I've heard she's a prime suspect but hasn't been arrested yet. If you get to Letterbrack this morning, you might have time to speak with her before chaos overwhelms her life."

I empathized with Julia Quinn, remembering how Georgina had been whisked away in the back of O'Shea's vehicle when the police had targeted her as the prime suspect in a murder.

Georgina didn't wait for my reply. Instead, she pushed a slice of brown bread toward me. "Hurry up and eat. I'm going to call Julia and arrange for your meeting."

CHAPTER 6

When I first arrived in Ireland, I purchased a used Renault touring car. Not knowing how long it would take to settle Dylan's Irish estate and sell French Hill Cottage, I'd figured buying a car made more sense than renting. Scarred with dents and scratches, the car drove like a tank, which I was grateful for when Georgina warned about the chance of heavy downpours and sometimes treacherous driving along narrow, winding roads. Not long after Georgina left, I changed from capri pants and Rocket Dog ballet flats into blue jeans and sturdy black sneakers.

As I navigated along the N59, which was about as wide as a pencil from Castlebar through Westport, along the Erriff Valley, past Ashleigh Falls, and into Leenaun, I struggled to keep my eyes on the road. The vista of lakes, mountains, waterfalls, and salmon fisheries captivated me. In Leenaun, where Killary Harbor lapped the road, I realized I'd entered County Galway. Soon after, the road lay between bodies of water, towering mountains, and dense forestry like a sandwich, leaving me feeling both sheltered and isolated. Finally, I glimpsed signs for Letterbrack Village, home to the Walled Serenity Garden and Kentmore Abbey.

Georgina had arranged for Julia and me to meet at the abbey's café for lunch. I arrived by 1:00 p.m. and found the tourist parking lot jammed with buses and cars. Worried about being late, I wedged the Renault into a grass strip between two other vehicles in front of a sign with an arrow indicating the way to the Walled Serenity Garden. When I stepped out of the car, I glimpsed the back of a lone figure gliding along the cement pathway toward a door in the wall. The woman's gray linen shift, which seemed to melt into the wall's granite, hung straight, stopping just above her ankles. Wavy salt and pepper hair barely touched her nape.

The breath snagged in my throat. *I knew that walk.* My knapsack slipped to the ground. I raced toward the woman, who, by that time, had reached the garden door.

"Mom!" I cried.

The woman must have heard me because her shoulders stiffened. Still, she didn't turn. Instead, grasping the door's iron handle, she pushed inward through the opening and vanished from sight as the door swung shut.

When I reached the threshold and pressed the handle, the door didn't budge.

"Hello," I shouted, pressing the handle again, unsuccessfully. I pounded on the arched cypress barrier, but I might as well have been butting my head against a brick wall. Finally, I inspected the surrounding, dampened granite stones covered with lichen and moss.

Unscalable and impenetrable—which also aptly described how I felt. Had I seen my mother? Was lack of sleep affecting my vision? Was her way of walking branded into my brain like a gosling imprinting itself on the first moving thing it ever sees?

The last time I thought I'd glimpsed my mother had been on a busy street in Dublin, over a year ago, when I'd almost been turned into roadkill. Ultimately, whatever or whomever I'd seen, I vowed to get into that garden. But first, I had an appointment to keep with Julia Quinn. Quite suddenly, taking her case appealed to me.

I gathered myself and my thoughts, returned to my car, and picked up my knapsack.

The abbey's Garden Café was snuggled between the flower and gift shops. When I entered the restaurant, I recognized Julia from Georgina's description. Julia stood and waved. I zigzagged around the tourist-crowded room toward her. When I reached the table, I hung my knapsack on the back of an empty chair and offered my hand to Julia.

"I'm Star O'Brien."

She nodded. "Yes, thank you for agreeing to meet with me." Julia's direct gaze put me at ease immediately. "Please take a seat," she said.

Georgina's description of Julia didn't quite capture the woman's style. Her blonde wavy hair cascaded to the middle of her back. A textured shawl in various teal shades rested on her shoulders above several layers of clothing. I immediately thought of Stevie Nicks and her bohemian skirts and dresses.

"I hope you don't mind. I've ordered two lemon parmesan kale and mixed greens salads for us," she said, indicating the to-go cartons at our place settings. "I haven't been able to tolerate much more than a salad in the last few days." She paused and gestured toward the sea of diners in the restaurant. "Summer season means we might wait over an hour before our order is served. I know the kitchen staff. We can easily transfer the contents onto the plates. Is that okay?"

I nodded and began, "I'm here at Georgina's request. I'm not sure how I can help, but I'm willing to listen to what you have to say."

A grin spread across Julia's face at the mention of Georgina. "She's been a friend of mine for ages." Julia's blue eyes blinked. "She cautioned me you might not be able to help."

"How did you meet Georgina? Did you attend school together?"

"No, not the same school. Georgina's a few years older than me. But our national schools organized trips to Knock Shrine in Mayo on religious holidays. Whenever the various school groups were at the shrine, friendships blossomed, especially when the nuns allowed us into the shrine shops to buy sweets." Julia chuckled and then sighed. "I must have a million prayer cards signed by friends I met on the retreats. Those were the innocent days."

"You sound regretful."

"Oh, life has gotten so complicated lately. I don't know why, but..." Julia hesitated before adding, "I've just been on a path that hasn't seemed very fulfilling. That's all."

I picked the kale out of the pile of mixed greens on my plate before pouring the dressing on the remaining greens and then said, "Georgina told me about your husband's murder. You're under suspicion." I kept O'Shea out of the conversation until I heard more from Julia.

She looked down at the table and, ignoring her salad, played with the blue-green porcelain salt and pepper shakers. When she raised her eyes to mine, she said, "Yes, I was in the vicinity at the time of Alex's death, which, according to the garda, makes me a prime suspect."

"In the vicinity, or did you find his body?" I wondered why she wasn't forthright. O'Shea had already admitted she'd found her husband and called O'Shea.

Julia heaved a sigh, swept the room with her eyes, leaned toward me, and whispered, "I found poor Alex. He wasn't breathing, but his body was warm to the touch." She shivered and gathered the shawl closer around her body. "I rang a garda friend immediately. I didn't know what else to do."

"Did you kill Alex?"

Julia gasped. Her hands dropped to her lap in an effort to

control the shaking. "No. I did not. But I know how it looks. That's why I need help. Someone hated Alex enough to end his life."

"Why do you think the police have focused on you?"

"Alex and I were in the middle of a messy divorce." Julia exhaled slowly as if taking time to consider what she said next. "To begin with, he was bent on ensuring I didn't receive any part of our home. Everyone in the village knew his position because he openly discussed our personal business with anyone who'd listen. Then, we had a bang-up argument one night in Charlotte's Pub. The pub patrons had ring-side seats to the spectacle." Julia took another deep breath and continued, "Naturally, the garda has focused on me. You know what they say. It's always the spouse."

"Does getting half or all of your house mean anything to you?" I asked, trying to gauge her potential motivation for murder.

"No." Julia seemed to relax, sitting back in her seat. "I own my business, and he'd agreed not to pursue any rights in that. But I understand how he felt about the homestead. More than three generations of Quinns have lived in the house. Also, there was his relentless dedication to nature. He loved his birdhouses and the property's walking paths leading to the woodlands. I didn't want to take any of that from him. But he didn't believe me. He thought if he could catch me in a relationship with someone else, he'd have me nailed, and I wouldn't be able to contest anything."

"Are you in a relationship?" I asked, noticing she hadn't touched her salad since she'd dropped her hands to her lap.

"No, but as I said, I have a friendship with someone I've known for years—since we were teenagers, really. I've always confided in him during life's pivot points. But"—Julia paused and stared out through the dining room's glass windows before continuing—"I don't know what will happen. He's the detective. I rang him when I found Alex's body."

"Where was this friend when Alex was murdered?"

"Close to where I found Alex's body. In fact, he notified the guards."

"Thomas O'Shea. He's the friend, right?" No wonder O'Shea wasn't bullying his way into the investigation.

Julia's eyes swiveled toward me. "How did you know?"

"Before Georgina became involved, O'Shea approached me. He believes you're innocent."

Julia exhaled a long breath of relief. "I haven't heard from him since I rang him about Alex. I was sure he considered me guilty."

"No, he's probably worried about what his superiors will say when they learn you are acquaintances. Who else was in the vicinity the day of the murder?"

"Gosh, just about everyone Alex and I know. I can make a list if you like. I'd just closed the shop, and the guild members had gone to the pub for a late lunch. I saw some of the people who work in the abbey café and gift shop heading for a walk in the woodlands. Because we live in the heart of unspoiled beauty, most of us take a walk every day."

"What's the guild, and how many members are there?"

"We're a group of artisans, artists, quilters, and knitters who pass our knowledge along to other people through classes, presentations, or just by being in the shop and answering questions. Members come and go, depending on what's happening in their lives. For some, guild activities are a hobby that fades away over time. But there are three people whose livelihoods depend upon their craft. Those three members help manage the guild activities."

"What about the abbey? Could anyone there have seen what happened?" I asked, thinking of the woman I'd glimpsed near the walled garden.

Julia shook her head of curls vehemently. "The abbey? No way. The few sisters who live there are retired and mostly keep a low profile other than Sister Meghan Brennan, who manages the abbey's properties." Julia's eyes blinked. "I saw Sister Meghan near the flower shop, but I can't imagine she'd have anything to do with Alex's death. I mean, I went to school at the abbey. We're talking about Franciscan nuns. They're the most reverential and respectful of nature human beings I've ever known."

"You went to school at the abbey. Is that how you met Alex?"

"I spent most of my childhood living in the abbey. You see, my parents were killed when I was a wee one, and, in those days, the religious orders fostered children."

My heart stood still for a moment. Julia had been fostered. Maybe not in the same way I'd been, but I assumed she'd probably experienced a loneliness similar to mine.

"You were never adopted?" I asked, thinking of my adoptive parents, the O'Briens. After my mother disappeared, I'd spent time in foster homes until the angels intervened, and I ended up in a foster-to-adopt-home with the O'Briens. They completed the official paperwork when I was ten. Unfortunately, two months after my eighteenth birthday, my life changed again. I was supposed to be with them that day. Getting the call about the Cessna's crash rocked my life. In one moment, I was alone again. But in life, the O'Briens had surrounded me with love; in death, their memories sustained me.

"No, I was never claimed." Julia's eyes blinked, but she managed a smile and continued, "I excelled in needlework and art. When I finished my secondary school courses, the sisters sponsored me at the National College of Art and Design in Dublin. After I graduated, I returned to Letterbrack and met Alex. By then, I'd decided I wanted to live in the west of Ireland.

I opened the shop as a way of paying forward the good I'd received by promoting the work of the area's talented artisans."

"What was it like? Living in the abbey?"

"Well, my life was different. Many of the students were orphans like me. Others were there for a brief respite away from chaotic home situations."

"I've read stories about the Mercy Laundries. Is that what you mean by different?" I asked, emphasizing the word *different*.

"Oh, no, not at all." Julia inhaled sharply and shook her head in denial. "The Franciscans are the kindest, loving group of women. In addition to the school, they've provided shelter to families who needed protection from abusive spouses or partners. I've never heard an ill word spoken about the order," Julia replied.

I sipped my tea, hoping to wash away the tart lemon dressing taste before asking, "Does the order still operate a respite program?"

Maybe the woman I'd seen wasn't my mother. Perhaps the woman had ignored me because she was worried about an abusive partner finding her.

Julia shook her head. "No. The school and the women's shelter are no longer operational. But you should ask Sister Meghan those questions. She oversees the café and the shops. Actually, you could say she's the face of the abbey and the order to outsiders." Julia raised her eyebrows. "Why do you ask? Are you thinking the former programs have a bearing on Alex's murder?"

"Get the heck out of my way," a man's voice interrupted our conversation.

I looked behind me toward the voice's source. Near the gift shop door, I glimpsed a male and female arguing. One of the man's hands was raised in a fist. I stood and pushed away from the table.

Julia's words stopped me. "Don't interrupt. Those two are

always getting into it with each other. An intervention won't work. Besides, Todd doesn't work here anymore. I expect Sister Meghan will show up any minute and politely ask him to leave."

Sure enough, a short woman not much taller than five feet, dressed in a brown Franciscan habit, approached the male. "Mr. O'Toole, that's enough. I must ask you to leave. I don't think your behavior is doing your case any good."

Todd pushed her aside and stormed out. You could have heard a pin drop in the dining room, where the guests sat frozen in place, utensils still in their hands.

Sister Meghan waved to everyone. "Please, continue. Enjoy your meal. Sometimes, people just have to let off a little steam," she said and then turned to the woman Todd had been arguing with and laid a hand on her shoulder. The woman shrugged, smiled, and exited the dining area. Sister Meghan whirled on her heel, her habit billowing out behind her, and retreated into the gift shop.

I imagined she wouldn't remain there for very long. If she were anything like my high school French teacher, Sister Regina, the abbey's Sister Meghan would probably follow this Todd character and give him a good talking to.

"Does this happen often?" I asked, sitting back down.

"A lot recently. Todd used to be one of the garden managers, but he was let go by the abbey board." Julia compressed her lips before continuing, "I assume I can reveal Todd was one of Alex's clients. Todd's suing the abbey board for breach of contract."

"Does he have a legitimate grievance?"

"I don't know. Everyone in the village knows that Todd was fired and that he'd hired Alex. Todd talks about his unfortunate circumstances almost every night at Charlotte's Pub, but Alex didn't share any details. He was meticulous about keeping client-lawyer conversations and documents to himself." Julia sighed. "Miss O'Brien, I've enjoyed our lunch, and I appreciate Georgina interceding on my behalf. But I suppose I'd be asking too much for you to take my case," she said, but her eyes begged differently.

The issues at the Consulting Detective, my last words with Lorcan, and Aunt Georgina's admonition about burning bridges raced through my mind, including the image of the woman I'd seen gliding toward the door in the garden's wall. "I don't know if I can help you, but I'll begin asking questions on your behalf."

Tears formed in Julia's eyes. "Thank you. You won't regret getting involved. I may not have loved Alex in the same way as I once did, but I didn't kill him."

"How was he murdered?" I asked, wondering whether the cause of death might help pinpoint the motive.

Julia hid her face in her hands, and when she looked up again, her cheeks were as pale as snow. "It was horrible. One of his eyes was gored out." Her eyes blinked, and she wept silently.

"And you didn't see a weapon?" I asked.

"Miss O'Brien, as soon as I realized Alex was dead, I rang Detective O'Shea. I didn't look for anything. I'd already seen more than I ever wanted to see in my life. I can't imagine who'd want to murder Alex in such a brutal way. That person must be brought to justice."

"I'll do what I can. First, I'll need a list of the three guild members as well as anyone else who saw you when you closed your shop."

"That's easy. May I email the names to you?"

"Of course."

"One more thing, can you point me in the direction of the trail you took the day you found Alex's body?"

"Of course, I'll draw a quick map." Julia's hands shook as she pulled a pen from her purse and made a crude sketch with lines and arrows on a napkin. "Have you ever been on the woodland trails?" she asked when she handed over the illustration.

"No."

"I'm sorry your first visit to Letterbrack is marred by death."

I didn't respond. Instead, I provided my business card, and then we rose from the table and left the restaurant together. Outside, Julia pointed out the path into the woods where Alex's body had been found.

CHAPTER 7

As soon as Julia disappeared from sight, I returned to the door in the walled garden where I'd seen the mystery woman. Once again, my entry attempts failed.

"May I assist you with something?" an imperious voice behind me said.

I turned, almost bumping into Sister Meghan, the Franciscan nun from the restaurant. My five-foot-six-inch frame towered over her by several inches. She wasn't obese but not thin. A brown rosary cord worn midsection over a full-length brown dress emphasized a curvy waistline. Her black veil encircled piercing blue eyes and a face free from wrinkles.

"Yes, actually, you can. I want access to the garden through this door, but it's locked."

"Of course, this access point is secured. If you want to see the parts of the garden on display to the public, you must purchase a ticket and enter just like everyone else."

My hand sought the phone holstered to my waist. "But I witnessed a woman walk through this entry about two hours ago. How did she get access?"

"Aren't you the nosy parker? From the sound of your accent, I'd say you're American. I know how much tourists want to get into every nook and cranny of the abbey. However, we are Franciscans. We live, work, and pray here. Not every facet of our life is open to the public."

I stepped back, somewhat surprised that a small package of a nun could be so forceful.

"I'm sorry, but I recognized the woman who entered the garden through that door. I just want to assure myself that I was correct."

"What is your name?"

"Star O'Brien. Julia Quinn has just asked me to investigate what happened to her husband, Alex."

My name-dropping worked to get Sister to drop her guard and see me as not so suspicious. Her face softened, and she stepped back out of my personal space.

"Poor Alex. He was a gentle soul when it came to nature. He didn't deserve to die at the hands of another human being. However, Miss O'Brien, the abbey had nothing to do with his death or murder, if we have to call it that. Whatever that child, Julia, has asked you to do, don't bring the abbey into it."

Sister Meghan turned away but pivoted for a moment to look back at me. "Also, if I were you, I'd stay away from locked doors."

With that, she made rapid strides toward the abbey entrance.

I watched her until she disappeared into the abbey. She may have warned me away, but I didn't plan to follow her orders. I wasn't in Sister Regina's French class anymore. As far as I was concerned, I was as determined to get inside as Sister Meghan was focused on keeping me out. I proceeded to the gift shop and picked up the free woodland walking trail map. Armed with the walk outline and the instructions Julia had provided, I made my way to the murder scene.

After about a thirty-minute walk, the manicured paths surrounding the abbey grounds gave way to mossy and luscious green ground cover beneath a densely forested area of pine trees. Bird twitter and song reverberated throughout the branches. Although I didn't see any, I thought I caught the scent of jasmine in the air. Then, without warning, the greenwood opened into a meadow. Adjacent to the meadow, a lake's pristine water gently lapped against the shore. I stopped moving, allowing my eyes to soak in the landscape's beauty. Who, I asked myself, had committed murder in an idyllic space where nature glistened and shone so brightly?

From my vantage point, I fixed my gaze on the middle of the meadow, where bits of paper and yellow tape surrounded a portion of the grass, marking the place where Alex's body had been found.

I approached what was left of the crime scene with mixed feelings of anger and sadness coursing through my being at whoever had desecrated this place. First, I perused the area, searching for anything the police might have overlooked, including access points other than the one indicated on the official trail guide. Next, I moved closer to the shoreline, where a section of the meadow receded, having been taken over by the forest. The mountain on the opposite side cast shadows on the lake's water. My observations didn't turn up any weapon or debris left behind by the murderer. I concluded that the meadow could have been accessed not only from the official trail but also from the woods and by boat. Julia was right; anyone could have gotten to Alex here.

Snap

A sound like brittle bones breaking crackled behind me. I whipped my body around and surveyed the forest while I listened for movement. Nothing. Not even bird twitter. Just the sound of the water lapping behind me. I pulled my car keys from the knapsack I typically carried everywhere and held them between my knuckles, ready to defend myself.

After a few minutes of relentless silence, I took a deep

breath, put my keys away, and retraced my steps back to the abbey. I was a few feet from entering the forest trail when I spotted a poor baby bird lying in the grass. I surveyed the nearby branches for a nest but didn't see one. How had this tiny songbird fallen? I pulled a tissue out of my knapsack, wrapped the tiny body in the paper, and carried the poor thing a little way into the woods. After placing the chick near the base of a tree where the ground's pine needles, leaves, and lichen offered protection, I said a silent prayer and then proceeded to find my way through the greenery to the abbey's parking area.

The shops and café were closed for the day, and a few straggling tourists ambled to the buses and cars. I stared at the door in the garden wall before striding toward it. The handle refused to budge. Frustrated, I returned to my car, threw my knapsack onto the passenger seat, and drove back along the N59 to Castlebar.

I found Aunt Georgina in the back room of her shop, sorting through a pile of fabrics.

"How was the meeting with Julia?' she asked as soon as she fixed her gaze on me.

"I'm taking the case."

Georgina's relief was evident in the smile that lit her face. "I knew you'd want to help. Where do we start? How do I help?"

"Honestly, Georgina, I have several selfish motives for agreeing to snoop around."

"Really? What's going on?"

"I glimpsed someone, a woman, in Letterbrack. She walked just like my mother. Her hair and height transported me to my childhood, watching my mother leave our apartment on her way to work."

"Star, you know...."

I opened my hand and reached toward Georgina in an effort to stop her from saying any more. "Don't. I just have to satisfy myself. The woman disappeared through a door into the Walled Sanctuary Garden. Not the tourist entrance but another door, almost hidden in the granite. When I tried to enter, one of the sisters warned me to mind my own business. If, by helping Julia Quinn, I get access to the abbey garden, then I'm going to do it. And"—I paused and considered the colorful fabrics, some of which were similar to the purple and green I'd seen reflected in the songbird's plumage—"the meadow where Alex was murdered is one of those thin places where Heaven and Earth come closer to each other... the mountains, the blue water, the cool forest air." I sighed. "I found a dead baby bird. The poor thing. I couldn't find its nest."

"Agra, you'll find your mother one day. I'm sure of it. Especially since you have Evelyn and whatever information she can provide."

"I'm supposed to meet her at a storage unit in Bohola, where she's stored our father's belongings."

Georgina tossed her scarf behind her and said, "Have you rung Lorcan? I'm sure he'd like to know you met with Julia."

I didn't answer her question immediately. During the drive back to Castlebar, my brain had replayed the dinner date with Lorcan repeatedly, in a loop. The iciness in his eyes when he shot a look at me. I'd never been at the receiving end of his anger. In fact, I'd never seen him angry—ever. I didn't know how I'd approach him. I'd have to admit I'd made a mistake—I never did that.

Georgina must have seen the hesitation on my face because she added, "Why don't you get a good night's rest? Perhaps you'll see Lorcan in the morning when you go for your walk along Cottage Road. Besides, the light of day changes everything." Georgina glanced at her watch and noted, "Speaking of daylight, I've got to get out of here. I'm meeting a friend for dinner. Will you be all right by yourself this evening, Star?"

"Sure. I'll call you later, Aunt Georgina."

WHEN I ARRIVED BACK AT FRENCH HILL COTTAGE, THE SUN HAD slipped closer to the horizon. Once inside, I checked my email and found the note from Julia with the names of three guild members: Anne Ford, Nigel Collins, and Rita Barrett. Julia had included a short description of each person and their artisan specialty. Anne created embroidery patterns, Nigel claimed environmental art as his prime focus, and Rita had won regional awards for patchwork quilts. I put the list aside to peruse later and called the Consulting Detective.

"I'm happy to hear from you," Ellie said.

"I called our clients on the list you provided. I got to all of them except for Mr. and Mrs. Lewis. That call went to voice mail."

"There's been a new wrinkle with the Lewis project," Ellie replied.

"What's going on?"

"They decided to take their business to Wanda King's information broker firm. I asked the Lewises to speak with you first, but they said they just weren't comfortable using the phone for status updates." Ellie's voice faltered. "I'm worried there will be more bad news, Star. Jim Hipple called. He wants to talk to you."

The dread I felt in the pit of my stomach increased when I heard Ellie's news, but I responded positively. "Ellie, nothing is going to happen to the Consulting Detective. Or to you and Phillie. I'll call Jim. Any idea what's up with him?"

"No, and I haven't seen him much lately. Whenever I've

bumped into him at the Daily Treat Diner in Ridgewood, he seems distracted, not as engaged as he usually is."

After retiring from the New York City Police Department, Jim moved to Ridgewood and founded All Towns Investigations, Inc. We were next-door neighbors and friends. Don't get me wrong, I still thought the police were inept, but when Dylan died, Jim had been a supportive friend, and his private detective skills and contacts within the police department had been helpful on more than one occasion.

"I don't want you to worry, Ellie. I'll keep trying the Lewises if only to tell them how grateful I've been for their business. In the meantime, please put Phillie on. I have a research project for her."

"Another murder mystery, Star?" Ellie asked. I could hear the disappointment in her voice.

"No, this time, the research is related to my mother. I want Phillie to look into a Franciscan abbey in County Galway."

"So, Evelyn Cosgrove has been helpful. She's put you on to what might have happened. I'm happy for you, Star."

Ellie and Phillie have supported my efforts since I founded the Consulting Detective. They held my hand when Dylan died and cheered me on in my search for my mother. I reminded myself often that I owed a lot to these two women. If I ever find my mother, these two dear friends will be over the moon for me.

"Something else happened, Ellie, unrelated to Evelyn. This will sound strange, but I was at the abbey and glimpsed a woman whom I would swear was my mother. I understand the abbey used to provide respite and protection for women and children in need. I want to know more."

"Thinking you saw your mother isn't strange, Star. We never forget what our parents look like, even if it's been years since we've seen each other. Hold on, let me get Phillie."

Phillie, Philomena Spring, was the Consulting Detective's

part-time technical guru, who managed our databases and assisted me with research. She spent the rest of her time blogging about women, technology, and innovation.

"Hi, boss, what's up?"

Like me, Phillie never wasted time on chitchat.

"Ellie will explain why I'm asking for this research. Can you look into adoption agencies, foster care, and women's shelter programs that have any association with Kentmore Abbey in County Galway? I'll send you the address. Go back as far as 1962."

"Isn't that the year your mother was born?" Phillie asked.

"Yes," I replied. "If you find anything, call me. Don't wait for email."

"Sure thing, boss. I'm already pounding the keys. Talk soon."

I ended the call and dialed Jim Hipple.

"Hipple." Jim's typical greeting sounded like it always did—retired New York cop-speak.

"Hey, Jim, it's Star. Ellie says you've been looking for me. What's up?" I asked.

"Not much. I just wanted you to know I've been a bit laid up. My blasted appendix acted up and had to come out."

"I'm sorry to hear that, Jim. Ellie's been a bit worried lately, and she thought maybe something dire was happening with you." I twisted the phone cord in my hand, picturing how much popcorn I'd seen Jim eat in the past, and wondered if that played a part in his need for surgery.

"Well, as I said, I won't be available for any snooping on your behalf for a while. I've got to keep up the image of a healthy person. Otherwise, some of the lowlifes I investigate in my business might think they can get the drop on me."

"Can you answer some questions?" I asked.

"Shoot," he replied.

"Have you ever heard of a police detective remaining involved in a case when they knew the suspect?"

"I've seen it happen. What? Are you tangled up with the cops in Ireland again?"

"I sure am. Someone I've repeatedly butted heads with in the past, but this time is different. He's asked me to conduct an investigation."

"Hmm." There was silence on the line as if Jim were thinking things over, and then he asked, "Did the person you're referring to inform his commanding officer of the connection?"

"I don't know, but I'll make sure to ask the detective when I see him."

"Well, if he did tell his commander, it would be up to the commander to decide whether there's a problem. Something like this can definitely put a twist on things at a trial. As a cop, I've always said transparency is the best policy."

"Thanks, Jim. This has been helpful. I hope you feel better soon."

We ended the call, and I made a note to ask O'Shea about how much he'd shared with his commanding officer.

FEELING RESTLESS, I EXITED THE COTTAGE AND STROLLED INTO the back garden. I stood in the silence, gazing at the rising moon. During previous stays, I'd barely had a moment to myself. Georgina stopped by almost daily and had gotten me involved with incidents that turned into murder investigations. I always seemed to bump into Lorcan when I looked my most unflattering self. In addition, the border collie, Ashford, had been a companion for a while. *Isn't it ironic!* You'd think I'd be glad for the respite, but that evening, I felt like the world's lone survivor.

I crossed to the other side of the lawn, stopped at the

Hawthorn hedges, and peered into the dense branches. Celtic mythology maintains that Hawthorn is home to the fairies. I wasn't a believer in lore, but for once, I wished a good fairy would appear and provide the answers to my dilemmas—all of them.

I had responsibilities at home in Ridgewood, New Jersey. But I'd become attached to this place and the circle of friends I'd made here. Traveling between New Jersey and County Mayo wouldn't cut it for much longer if what Ellie feared became a reality. I couldn't let my business fail, but I was torn by the need to see the search for my mother to a finale. Once I confirmed whether the mystery woman at the abbey was or wasn't my mother and determined if Evelyn had any helpful information, I'd cut the cord to this place, pack up, and head west across the Atlantic.

Yeah, I might not have believed in the lore, but I could use some fairy dust. I sent a silent prayer up to the moon for guidance and returned to the cottage.

When I was ready for bed, I picked up my phone and checked for calls. Nothing. I guessed Georgina was still somewhere having dinner. And, Lorcan. Well, he'd been angry. I looked forward to seeing him in the morning and letting him know I'd honored his request.

CHAPTER 8

F riday morning, I'd power-walked along Cottage Road without coming across Lorcan, and he hadn't answered his phone. An unsettled feeling took hold of me, but I needed to get to Letterbrack. I moved quickly as I showered, dressed, grabbed my knapsack, and drove toward Connemara.

Halfway between Leenaun and Letterbrack, the N59 was closed with police panda cars littered across the road. Impatient for action and with no other viable alternative access to the village, I sprang out of my car and approached another driver who stood on the road, waiting.

"What's going on?" I asked the young woman whose child was playing with a stuffed bear at the side of the road.

"The usual annoyance, I suspect. Some lorry has driven off the road. Before long, the guards will get the mess cleaned up, and we'll go on our way." The young woman tilted her head and seemed to assess me. "Are you a tourist?"

"Not really, but I'm on my way to Letterbrack. I'm guessing you often get a slew of what you call visitors along this route."

"Arrah, yes. I work part-time at the abbey's gift shop on weekends," she replied, glancing at the toddler, "when my husband is home and can keep Sarah there busy for a few hours. I just thought with your American accent...."

"I understand. I'm visiting a friend of mine, Julia Quinn."

"Julia? From the Connemara Crafters shop? Well, good luck. I heard she's the prime suspect in her husband's murder."

"What do you think?" I asked, interested in what the locals thought about Alex's death.

"No way. Julia is an artist and one of the kindest people I know. We carry her designs in the shop. She's in and out all the time, replenishing supplies. Although she's seemed a bit distracted over the past several months—always in a hurry. Even missed delivering some of the goods clients had ordered. I had to ring her and give a reminder."

"Did you ask her what's been bothering her?"

"Lord, no, I'm a part-time clerk, and with all the brouhaha over the former manager, I've kept my head down. I don't want to get fired." She cast a glance at the child. "I need this job."

"Yeah, I heard something about one of the managers who oversaw work in the garden. I imagine you'd have to do something pretty horrific to get fired by the Franciscans."

"I don't know what happened, but I've heard money was involved. I know one thing for sure—Todd's out of a job." At that moment, the panda cars started moving. The young woman strode over to the toddler and hoisted the child into her car.

I returned to my Renault and followed along, like a train car, with the rest of the traffic until I reached Letterbrack's village green. Julia's shop, which opened at 9:30 a.m., was already full of tourists filling up on organic, tweedy, and woolen yarns along with other knitting supplies and guidebooks about dyeing and texturing yarn. I quickly parked behind a commercial pickup truck and walked toward the shop.

"The shop's chockablock. You might want to wait until the lunch crowd heads over to the abbey's eatery. That's if you're planning on doing any serious shopping." The words belonged to a male in his mid-fifties with brown wavy hair.

"Are you waiting to go in?" I asked.

"Me, no. I've had my fill of Connemara Crafters," he replied, emphasizing the word, *Crafters*. "The wife makes quilts. She claims she's an artisan," he said, folding his arms across his barrel-shaped chest.

"Then you live in the village?" I asked, noticing his boat shoes and the heavy, padded green jacket he wore.

"I run the local salmon fishery," he replied, pointing at the pickup truck I'd parked behind. "I'm just waiting to see my wife before she gets all tangled up in her quilting gloves this morning."

I glanced at the truck and noted the name Atlantic Salmon Farms on the side panel. Pails, fishing equipment, shovels, and several tote bags filled with a variety of nasty-looking hooks and spears filled the cargo bed.

"I'm Star O'Brien. And you're...?"

"Brendan Barrett, and from your accent, I'm guessing you're the American snooping around for Julia."

"And you learned this from...?"

Brendan's eyes glared at me. "Everyone knows everything around here. It's a fact of village life. Julia told her precious guild members that she'd gotten some Yank to help her. Before you ask me anything, you need to know: I don't want no part of Julia's schemes. Why the guards haven't arrested her yet is a mystery to me. I'm sure she murdered her old man."

"Is that so? Why do you believe Julia murdered her husband?"

"Those two were always getting into each other's knickers over everything. Oh, yeah, everyone thought they were just the loveliest couple: her, the artist, and him, the lawyer. But I can tell you because I've lived in the village all my life, Julia married him for his money. And him? Lord knows what got into his head when he met her." Brendan stopped speaking, scanned the space around us, uncrossed his arms, and leaned in closer to me. "I saw her heading into the woodland walk that day. She carried one of the precious tote bags she sells in the shop. You take it from me. She was sneaking around on her husband." Barrett stepped back and fixed me with a stare. "She was in the eatery early in the morning buying up prepared sandwiches and biscuits."

"You saw her? Which path did she use?"

Brendan pointed to a stretch of beaten-down grass.

"I don't see a walkway there."

"Of course not; the paths are for the bloody tourists, so they don't get lost in the woods. But those of us who live here know all the ins and outs of the greenwood. We don't need trails."

"What time did you see Julia in the café?"

"Well, early. I was on my way to the fishery and stopped for a to-go coffee. I'd say about half eight in the morning"—he paused and then continued—"then later in the day, when I stopped to pick up a sandwich at one p.m., I saw her making her way toward the woods."

"When did you hear about what happened to Alex?"

"Not 'til the evening. I finished at the salmon processing plant, went home, showered, and headed to the pub. That's where I heard about Alex."

"I'm surprised the guards weren't in the pub, taking witness statements."

"Oh, you don't know us, Miss O'Brien. Letterbrack is a crossroads between the mountains and the Atlantic Ocean. Throw in the Walled Serenity Garden, and you have yourself a major tourist attraction. The guards have been interviewing people on the hush-hush. No need to get visitors riled up when we know who the victim and the perpetrator were." Brendan took his eyes off me to focus over my shoulder. I twisted around and noticed a woman advancing along the sidewalk toward us.

She carried several tote bags, and I assumed she must be his wife.

When the woman drew nearer, Brendan broke away from me and rushed to her side. His six-foot frame towered over the woman as he bent to whisper in her ear. She threw a brief glance in my direction before turning her eyes back to her husband. Brendan patted the top of her head and proceeded to climb into his truck, waving at her as he pulled out of the parking space. She remained where she was, scowling at the rear end of the pick-up as it vanished from sight.

"Star," Julia's voice called from the doorway of the shop. I turned and moved toward the shop.

She held the door open, and I walked inside before hanging my knapsack on the edge of a table with catalogs for ordering patterns and various knitting supplies.

"Good morning, I'm glad you're here. Why don't you take a look around while I do a bit of tidying before the next wave of tourists arrives?"

I moved quickly throughout the space, noting several comfy chairs and woven baskets filled with yarn, cloth swatches, needles, and embroidery threads. Disorganization seemed to be the shop's unifying theme. The tote bags Brendan had mentioned, similar to the ones I'd seen his wife carrying, were strewn throughout the room on tables and displayed on the spindles and pegs of a wooden coat rack. A sign over the coat rack indicated a monogram could be added to your purchase if desired.

A double-wide window at the back half of the shop provided a view into a small garden with what looked like herbs and lettuce heads. Unfinished sewing and knitting projects lay atop two oak kitchen tables near the window.

"Quite an eclectic space," I said to Julia when she began straightening one of the tote bag piles.

"The tourists love these things, but sometimes people wreck the displays, rifling through them."

"Have you heard from the guards yet?" I asked, looking out the storefront window at the cars that lined the street. The woman Brendan had spoken with was no longer visible.

"Of course, they interviewed me as soon as Alex's body was found. I've been expecting them to arrest me, but they're probably amassing evidence. I wish I knew more about what's going on. The sooner the guards talk to me about evidence they may or may not have, the sooner I can explain myself."

"There was a man outside named Brendan. He seems to think you're guilty, Julia."

Julia bent and fluffed up the pillows on the comfy-looking chairs. "Was he about six feet tall, wearing a padded jacket?"

I nodded and said, "Drove away in a pickup truck."

"Oh, yeah, Rita's husband. He was one of Alex's clients." Julia sat on one of the armchairs and sighed. "I guess everyone in the village has been a client of Alex's at one time or another." She shook her head. "Who knew employer-employee relations was such a hotbed of litigation? But I don't know why Brendan believes I could have killed Alex."

"Once the police determine time of death, they're going to want an alibi. What did you do that day?"

"Me? I was here, of course. I left the house at eight a.m. Alex was home in his study—alive. I didn't leave the shop again until well after one p.m. when I closed for lunch until two thirty p.m. The tourists usually visit the shop after they've been through the gardens, and I wanted to be back by then. I found Alex at about two p.m. Why?"

"Brendan claims he witnessed you walking into the woodland with a hefty tote bag." Julia's eyes blinked, but she didn't respond. "Julia, I can't help if you aren't honest with me." Her silence told me all I needed to know. O'Shea's desire to keep his involvement in the case quiet suddenly made complete sense to me. "You and Tom O'Shea are having an affair, aren't you?"

Her cheeks blushed from rosé to a merlot red before she said, "We're friends, old friends, but lately, the relationship has moved to a deeper level."

"Did Brendan see you walking into the woods, Julia?"

"I don't know if he saw me or not. But, yes, I walked into the woods. I'd picked up some sandwiches for Tom and me."

"When were you going to tell me?" I demanded. When, for that matter, was Tom O'Shea going to tell me the truth? I'd have to talk to him again and let Lorcan know his so-called friend wasn't as forthcoming as Lorcan might want to believe.

"I didn't want to say anything to you yesterday. After all, I didn't know if you'd really show up here again. I didn't want you to think I was guilty."

"Oh, that makes all the sense in the world. You and Tom kept information from me; a witness claims to have seen you going into the woods, but you want me to think you're innocent," I said with a hint of sarcasm. "Julia, if I'm going to help you, you've got to tell me everything. Is that clear?"

"What else do you want to know?"

"For starters, what time were you in the woods that day? And where in the woods did you meet Tom?"

Julia's eyes blinked, and her mouth twisted into a grimace before she answered. "Sometime between one thirty p.m. and the time I found Alex. Honestly, I don't know the exact time," she said, shrugging her shoulders. "Tom and I always meet in one of the meadows. It's a short walk from the back of my property, through a stand of trees, to a small clearing. But that day, I was running late, and Alex was working from home. I didn't want him to see me, so I took a longer route through the abbey woods to get to Tom."

"I see. Do you and O'Shea usually meet where Alex's body was found?"

"Yes, but I have no idea why Alex was there. He normally stayed within our property boundaries. He's got birdhouses and feeders all over the garden, which he spent most of his time tending to."

Julia picked up a tangled skein of wool and squeezed it like a hand-held stress ball. "Something or someone lured him to that spot. That must be what happened."

"How did O'Shea usually get to your meeting place?" I asked, certain he wouldn't have chosen to trek through Alex's backyard for a clandestine meeting with the man's wife.

"He normally parked on one of the roads leading into the village. It's common for people who might be going fishing to park near a man-made walking path to get to one of the many lakes. He usually got there ahead of me. Sometimes, I was delayed because of tourists still in the shop."

"Were you delayed the day you found Alex?"

"Yes—"

"Julia, are you okay?" The shop door crashed open. The voice's owner, a muscular man of about twenty-five with raven black hair flowing well past his shoulders, rushed over to Julia's side.

"Nigel, I'm fine," Julia said, patting his arm and turning back to me. "Star, this is one of my most promising artists, Nigel Collins."

Nigel barely glanced at me. Instead, his eyes remained focused on Julia. "I just met Rita Barrett. She said the guards suspect you of murder. I'm not letting them near you," Nigel said, flexing his shoulders in a show of strength.

"Nigel, stop. Listen to me. All is well. You can help by talking to Miss O'Brien here. She needs to know more about Alex and why someone might want to murder him. The more we tell her, the easier it will be for me. Do you understand?"

Nigel shifted the artist pad he held into his left hand and offered his right to me. I accepted, noticing the strength of his grip. "I'm pleased to meet you, Miss O'Brien. But I want you to know right from the start—Julia's innocent."

"Well, if that's the case, my job here will be brief. But in the meantime, I'd like some more time with Julia, alone."

Nigel nodded. "Julia, will you be okay?"

"I'll be fine. Get back to work. I want your portfolio completed in time for the exhibition in Dublin."

"He's a dote, isn't he?" Julia said to me after Nigel exited the shop.

"He has a major crush on you," I replied, wondering if Nigel's infatuation with Julia was enough for him to murder her husband.

"I know, but there's a certain young lady in the guild who adores him. One of these days, he'll realize that, and his fixation on me will end. So, let's continue our discussion."

"So, you were saying you were delayed closing the shop at lunchtime?"

"I think so. Honestly, I don't remember much. I know it was after one p.m. because I was helping a tourist match a swatch of cloth to the dress she wore. I remember her glancing at her Apple watch and saying, 'Oh, I'm going to be late for my lunch appointment.'"

I walked over to the wall where floor-to-ceiling shelving was filled with skeins of yarn. Drop lights highlighted the variety of shades like a rainbow arc after a storm.

"This is all very pretty," I remarked. "I see why Georgina enjoys working with you."

"Ah, yes. Georgina and I are two kindred spirits when it comes to design. Once in a while, we have our creative differences, but"—Julia laughed—"Georgina usually persuades me to her way of thinking."

"I'm beginning my investigation with Sister Meghan. What more can you tell me about her and the abbey?"

Julia's lips pursed, and her eyes widened at my question.

"Why would you want to speak with her? Besides, I saw her in the café the day Alex was murdered."

"Oh, what time was that?"

"When I went to pick up the sandwiches. Like I said, I don't remember the exact time. Anyway, I can't imagine her embroiled in a murder."

I glanced out the shop windows toward the abbey and garden walls. "Let's just say I'm naturally suspicious, especially when someone tells me to keep my nose out of his or her business." I didn't mention how impatient I was to get a look inside the garden section that was off-limits as soon as possible.

Julia sighed. "The guild members are nervous about your involvement. Until yesterday, we were all happy and on good terms with each other. I know you need to ask questions, but I don't know if the guild members will understand." Julia glanced at her watch. "Most days, Sister Meghan is in the section of the garden that is open to the public at about this time. She gives an informative herb garden tour. If you hurry, you can buy a ticket and get in with the group."

"Thanks. I'll see you later," I said, and then grabbed my knapsack and ran out the shop door toward the ticket kiosk I'd seen when I parked my car.

CHAPTER 9

An undulating wave of color and perfumed air greeted me when I burst through the official gates into the Walled Serenity Garden. Raised beds filled with herbs, flowers, and vegetable plants dotted the landscape. In the distance, I glimpsed Sister Meghan with a group of about six tourists. I ran across the luscious, green lawn to join them. Sister's mouth flattened into a straight line when she saw me stop at the assemblage's edge.

"Some of the plants in the garden date back to 1880," she said, raising her left hand to indicate the entire garden.

"What about the gardener's house?" a tour group member asked, pointing to a bungalow-style building at one end of the garden. "Does anyone live there?"

"The cottage has been restored according to its original plans. You'll also notice the solar panels on the tin roof. That's an improvement you wouldn't have found in the nineteenth century. It's one of many upgrades we budget for each year using the entrance fees we collect from visitors like you." Sister Meghan smiled at the group, but from where I stood, I could see her eyes focused on me like a laser.

"You didn't answer the question, though," I stated, pointing at the structure. "Does anyone live there?"

Sister Meghan ignored my question, choosing to continue with her tour speech. "Of course, we have gardeners and local volunteers who donate time and expertise caring for the property, and several Franciscans tend to the vegetables and herbs."

"I read somewhere about a separate space, called the kitchen garden, in most of these seventeenth- and eighteenth-century estates. Does the Walled Serenity Garden have a separate kitchen garden apart from this one, Sister?" another tour group member asked.

"Yes, there was a place for growing medicinal and vegetable plants in the late eighteen hundreds, but that particular area hasn't been cultivated in years. Nowadays, we grow all our vegetables and herbs in this part of the property," Sister Meghan replied. She glanced at me before adding, "And the original kitchen garden is not open to the public. Stinging nettles and thorn bushes pose a tangled danger." Then, a brilliant smile lit her face when she said, "I wouldn't want anyone wandering in and getting hurt. Shall we continue with the tour?" she asked, turning toward a large rectangular raised bed planted with herbs.

The group grew silent and obediently moved behind her. "I hope you enjoy lunch in the Garden Café while you're here," she continued. "The salads and vegetables on the menu are what you call farm-to-table. The dwarf beans, endives, and radishes originate in the greenhouse and then are planted, grown to maturity, and picked each morning for the day's menu offerings. I personally recommend the beet salad."

While Sister Meghan continued her speech, indicating herbs like parsley, chives, rosemary, and thyme, I inched closer to her. Julia may not think Sister Meghan could murder someone, but I wasn't about to take Julia's word for it. In contrast to the sandals I'd seen on Sister when I'd encountered her yesterday, she wore a navy slip-on boat shoe similar to what I'd seen on Brendan Barrett. Then, I spotted mud on the back edge of her habit. Brendan's comments about the area's residents knowing all the ways in and out of the forest crossed my mind. Certainly, based on what I'd seen of the mysterious garden door yesterday, I was sure there might be other egresses from the garden that weren't visible to the general public.

"Thank you for your interest in our little part of Heaven on Earth." Sister Meghan's words broke into my thoughts. "Please stop into the gift shop after you've had lunch, where you'll find tea towels imprinted with the herbs featured in the garden. Also, there's a beautiful selection of soaps scented with the garden's flowers."

As the group dispersed, Sister Meghan marched over to me. "I thought I told you yesterday not to involve the abbey in your investigation."

She might have been shorter than me in stature, but Sister Meghan's face got inches away from mine—again.

"With or without you, I'm helping Julia. If you and the people of Letterbrack can't answer questions regarding who might have wanted Alex dead, Julia stands a good chance of being convicted of murder. Is that what you want, Sister?"

"I have responsibilities, Miss O'Brien, to this abbey and the people who live within its walls. What in the world can I tell you that will make a difference to the investigation the guards are conducting?" Sister Meghan touched the rosary cord at her waist. "What kind of credentials do you have that give you the right to show up here in our village and begin asking questions?"

I didn't respond immediately because I was peering at Sister Meghan's ankles. When she repositioned her cord, her habit rose an inch or two to reveal what looked like black leggings or yoga pants—mud splatter, boat shoes, and leggings.

Usually, I wouldn't have questioned the leg coverings, but summer was in full swing, and even if the weather was chilly, which it wasn't, I'd have thought the brown habit would have provided enough warmth. Obviously, Sister Meghan had to be considered a suspect, especially in light of the way she seemed so determined not to be questioned.

"I've dealt with the police all my life, Sister. Julia told me about her parents. I know she grew up in this abbey. You must care about her. Otherwise, why would the abbey have supported her through school?" I hesitated and then continued, "I lost my mother, Sister, when I was six years old. The police said it was a case of abandonment. But I've never believed what the police said and continue to say about my mother and others who appear guilty but are really innocent. That's why I'm here, Sister... to prove Julia's innocence and, I warn you. I want to know what's in that garden you're so carefully protecting." I pushed my face closer to Sister Meghan's. "Who was the woman I saw yesterday?"

Sister's face reddened, and she glanced behind me at the official garden exit. "I have no idea what you're talking about. If you have questions about Julia and Alex, I'll answer them, but you must make an appointment to see me in the abbey. I want my secretary present when we meet." With that, Sister Meghan bustled away.

I pulled the map of the garden's layout from my knapsack and walked the area's perimeter. When I came to the gardener's house, I pressed my nose against one of the windows and peered inside. A narrow cot was pushed up against the far wall. A linen dress, belt, and long-legged pants lay strewn on the bed's mattress. I couldn't tell if the clothing was curated for looks or actual garments used by someone. Recalling what Julia had said about the abbey providing respite, I could understand Sister's reluctance to share information with the public. I'd just have to convince her I was different.

In the meantime, I continued my inspection along the garden wall, looking for doors other than the one used by the tourists. If there was a door here, it was well disguised, but that didn't mean I wouldn't find an entrance. What had Ralph Waldo Emerson said? "Every wall is a door."

My thoughts turned to Lorcan and his engineering mind. In addition to being the heir to his father's estate and several business ventures, Lorcan owned patents to several inventions. If anyone could identify hidden sections of this garden, it would be him. I looked forward to getting him involved, and if I were honest with myself, I was feeling sad and disconnected since we'd argued. I hoped he'd gotten over his anger.

Once I'd completed my circuit of the garden, I exited and walked to the abbey's entrance. A sense of quiet and cool air greeted me when I entered the official visitor's foyer. Two large mahogany doors on one end of the foyer stood open, displaying a sweeping vista of the Connemara mountains. I couldn't help but compare what it must have been like for Julia to grow up here compared to my early years in foster homes, passed off from one to another until the O'Briens adopted me. I wondered what they might say if they knew I had a half-sister, imagining they'd have been overjoyed. The soft sound of a bell in the distance interrupted my thoughts. I turned away from the panoramic view, strode to another set of doors set into the opposite end of the hall, rang the doorbell, and waited. A younger, slimmer version of Sister Meghan dressed in a brown habit answered the door.

"May I be of assistance?" she asked.

"Yes, my name is Star O'Brien, and I'm here to make an appointment with Sister Meghan." I passed a Consulting Detective card to the young woman.

"Oh, yes, of course. Sister told me you'd be calling. I'm Sister Evangeline, Sister Meghan's assistant. Wait here, please." The door closed.

A few minutes later, Sister Evangeline appeared with a large, hard-covered book and pen. "Let me see. Sister has free time next week on Thursday morning. Can you be here at eleven a.m.? Sister usually inspects Serenity Chapel. She'll meet you there."

"My plans are pressing. Next week doesn't work for me. How about tomorrow morning?"

"Oh, no, Miss O'Brien. We don't work that way here. Sister Meghan's calendar is filled with all kinds of appointments and meetings. Next Thursday is the best I can do with her calendar. I'll just pencil you in."

"But why are we meeting in a chapel? Why not meet here in the abbey?" I asked, wanting desperately to get inside.

Sister Evangeline's blue eyes regarded me with a smile on her lips. "I can tell you are anxious, Miss O'Brien, but we don't work according to the world's tempo. We follow a more measured and mellow cadence." She closed the appointment book. "I apologize, but I must leave you. Sister needs me to word-process some notes for her, but please enjoy the grounds and natural environment." She began to close the door, but I planted my foot in its way.

"You mentioned the garden. I'd like to explore some more and understand how the garden fits into the overall landscape. Are there documents or maps other than what's in the gift shop? Sister mentioned a kitchen garden. I'd like to know more about that."

"Oh, Miss O'Brien. I'm afraid I can't help you. Besides, some doors are best left closed," she replied, gently using her foot to move mine out of the way before shutting the door.

Frustrated and angry, I returned to Julia's shop. The bell over the shop door rang when I opened it. Julia moved from behind the register, signaling me to follow her to the worktable. Nigel and the two women at the worktable in the rear of the shop stopped what they were doing, glancing at me and then at each other.

"Everyone, I want to introduce a friend of mine, Star O'Brien. She's going to help us figure out who would have wanted to murder Alex," Julia said. A hush fell over the group. Three pairs of eyes locked on me. Finally, Nigel spoke. "I'm ready to do anything I can to protect Julia."

A gasp escaped from a young woman's lips. "Nigel, we have no business getting involved in this scheme. What would happen to your art school career if a murderer set their sights on you? Besides, I think Julia is well able to take care of herself."

"I don't think we've met before," I said to the young woman.

Her lips moved, but her eyes never left Nigel when she quietly said, "Anne Ford."

Rita Barrett, whom I recognized as the woman Brendan had patted on the head, spoke up. "What qualifications does she have?" she asked, staring at Julia. "Do you know anything about this woman, this American? What can she do that we can't do ourselves?"

"If it's any solace, Rita, Georgina Hill is Star's aunt. I know you've met Georgina before. Georgina's a friend, and she recommended Miss O'Brien."

"I run an information broker consulting company. Most of the time, I search for missing heirs, marriage licenses, and the sort." I stopped and pulled several Consulting Detective cards from my knapsack and placed them on the table. "But I've also been involved in some murder mysteries. I admit I'm no Miss Marple, but sometimes people are more comfortable talking to me about the victim. Sometimes, they share information that the police might not ask about, or the interviewee might not want to tell the police."

"Hmm," Brendan's wife said, "I think you're in for a shock, Miss O'Brien if you think the locals are going to open up to some American."

"Look, I'm here to give Julia support. That's all. I'll be asking each of you to tell me about Alex. You're not required to tell me your deep personal secrets." What I didn't say was secrets might be the reason Alex was murdered.

"Tell you what, Star is going to interview me first," Julia said. "If I don't like how it goes, or if I think she's not being sensitive or might reveal secrets, I'll let you know. But listen to me; I need your help. I'm in trouble. If we don't come up with a reason for the guards to consider other persons of interest, my shop, *our* work here, will come to an end."

Nigel rose and walked over to Julia. "I'll be at the abbey's dining room getting a bite to eat if you need me." Then, he left, joined by the rest of the group, who gathered up tote bags and pieces of paper covered with color markings and diagrams.

"Well," Julia smiled. "That went just about how I thought it would," she said after she locked the shop door and turned the *Open* sign to *Closed*.

"If you think so. Okay, let's begin."

CHAPTER 10

A light drizzle was smearing the windowpanes when Julia closed out the register and printed the paper receipts. "Please, take a seat. I'll just be a moment," she said, moving behind a screen at the back of the shop.

Impatient to begin, I remained standing and thumbed through the craft magazines addressed to Julia strewn across the oak worktables. I made a mental note to ask Phillie to dig into the shop's revenues. The large inventory of woolens, needles, and various carryalls like the monogrammed totes probably cost a good penny to keep in stock.

"Here we go," Julia said, hefting a large tray with a teapot, cups, and a plate of cookies. She placed the tray on the table and pointed at the chocolate-covered biscuit triangles. "Sister Meghan supplies me with the chocolate queen cake. They're baked here in the abbey. Please, sit."

I sat while she dropped an Earl Gray tea bag into one of the cups and poured steaming hot water over it before passing the brew to me.

I took a sip and began with my questions. "Sister said that Alex was a kind soul. What's the significance of her description, if any?" I asked.

Julia sat back in her chair, taking a few moments before she said, "I can see why she'd describe him that way. He absolutely loved nature and the beauty of this Connemara landscape. However, if he thought someone was destroying the environment, he quickly turned from Dr. Jekyll to Mr. Hyde."

"Have there been issues with the environment? Has he taken on any cases that might have made someone angry about his looking into things?"

"Not that I know of. He never discussed his litigation cases with me. He prided himself on his oath and client privilege. But getting back to his love of nature, he served on the abbey's Conservation Foundation." Julia paused to bite into one of the queen cakes. "Sister Meghan presides over the board."

"Hmm, she seems to have a hand in everything around here, doesn't she?"

Julia laughed. "I'm guessing you might have come under the scrutiny of her piercing blue eyes?"

"She definitely packs a wicked scowl for a diminutive nun," I replied, thinking of how Sister Meghan's eyes never left mine when she'd lectured me. "By the way, I noticed yoga pants and mud on the hem of her habit. Is it customary for the sisters to wear yoga pants?"

Julia nodded. "She inspects the scenic trails every day as part of her dedication to the abbey's preservation role." Julia smiled. "I wouldn't be surprised if she meditates outside in one of nature's nooks and crannies. 'Prayer and nature are prime ingredients of the spiritual life' is what she used to tell us children growing up in the abbey."

Sister Meghan walked the paths. I hoped the police had confirmed her whereabouts the day of Alex's murder, making a mental note to check with O'Shea. I also added the foundation members to my interview list.

"Interesting that you mention the local conservation efforts.

I found a dead bird yesterday when I visited the murder site. I couldn't find a nest, though."

Julia rubbed her hands together and dusted crumbs off her lap. "You visited the site. I wasn't sure you would. I saw you head over to the abbey after you left here." Julia blinked. "I don't think I can ever go back there again. What a sacrilege. To murder someone in the most sacred places or anywhere in Connemara."

I didn't disagree, but then murder is always a desecration —anywhere.

Julia continued, "I wonder if you found a songbird. Alex was quite focused on nurturing the region's bird life. You'll have to visit our home." Julia paused and then said, "I guess my home now. The back lawn is filled with birdhouses, and the bird song is quite beautiful—enchanting, really." Julia's voice cracked on her last words, and her eyes filled with tears. "I may not have had romantic feelings toward Alex anymore, but I loved him as a human being. How could I not?" She rose and reached for a tissue box near the register. "This is all so upsetting," she sobbed, wiping her face. "Do you have any more questions? I want to go home."

"We should continue. Time is not on your side, Julia. The sooner I know about Alex and potential motives for his murder, the sooner I can help you."

Julia sighed and replied, "I just can't handle this. I have to make arrangements for Alex's burial—whenever that will be, and heaven knows when the garda will arrive at my door to whisk me away. Please talk to the other members of the guild. They can tell you more about Alex."

"Let me help you, Julia," I said, picking up the tea tray and carrying it behind the screen where a mini-refrigerator and sink filled the tightly arranged kitchen. I emptied the cups, placed them in the sink, found some Saran Wrap for the leftover biscuits, and wiped down the counter. When I turned to leave, I noticed the needles thrown into the garbage receptacle.

"Do you recycle in the village?" I asked, returning to the table where Julia stood, tidying up the magazines.

"Sure do. Why do you ask?"

"There are needles for knitting in the trash. Aren't they constructed with aluminum or steel? The needles should be in a separate recycle container, right?" My thoughts went to Castlebar, where the town required separate garbage and recycling containers.

Julia shook her head. "That's funny. How'd they get there?" She moved behind the screen and emerged with a set of long, narrow, circular needles in her hand. "I can't believe someone in the guild threw these into the garbage. I'll have to say something when we meet again." She took the paper towel she held in her other hand and wiped whatever liquids had been in the trash off the needles. "These are still perfectly good," she declared, placing them on the table.

"What's the name of the pub where Todd hangs out?" I asked, pulling my cell phone from its holster and looking at the time. I wanted to get home to call the Consulting Detective.

Julia wrinkled her brow and bit her top lip. "Are you planning to interview people at the pub? I don't think that's a good idea. The locals aren't friendly toward strangers, especially when the stranger is asking questions. It would be better if you met people here."

I thought about Brendan, who said Julia and Alex often fought at the pub. Was that behind Julia's desire to stay away from the pub?

"Julia, you asked me to dig into what might be the motive for Alex's murder. I will ask questions, and hopefully, one of the answers will lead to why someone harmed a 'gentle soul of a man' as Sister Meghan described your husband."

I didn't wait for Julia's answer; I hefted my knapsack and

headed for the door. "It's up to you whether you want to be there. But either way, I'll return this evening."

~

BACK IN FRENCH HILL, THE LANDLINE'S MESSAGE MACHINE flashed. Three messages. The first one was from Phillie. "Hi, boss, give me a call. I've dug up the info you asked for about the women's shelter."

I punched in the Consulting Detective's number. "Consulting Detective," Ellie's voice announced.

"It's Star, Ellie. Let me speak with Phillie first, and then I'll come back to you."

"Sure, hang on while I transfer you."

"That didn't take long. I left that message a few minutes ago."

"I just got home. Go ahead. What have you got?" I grabbed my Mead composition notebook, ready to take notes.

"Information is sparse, but I think you'll like what I found. Here goes. The abbey provided shelter for battered women and children during the 1970s. I came across an old clipping from a local newspaper about the abbey providing stop-gap measures for abused women who didn't qualify for the niche social services offered by the government."

Phillie's words made sense. The abbey had taken in orphans. Why not take in women and children in need of protection from violent abuse? "When did the abbey stop providing shelter?"

"Sometime in the 2000s. The government-funded social services had stepped up, so the sisters began investing their efforts in tourism. A major government grant provided the money to revitalize the Walled Serenity Garden. That's all I have, boss. As is the case with most shelters, names of women seeking protection would have been anonymous."

The abbey may no longer offer respite services, but in my mind, Sister Meghan was hiding something. What if she were still helping women but not reporting it to anyone? Maybe I was way off base, thinking the mysterious woman was my mother. I've been wrong before—often. What if my questions and snooping around endangered someone who sought protection from violence?

"Thanks, Phillie. Please email a summary of what you have, and here's another project for you."

"I'm ready."

"Dig into a business in Letterbrack called Connemara Crafters. See what you can learn about management, liens, revenues, etc. I don't know if an Irish Better Business organization exists, but if so, check for any complaints. Finally, conduct a search about a lawyer in Letterbrack who was named Alex Quinn."

"Easy peasy, boss. You said 'was.' Is this Alex guy the murder victim?"

"Yes. Julia is his wife and prime suspect. I'm working with her. Thanks, Phillie. You can put Ellie back on."

"Did you get to Jim Hipple?" Ellie asked as soon as she came on the line.

"Yes, and there are no worries, Ellie. He had appendicitis and was laid up for a while. He just didn't want people to know."

"What? Why on earth wouldn't he have told us? I like to think we're among his best friends. Ralph's just been hanging around the house in between job interviews. If we had known, he could have done something useful and helped Jim out while he was recuperating."

"Ellie, calm down. Jim explained he didn't want anyone to think he might not be as fast on his feet as he used to be. He promised to visit you and Phillie in the next few days."

"Oh, good." Ellie's voice quietened. "I'll bake one of my pumpkin breads and send it home with him."

"Make sure Skipper's in his cross pen when Jim arrives. I imagine he'll be pretty sore for a while. You know how much that Schipperke loves him. The last thing Jim needs is to have a ball of fur launched at him."

"I hope things get back to normal soon. We've just gotten a few requests for services. Do you think you can take a look at them?"

"Of course. Email the specifications and Ellie, I promise things won't always be like this. If whatever Evelyn shares with me doesn't lead me to my mother, I'm ready to concede I may never find her."

"Oh, Star. No."

"I don't want you and Phillie worrying. I'm committed to you and always will be. You're my family," I said, also thinking of Georgina, Marcella, and Lorcan on this side of the Atlantic. I didn't know how I'd manage to embrace my extended universe of friends, but I vowed to find a way.

"You know how we feel about you. I'll get this information to you ASAP; if you agree to take the cases, I'll have the contracts sent to them for review and signature."

"Okay, we'll talk soon," I said and ended the call. The next two messages were from local businesses selling lawn and garden services. Finally, I dialed the number O'Shea had scribbled on a piece of paper when he'd visited.

"O'Shea," he said, picking up on the first ring.

"We need to talk. I have questions. You better have answers."

"Understandable, but not in Castlebar or your cottage. Can you meet me in Westport at Curry's Bakery?"

"I know the place, but doesn't it close at two p.m.?"

"Sorry, how about at the Aldi in Westport? There's a coffee bar, and they'll be open for sure."

I paused for a moment, contemplating the fact that O'Shea had used the word *sorry* out loud. He must be desperate. "Give me forty-five minutes," I said, glancing at the time on my iPhone.

"Thank you." O'Shea's voice softened, sounding relieved.

"Don't thank me yet. This entire investigation isn't sitting right with me," I replied.

"I know. I'll see you there."

We ended the call, and finally, I dialed Lorcan's number, which went directly to voice mail—again. I reholstered my phone, trudged into the kitchen, and stared out at the horses grazing in the field behind the cottage. Finally, I yanked the phone out of the holster, swallowed my pride, and dialed.

"Marcella, here."

"It's Star. How are you?"

"As well as I can be, seeing my son has left the country again."

Heart pounding, stomach knotting, and phone-clenching bodily reactions cascaded through me along with a rush of feelings—sadness and abandonment.

"Oh, Marcella, I'm sorry," I said.

"Well, my dear, he was called back to the wind project in Wyoming. But in my opinion, he might not have left this soon after his return if he wasn't angry. In fact, I've never seen him so emotional."

I didn't want to ask, but I knew I had to. "Was it a work issue? He's mentioned how involved he's been in solving the wind turbine problem."

"No." Marcella's voice rang stridently in my ears. "The problem is much closer to home. He's in love with you, Star. He hasn't said so in words, but I can see it, and you, I don't know what to say to you." Her voice quieted, and then she said, "He was hurt and disappointed when you refused his request to lend O'Shea a hand. Lorcan has given up all hope of you ever reciprocating his respect."

At that moment, my emotions got away from me. Tears trickled down my cheeks, and my chest felt like a deep crater had opened.

"Star, are you there?"

I took a deep breath. "Yes, I'm sorry."

"Sorry won't cut it anymore. Since the first time I met you, I've admired your strength and independence. I know that underneath the hard-shelled veneer, you're hiding hurt and vulnerability. But in my opinion, it's time to allow yourself to love and be loved. I love you, Star. Georgina loves you, and my son loves you. A word of advice, if I may...."

"Yes."

"The next time you hear Lorcan's voice. Listen. Listen to him with your heart, and don't let him go again." Marcella's voice cracked on those last words. "I have a fundraising event I'm planning for the Castlebar Library. I need to pop off this call. Say hello to Georgina if you see her before I do."

Marcella ended the call.

I wiped the tears from my face, all the while thinking of her words... a lecture if I were to admit it. I deserved what she'd said. I regretted my last conversation with Lorcan. I wondered how long he'd be away and if I'd ever have a chance to make amends. I rested my hand on the kitchen chair where he usually perched himself, picked up my knapsack, and headed to Westport.

CHAPTER 11

Westport's Aldi store was conveniently located on the outskirts of County Mayo's coastal tourist destination. A left turn at the first traffic light in town deposited me into the store's oversized parking lot. I found O'Shea seated with his back to the entrance at the furthest corner of the coffee shop.

"You have a lot of explaining to do," I said, hanging my knapsack on the back of a chair. O'Shea didn't answer immediately, but the scar on his face deepened, telling me all I needed to know. "Don't be angry with me, O'Shea. You asked me for my help."

He shrugged and nodded in agreement. "I know. I can't ask my partner, Keenan, to put his career on the line for me. You're the only person I can turn to for help," he said, picking up a teaspoon and tapping it on the table.

I'd never seen this side of O'Shea before. The man sitting across from me radiated fear and doubt in contrast to his usual self-assured behavior.

"Have you shared with your commander or whatever the title is in Ireland that you've invited a civilian into the investigation?"

"No. I haven't told him I've asked the American amateur sleuth, Star O'Brien, to do what I cannot do."

"But you did tell him about your relationship with Julia, right?"

O'Shea nodded. "I've communicated up the chain regarding my relationship with the victim's wife. I promised not to have any direct involvement with Julia or the case." O'Shea paused and then asked, "How is Julia holding up?"

"You don't know?" I asked.

"No, we haven't spoken."

"Why didn't you tell me upfront about your relationship with Julia?" I continued with my questions, leaning back in the chair to get a better view of O'Shea's reaction.

O'Shea shook his head. "Fear, confusion. For goodness' sake, I've never been this close to a suspected killer in my life. I didn't know how to handle this. I love Julia, and at the same time, I mustn't allow feelings to overshadow judgment."

I silently empathized with O'Shea. The losses I've suffered are the reasons I work hard at not getting involved.

"If I'm going to help you, you have to be completely honest with me."

"Okay."

"First, where were you when Julia phoned about Alex?" I asked, pulling my Mead notebook from the knapsack and glancing at the notes I'd already written.

O'Shea dropped the teaspoon onto the table and fidgeted in his chair. "Why does that matter?"

My mind raced with the sheer stupidity of O'Shea's question. "You're in a relationship with Julia, and you happened to be in the vicinity when Alex's body was discovered. This makes you a suspect. Are you so egocentric you believe the police will give you a pass?"

O'Shea raised his hands and held both sides of his head.

"This whole thing is a bloody nightmare. I called the crime in, and I have an alibi."

"So, you can prove your whereabouts," I stated.

"Yes, I had an appointment for service on my car. The receipt is timestamped, as is another receipt from a local coffee shop." There was a long silence, and then O'Shea said, "At the moment, my boss is giving me leeway."

"Oh, yeah, right. Another case where the police are standing back and not ferreting out the details." I pulled my phone from its holster and placed it on the table in front of me. "Let's start at the beginning. What were you doing in Letterbrack that morning?"

"Julia and I usually meet up in that meadow every Wednesday." O'Shea took a deep breath. "Most times, we'd go for a walk through the woods. Julia would bring a sandwich or such from the abbey's restaurant. We'd talk and enjoy the quiet beauty."

"Where was Julia when you arrived? And why was her husband there?"

"I don't know why Alex ended up in that meadow. Julia and I have been careful, especially since they were in the middle of a divorce. Alex was trying to catch Julia cheating with another man—something he could use against her in the divorce settlement." O'Shea stopped speaking.

"I wonder if he was having Julia watched," I said, thinking of Jim Hipple's private investigation business. He was often called upon to track someone's movements related to digging up dirt on a spouse. "You haven't told me everything. Was Julia there?"

O'Shea turned his head to look at the sound created by two women who sat at the table behind him. He leaned in over the table. "Not when I arrived."

"Her husband just happened to be in the place where you

and Julia usually meet. What did Julia say about this unusual coincidence?"

"I haven't discussed Alex's murder with her. When she got to the clearing, she rang me." O'Shea shook his head. "I was delayed getting to Letterbrack, but I was nearby. I told her not to touch anything and return to her shop. When I arrived, I examined the body, determined life-saving assistance was useless, and then I got out of there as fast as I could."

"What happened next?'

I drove to Leenaun, rang the local garda station, and continued onto Castlebar, where I met with my superintendent."

"Why not report the body when you found Alex? Why drive to a neighboring village when you could have made a call from your car?"

O'Shea huffed out a sigh. "I panicked. The woman I love had just found her dead husband where she and I had our trysts. I wanted to get away from the scene before I made my report. I knew I hadn't murdered the man, and I believed Julia hadn't either."

"Gee, O'Shea. Are you sure you're a detective?" I asked, not quite believing this was the same man who'd been an obnoxious oppositional force against me in the past. "Why make an anonymous tip if you planned to tell your supervisor right away? I think you're hiding something, or you're leaving things out."

"Neither," O'Shea insisted, his scar deepening as his face flushed crimson. "I've already said. I wanted to get as far away from the crime scene as possible. After I reported the incident, I went directly to Castlebar and met with my superintendent. After that, I texted Julia and asked her to cooperate with you."

"So, you told Julia about me before you asked for my help? That was a bold move on your part, O'Shea, especially when you weren't sure I'd want to get involved."

"That's why I contacted Lorcan. He promised to talk with you on my behalf."

I wondered if Lorcan would have interceded if he'd known the extent of O'Shea's involvement. "Lorcan is your friend. Did you lie to him?"

"I told him everything. He wasn't thrilled, but he agreed to speak to you." O'Shea glanced everywhere except at me. "I asked him not to tell you about my relationship with Julia until I did."

I touched my phone, wishing with all my heart Lorcan's name would pop up on the display. I wanted to talk to him. No, I admitted to myself, I *needed* to talk to him.

"You believe Julia is innocent. Who, then, wanted Alex dead?" I asked, leaning closer to the table.

"I don't know. I keep thinking it has something to do with his legal cases. He mostly specializes in corporate and human resource litigation cases. But who in Letterbrack would be motivated to kill over the kind of case that usually settles before litigation?" O'Shea took a sip of what, by that moment, must be an ice-cold tea from his cup. "Whoever did this, they were angry." O'Shea placed the cup down on the table. "You wouldn't normally be privy to what I'm about to tell you, but it was a nasty attack. The medical examiner believes someone pierced his eye with a sharp instrument." O'Shea closed his eyes as if to blot out what he had seen.

"Has the weapon been found?"

"Not yet. I didn't come across anything that might have inflicted what I witnessed." O'Shea looked down at the table. "Any kind of a common tool like a screwdriver or even a garden tool like an asparagus knife might have been used. The Connemara region is a big farming and tourist area." The scar on O'Shea's cheek deepened. "The poor man was laid out there in the middle of a grassy meadow with bird song in the air around him."

"What about a thin gauge knitting needle?" I asked, thinking of the needle I had found in the trash at Julia's shop.

O'Shea opened his eyes and nodded. "Yeah, the medical examiner said the instrument was extremely narrow, which knocks down my asparagus knife theory. I hate to say it, but Julia's shop sells a healthy number of different knitting and crochet needles. The instrument was long enough to damage the brain. The poor bloke died instantly."

Anger and murder often go hand in hand. I've found in my missing persons cases that anger builds over time if family members have been affected by the missing person's absence. But this didn't sound like that kind of case. Although I've been called upon several times to get involved in investigations I wouldn't usually get tangled up with, none had turned out to be as gruesome as this one sounded.

"That's it? With all your training, you didn't notice anything else out of the ordinary?" I asked.

"No, and that's what's so weird. I didn't find any signs of a struggle or any other evidence of a crime. Just a body that seemingly fell from a stab wound. It doesn't make sense," O'Shea replied, squirming in his seat.

"Has the medical examiner determined the time of death?" I asked.

"Not yet, but I estimate Alex was killed sometime between eleven a.m. and two p.m. His body was warm, and rigor hadn't set in, so I'd say not long before Julia discovered him." O'Shea sighed. "Are you going to work with me or not?"

"When I walked the meadow, I found a baby songbird just a few feet into the forest that borders the meadow. Julia said Alex was on the nature conservation board."

O'Shea nodded. "Yeah, he was very much into Connemara's natural beauty and was especially interested in birding. But I don't think a dead bird is connected to his murder, and he definitely wouldn't have done anything to cause a bird to fall from a nest."

"Well, I'll have to talk to someone at the foundation. Maybe the group made some land developer angry."

O'Shea's face relaxed. "So, you will work with me."

"What do you know about the abbey?"

"It's a huge tourist attraction, especially the Walled Serenity Garden. The government invested in refurbishing the garden several years ago and then opened it to the public." O'Shea's face paled. "If a tourist did this, I don't have a prayer in heaven of clearing Julia's name."

"The head nun, Sister Meghan, didn't seem all too happy to have me snooping around. She warned me not to get the abbey involved."

"Aye, she may not cooperate with you. But she will respond to whichever detective is assigned to the case." O'Shea paused and then continued, "You haven't answered my question. Will you help me?"

"Yes, but not because I've suddenly taken a liking to you, O'Shea. I *like* Julia. We have a lot in common. Besides, I regret not agreeing to Lorcan's request in the first place."

"I was disappointed when Lorcan told me you said no," O'Shea replied. His eyes sought mine. "Why'd you change your mind? You said you like Julia, but you hadn't met her until you went to Letterbrack."

"Aunt Georgina intervened on Lorcan's behalf and convinced me to at least talk to Julia." I didn't mention my personal reason for wanting to spend time in Letterbrack—the woman I'd seen slip into the garden.

O'Shea leaned back in his chair. "Georgina. Aye, of course. She's been an influence on all our lives since Dylan, Lorcan, and I were young lads."

I'd forgotten how far back Lorcan's relationship went with

O'Shea, which made me feel even worse about turning down Lorcan's request.

O'Shea pushed his cup away and got to his feet. "Okay, I'll talk to my supervisor, and I promise I'll share whatever information I can. To a limit," he warned before finishing the conversation with, "Ring me when or if you find anything suspicious, and Miss O'Brien, thank you. I'll be in touch when I hear anything more about the weapon."

I remained behind, making notes in my Mead composition book about our conversation. My list of potential suspects included O'Shea, Julia, and Sister Meghan. The mysterious woman was number four. Todd was number five. The list was small, but I expected to add more names after I'd visited the local pub. O'Shea and Julia were the headliners. Too often, a love triangle resulted in one of the three people involved eliminating the opponent.

I didn't know yet if that was the issue in this case. But the polished, blue-suited detective I'd usually dealt with in the past seemed to have undergone a transformation. I had no doubt he'd hide information that would make Julia look guilty. Either he was desperately in love, or he was protecting a murderer. I wasn't sure he'd share every tidbit of information he gleaned from the police about the case. But I knew him well enough from having to deal with him in the past that he'd come through in the end. As I rose from the table, my phone's screen displayed Evelyn's name. My thumb pressed the green button. "You're back. When can we meet?"

"I'll be passing the storage facility on my way home from Dublin. I can meet you there."

"Absolutely," I said, slinging my knapsack over my arm. "Where?"

"Bohola, the village isn't far beyond Turlough. On the N5. Do you need directions to the storage company?"

"No, I'll find the place. I'm in Westport. About forty-five minutes away."

"That works for me. I'll probably get there before you. See you then, Star."

As I drove back toward Castlebar, I considered what O'Shea had and hadn't told me. When I first arrived in Ireland, I never expected to find myself enmeshed in a series of murder mysteries, but Dylan's aunt, Georgina Hill, had pressured me to use my information broker skills to clear the victims' reputations.

O'Shea and his partner had been the lead detectives in each of those cases. From the first time we'd met, he'd made his opinion clear. I was an American butting her nose into places I didn't belong. But I'd persisted because, as O'Shea had reminded me, I was a voice for the dead, the missing, and the lost.

I'd come to Ireland to claim my inheritance and to scour Ireland from end to end in the search for my mother. Much had happened since my first arrival in French Hill. I'd met Aunt Georgina, Lady Marcella McHale, and Lorcan. I'd never expected to learn that I had a half-sister. I knew my father's name. My universe of friends and family kept expanding.

THE TRAFFIC CIRCLE LEADING FROM CASTLEBAR ONTO THE Turlough Road was jam-packed with end-of-work-day traffic. While I awaited my turn to drive around the circle, I tuned the car radio to MidWest's station. Alex's murder was mentioned with a note that the Letterbrack garda unit was handling the investigation. The investigation was out of County Mayo's jurisdiction. I wondered if that would have been the case if O'Shea wasn't involved with Julia. Maybe the higher-ups continued to shield him. I expected I'd know soon enough when I got under the nose of the detective in charge of the case.

The horn blast behind me jolted me out of my thoughts. I stepped on the gas pedal and navigated around the circle onto the N5. When I passed by the entrance to the Turlough Museum, I remembered the day Lorcan had introduced me to Evelyn at Rooster's. I'd smiled up into his eyes and knew then that I had more than friendship feelings for him. I only hoped I'd have another chance to show him I'd changed. Meanwhile, I drove toward Bohola and whatever information awaited me there regarding my mother.

CHAPTER 12

A few miles past Turlough Village, I spotted a smoke plume rising into the air. As I neared Bohola, the column of smoke became wider. I sped up when the firetrucks came into view, but the traffic-calming speed bumps on the outskirts of the village hampered my progress. Finally, I pulled onto the road margin, turned off my car, and ran toward the Extra Space Storage facility sign where the fire trucks were pulling away. *Oh, no*, I said to myself, picking up the pace. I looked around for Evelyn's car and then realized I didn't know the make or model. A group of people congregated outside the facility's visitor office. Evelyn wasn't among them.

A young woman wearing a name tag, identifying her as the facility manager, stepped out of the office as I approached and said, "If you've come to rent a unit. I'm afraid you'll have to wait. I've got to update my regional manager about this incident."

"What happened?" I asked.

"Someone's container had a wee fire." The young woman shook her head and cast a glance at the people milling around. "Unfortunately, some clients are pack rats. A fire starts easily when the stored materials probably date to the 1600s. I've been telling the head office we need to install more smoke detectors and fire sprinkler systems."

"Do you know who owns the unit that was damaged?" I still didn't see Evelyn. *Please, don't let the damaged unit be hers*, I said to myself.

"The owner of the scorched unit isn't here."

"I'm planning to meet one of your clients, Evelyn Cosgrove. Has she arrived? Was anyone inside the units when the fire broke out?"

"I'm the one who called the fire brigade," a frail-looking man with thin wisps of hair said. "I'm sure the units were empty. The brigade required the manager here to open all the doors just to be certain."

"Everyone is supposed to log in here at the office before heading back outside and walking or driving to their storage unit," the manager said.

"Can you check the sign-in sheet?" I asked.

The young woman stepped back into the office, pulled a binder from the countertop, walked back outside, and opened the three-ring notebook. Shaking her head, she said, "I don't see the name of the person you're asking about in the log."

I breathed a sigh of relief just as a compact Saab drove into the parking area. The vehicle had barely stopped when Evelyn jolted out.

"Star, is everything all right? I'm sorry I'm late." Evelyn's eyes swept the crowd and the open roll-up, garage-type doors beyond the iron security gates. "Why are all the storage doors open?"

"There's been a fire. Which one is yours?" I asked.

"Oh, no." Evelyn turned to the manager. "Please open the gate. I'd like to check on mine."

"I think the unit adjacent to your space is where the fire occurred. I have to call headquarters and get operational approval to open things up. Just give me a few moments."

The manager walked into the visitor's office. I watched her pick up a phone and begin a discussion. Within minutes, she hung up and walked over to her computer. When the gate swung open, a collective sigh of relief passed over the group.

Evelyn broke into a run. I followed her. The air stank with smoke, and bits of papery ash swirled around the ground, briefly rising before falling again. Finally, Evelyn stopped in front of the unit where the fire had occurred. I felt my heart rise and fall like the bits of ash swirling up and down above the macadamed ground. I also felt my suspicions grow about the convenience of a fire close to Evelyn's unit on the day I was set to visit, but I pushed the thought to the back of my mind for the moment.

"Thank God, my unit is okay," she said, pointing to the adjacent cell.

I walked toward the space, taking a look inside. The room was crammed with vintage furniture, cardboard boxes, and tables stacked high with papers. Framed paintings lay along one of the side walls.

I pointed to the pictures. "He liked paintings."

"Yes, most of them are of the Atlantic Ocean looking out toward America. I never understood why he liked the image, but in retrospect, I think he may have been thinking about your mother. And wondering...." Evelyn's voice trailed off.

My stomach twinged, and my heart sank. Why hadn't I known my father still walked this planet? Why hadn't my mother ever told me his name?

"If you like, why don't you look through the paintings? I don't have room for them at my place, and at some point, I plan to auction off the furniture and other household decorations. I held off while searching for Maggie O'Malley, but that's no longer necessary." Evelyn smiled.

"I'd like that, but first, let's look at the letter you mentioned." A frown crossed her face when she pulled open a metal cabinet and rooted around in a bunch of folders. "I thought I put the letter in here," she mumbled.

I grasped the phone clipped onto my jeans. "Where is it?" I asked, stepping closer to her side.

"Wait." Evelyn moved farther into the space toward a mahogany table. She slid the top aside to reveal a drawer. Inside, I could see a stack of letters. "Here it is," she said, pulling a plastic letter protector from the pile. "Funny, I don't remember putting the letter in here with his business correspondence." She handed a sheet of paper, yellow with age, to me.

My hand shook as I reached for the delicate item. The first thing I noticed was the browned and crinkly edge, as if the paper were hundreds of years old. I assumed the paper was almost as old as the number of years my mother was missing. When I unfolded the letter, I realized the reason for the missive's antique look. The letter was dated 1986—the same year my mother disappeared.

"Was there an envelope?" I asked, although I already knew the answer. If Evelyn had an envelope with a return address, the years of searching would have ended long ago.

Evelyn shook her head. "No, I hunted through every bit of his belongings for any envelope or scrap of paper that might have an address on it but didn't find anything. Look, I'm going to step outside for a few minutes. I've read the letter. You might want privacy."

I nodded, and because, at that moment, I couldn't trust my emotions, I sat down on one of the armchairs that didn't have belongings piled on the cushion.

"Call out for me when you're ready," Evelyn said. She touched my shoulder and walked out of the unit.

I lowered my eyes and read the script.

My Dearest Mícheál,

By now, you know I've left my beloved Dooega and Achill.
Leaving you and all our love behind was the saddest day of
my life. But I left with something even more precious than
the love we shared. Mícheál, I'm pregnant with the sweet
expression of our love. I couldn't tell you because I knew
you'd want to make things right, and I can't let you do that.
You deserve to go to university as you planned and become
the successful mathematician that I know you will be. Also,
my dearest, I couldn't face the disgrace and whispers the
island people would throw around when they learned I was
carrying a child. So, I've decided to go to New York, where I
will stay in a community home for pregnant women until the
baby is born, and then I will find work. I want you to know I
will always love you, and I will love our innocent child even
more. Don't be afraid for me. I will do the best I can, and
perhaps someday we'll be together if only to say hello to each
other, and so you can smile upon our child and say, "I am
your father."
Until then, be brave, go to university, and have a wonderful
life knowing that whatever happens, you are loved. Your
Maggie forever.

I set the letter aside in case the tears streaming down my
face damaged or erased the faded blue ink. For once in my life,
I didn't control the sobs racking through my body. My poor
mother. How scared she must have been leaving the only place
and people she'd ever known, and, in her leaving, she'd
demonstrated her deep love, courage, and strength.

I'd spent most of my adult years searching for my mother.
I'd found part of her in this letter where she poured her heart
out to my father. Deep in my soul, I'd always known that she'd
never abandon me. If I never found her, at least I'd be
comforted by the words she'd written. I reached for the letter
again, gently folded it back into the pocket protector, and

stored it in my knapsack. I planned to put the letter with the Bible my mother had left behind when she'd disappeared. I'd always wondered why the back pages where births, deaths, and marriages would have been listed were ripped out. I had one answer to my questions. She'd let him know about me but not where to find me. Had my mother wanted to hide something? My questions regarding her disappearance continued to loom large in my life.

Finally, I stood, took a deep breath, and walked over to the stack of paintings. One by one, I disassembled the pile until I came to an oil depicting Achill Island's Keem Bay. In the picture, the bay opened up to the Atlantic Ocean beneath a blue sky. I put the painting aside and reassembled the stack. Then, I swung my knapsack over my shoulder, picked up the Keem Bay painting, and emerged into the daylight.

Evelyn stood with her back to me, her cell phone pressed to her ear.

"I'm ready."

When she heard my words, Evelyn ended the call, approached me, and tried to wrap her arms around me. But when she couldn't get past my knapsack and the painting, she patted me on the arm.

"I'm sorry you had to read that letter. In a different time, under different circumstances, your mother might have been able to stay with my father. But then, I might not have been born." Evelyn dropped her hands and stepped back. Her hazel eyes held mine. "We have a lot of time to make up for. We may have different mothers, but we are our father's legacy. Let this be a new chapter in our lives."

My heart twinged at her words. I nodded, realizing for the first time in such a long time that I actually had a blood relative in my life—a sister. I vowed to cherish our relationship for whatever remaining time I had left in Ireland before I returned to the States.

"Do you fancy going to Costa Coffee in Castlebar?" Evelyn asked. "Although I know it will be a peppermint tea for you, my dear sister."

I nodded and said, "I know where the place is. I'll follow in my car."

Evelyn closed the storage unit door and walked to her car. I placed the painting on my back seat, and we headed to Castlebar.

❧

WHEN WE ENTERED COSTA COFFEE, EVELYN TOOK MY KNAPSACK and went to find a table while I placed our beverage order: an herbal tea for me and black coffee for Evelyn. I asked the person behind the counter to add brown scones with butter and blackberry jam to the tray, as well.

"I have some news," Evelyn said once we were seated and finished eating. "I'm returning to London tomorrow. The crew has found a huge cache of artifacts at the Charterhouse Square dig site."

"Oh, I hoped we'd get to spend more time together," I said, not hiding my disappointment. Here I was, the fiercely independent Star O'Brien, just getting used to the idea that I had a sister, and said sister was about to put some distance between us.

"I know, but I'm the dig director. Besides, whenever I'm in London, I'm on the lookout for information regarding what happened to my husband." Evelyn pushed her coffee mug away and sighed. "We were happy, and then one evening, I arrived home to find the place empty."

Phillie had dug up background research on Evelyn's husband, an investigative journalist. His disappearance remained unsolved.

"I wish I could help you," I replied, wondering why the

people in our lives, my mom and Evelyn's husband, just seemed to disappear without a word.

"I know, Star, but I won't be gone long. Just a few weeks, and then I'm back to Dublin for a conference with Dr. O'Dowd. You and I will meet up then. In the meantime, here are the keys to the storage facility, just in case you want to look through everything again."

I didn't think I could face the reminders that my father had been alive for many of my adult years. I took the keys and buried them in my knapsack.

CHAPTER 13

Georgina arrived at French Hill Cottage shortly before 7:30 p.m. on Friday evening. I was still getting dressed when I heard her call out my name from the kitchen. "Star, hurry up, loveen. If we don't get going soon, the pub will be chockablock with locals. We may not be able to get in."

I took one last look at my short-cropped ebony hair, picked up my knapsack, and walked through the living room into the kitchen. "Oh, my, you look different," I said when I took stock of her attire for the evening. In a departure from her usual green and gold wrap dresses and complementing scarves, she wore pressed blue jeans with a crisp white linen sonnet blouse. The cloth-covered buttons ended in a V-neck collar, and tiered ruffled sleeve cuffs rose above a sporty watch. Her sneakers were sage green.

"I guess we've never gone to a hooley together." Georgina tilted her head, assessing my black jeans, black T-shirt, and black high tops. "What are you planning? A break-in?" She laughed. "Come on, Star. Let's get going."

We didn't speak much during the drive from Castlebar to Letterbrack, twilight on the narrow, twisting N59 requiring all my attention. When we arrived in the village, Main Street was lined with parked cars.

"There's a parking lot behind the local church." Georgina pointed to a narrow lane. "Turn down here. We'll park the car and walk to the pub. Thank goodness, it's a beautiful evening."

The Charlotte Evans Pub, named for its owner, was between Julia's shop and a bakery. Tables and chairs lined the sidewalk in front of the pub. Couples and groups of young people sat outside, holding wine glasses and beer mugs. Music emanated from within. I pushed the door open, held it for Georgina, and surveyed the room, searching for Julia. I finally spotted her at a table with Nigel and several familiar faces from her shop. I tapped Georgina on the elbow and directed her to join the group at the table. Meanwhile, I approached the bar and patiently propelled my body through the crowd until I reached the woman serving up the beverages. I'd already perused the pub's website and recognized the owner's face immediately.

"What can I do you for, love?" she shouted.

"A diet ginger ale for me and a white wine for my companion." I indicated the table where Georgina had taken a seat, which I could still see despite the influx of people coming through the pub door.

"Coming right up, but if I were you"—Charlotte nodded in Julia's direction—"I'd keep my eyes on my drink. You're keeping company with a murderess."

"That's interesting. I'd like to speak with you about your opinion." I pulled a Consulting Detective business card from my jeans pocket.

Charlotte picked up the card and flicked it onto a pile of cards on the counter behind her. "Sure, anything I can do to bring justice for Alex. Give me about fifteen minutes. My relief bartender will be here shortly. I'll meet you outside." Then, she planted the drinks in front of me and demanded ten euros.

I complied, picked up the glasses, and plowed my way through the crowd to the table. I handed the wine glass to Georgina and held onto my soda until I'd positioned myself on the only empty chair. At that moment, I spotted Rita Barrett, the other guild member, come through the pub door. Getting to my feet, I waved, indicating my chair, but Rita scowled, turned abruptly, and left the pub. Once more, I sat down in time to hear Nigel's remarks directed to me.

"Julia tells us that you inherited a cottage in Ireland," Nigel stated, fixing his gaze on me. "Property ownership must be nice."

I sipped my ginger ale, surveying him over the rim of the glass. I hadn't expected to be interrogated. "Yes, I did," I said without elaborating. "What about you? Do you live near the village?"

"I'm a member of the tenant class. I rent the flat over Julia's shop."

"So, you have a bird's eye view of comings and goings around the shop area?" I asked.

"I wouldn't say that exactly. I have an easel set up at my window, where I usually sketch and work on my art pieces. I focus on environmental realism in art, so I spend a good amount of time looking out my window when I'm not working outside."

"Connemara certainly seems like a good candidate for your work. Did Alex ever talk to you about it?" I asked, thinking about Sister Meghan's description of Alex as a nature lover.

"Several times, actually. He asked if he could see my portfolio. He was especially interested in my woodland scenes."

"Did he say why?" I asked.

"No, he looked and then said, 'You've got talent, young man.'" Nigel's face paled. "I never thought to ask him about his birding hobby, and I regret that."

"I've been telling Georgina that I'm working on several

textile designs she might want to incorporate into her dresses," Julia commented, changing the subject.

"Why don't you bring the samples to the Golden Thread, and we'll have lunch?" Aunt Georgina said. "Summertime is perfect for bright colors and floral designs."

"Oh, I'm so glad we're talking about work and not what happened to...." The young woman I'd met in Julia's shop, Anne Ford, stopped, covered her mouth with one hand, and shot a wide-eyed look at Julia.

"I'm pleased also," Julia said, raising her glass to the young woman. "I know Star plans to speak with each of you, but for this evening, let's just enjoy each other's company. This terrible event will be righted. How, I don't know, but it will."

For someone who'd just stated she'd rather talk about work, Anne proceeded to ask Julia about the case. "Don't the garda believe you're the murderess?"

"I'm under consideration as a person of interest, but so far, that's all I am," Julia said and then turned to me. "Anne is another talented member of the guild. Her embroidery patterns are carried in arts and crafts shops all over Ireland."

"How do you create your designs?" I asked.

Anne smiled and leaned against Nigel before replying, "I select textured fabric from Julia's shop, and then, using needles and sometimes thin wire, I decorate the cloth with an art design."

"So, if someone purchases your patterns, what do they get?"

"My work comes packaged with thread, hoop, and the material with the art design embedded."

"Where does the thin wire come from?" I asked, thinking about Anne's use of a *thin wire* and O'Shea's report about a sharp implement as the murder weapon.

Anne shook her head at my question. "I have a reel of it in my studio. The do-it-yourself stores carry loads of it. Why do you ask?"

A blast of cold air blew through the pub when the emergency exit door burst open. Todd, the person I'd seen in the abbey's restaurant arguing with an employee, appeared. He stumbled into the room, bouncing against one table after another until he landed at ours.

"You have some nerve appearing in public." He slurred his words, wiping the back of his hand across his mouth.

Everyone's face at the table froze. Julia got to her feet and placed a hand gently on his arm. "Todd, you don't know what you're doing. Have you eaten? Why don't you join us and have a sandwich?" Julia managed to ask before Todd slapped her hand away.

"There's plenty of room. Pull up a chair," Georgina said, glancing at Nigel and Anne.

"Yeah, Todd, come on and join us," Nigel said.

"Oh, right." Todd's upper lip curled as he replied, "The great lady, Julia, taking pity on the out-of-work, fired, drunken, former abbey garden manager. I know what you're all thinking."

I rose and moved next to Julia.

"Who are you?" the man hiccuped.

"I'm a friend of Julia's, and I must ask you to leave."

"Yeah, Julia's got friends in high places, just like that husband of hers. He thought he could just throw me to the curb. But I won't go quietly. He got his comeuppance, and you will too, Miss Julia."

At that moment, several men moved from the bar and surrounded Todd. Charlotte Evans joined them and said, "Arrah, come on, Todd, you've had a few too many. Come on, lad, we'll get you home. You're not going to be happy with yourself in the morning." The men, bouncers, I assumed, strong-armed Todd and escorted him through the front door. Charlotte followed along and then, after a few minutes, returned alone.

When I approached the bar's counter, she waved me away and said, "I'm in no frame of mind to discuss Alex, Julia, or anyone else."

"Does he usually behave this way?" I asked, tilting my head toward the door where Todd had exited.

"He's been out of control recently. Something went down between him and Alex." Charlotte grabbed a cloth and began wiping down the countertop. "I'm sure she's involved," Charlotte continued, casting a glaring look at Julia. "If you want to talk, you'll have to come back when the pub is closed. Probably best to be here at about ten a.m."

"I'll see you then." I rejoined the group at the table, where I posed the same question I'd asked Charlotte. "Does this happen often?"

"He's been under a lot of pressure since he lost his employment. Most people don't know he's a diabetic. Liquor and low blood sugar are not his friends," Julia replied.

"We've all tried to be supportive. Letterbrack is a small community. We've known him for most of our lives," Nigel added.

"I saw him arguing with a female employee at the café. What happened between them? Why did Sister Meghan dismiss him?" I asked, turning to Julia, who'd retaken her seat. "What did Todd mean about being 'thrown to the curb'?"

"I don't think we should discuss Todd here. Conversations like this one are easily misconstrued if someone overhears," Julia added quietly. "I've had enough for this evening. I suggest we all get a good night's rest and reconvene at some point tomorrow. I'll fill you in then, Star." Julia rose and wrapped a shawl around her shoulders.

"I'll walk you to your car," Nigel offered.

"I'm fine, Nigel. Why don't you walk Anne to her car? Good night, all." Julia drifted away from the table and out into the evening. Nigel offered his arm to Anne, who readily accepted. Georgina and I followed them out onto the sidewalk.

The cool, moist air felt wonderful after being inside the pub for two hours. Georgina linked arms with me as we strolled through the streets to the parking lot. "You and I have to do this more often," she commented.

"You know I'm not into pubs and evenings out," I replied, "but I'm glad you were with me."

"Sometimes, you're too serious, Star. I hope at some point your life will be filled with lighthearted fun."

Instead of answering, I picked up the walking pace until we arrived at our car. During the ride home, Georgina brought up the subject that I'd hoped she wouldn't.

"Have you heard from Lorcan since your disagreement?"

"Not a word, and I admit I missed him tonight," I said, remembering the evening we'd visited a pub in the Neale and other companionable rides we'd taken, like in his Piper Cub airplane. I shook my head. "He's such a practical, logical person. I never expected him to react the way he did."

"He's a man, Star, and he's fallen in love with you. Can't you see that?" Georgina's voice sounded edgy.

I gripped the steering wheel as I maneuvered the N59's twists and turns. "Georgina, I'm attracted to him, and that's why I have to stifle my feelings."

"For heaven's sake, woman, what are you talking about?"

I didn't answer Georgina directly. Instead, I said, "You know, settling Dylan's estate and using the time to search for my mother was why I came to Ireland. I've never had any intention to make French Hill my permanent residence. Ellie and Phillie need me back home."

"I know long-distance relationships are difficult, especially one that would span two continents. But that said, I believe Lorcan would understand and accept your commitments to your business and relationships in New Jersey. You might think about giving it a try." Georgina paused and then asked, "What are you afraid of, Star?"

"Hurt, getting hurt again."

"Star, you should know by now that life is full of hurts and disappointments. But life is full of joy and wonder as well. I hope you change your mind about leaving Ireland," Georgina said softly. "Promise me whatever happens, you'll try to find peace for yourself."

I nodded. "I appreciate your advice, Georgina." Wanting to bring the topic to a close, I asked, "Did you hear anything about Alex's murder while I was busy talking to Charlotte Evans?"

"Everyone seems to think the gruesome attack was the work of some deranged tourist hiking the Connemara trails."

"Of course, blame the incident on an outsider, a stranger."

"I don't know, Star. The residents of Letterbrack seem like a close-knit community. I think they'd suspect if they had a murderer in their midst."

"Not necessarily, Georgina. The guilty party's character is often hidden in a web of lies, which the local folks may not recognize." By this time, we'd driven into Castlebar. I glanced at Georgina and said, "Charlotte Evans seems to think Julia is the guilty party."

"Did she say why?"

"No. Todd's entrance caused a distraction. I'll get back to her in the morning. I noticed the guild member Julia had identified as Rita Barrett made a U-turn out of the pub when she spotted me."

"I didn't see Rita. But as I said earlier, the locals are apprehensive of an outsider asking questions. Especially when people are always worried about avoiding the tax man."

"You know that for a fact?" I asked.

"Oh, yes, Julia confided in me that the group has been hiding income, and in Rita's case, from her husband, Brendan, as well."

"But I don't think that's a motive for a gruesome murder, Georgina. Besides, Alex is a corporate attorney, not a tax lawyer. Why would hiding taxable income have anything to do with him?" I said as I turned onto the grass verge near the barn at French Hill Cottage.

"Probably nothing, but as I said, people are suspicious of strangers. Sometimes, where there's one secret, there are others. Maybe while he was pursuing Todd's case, Alex got close to something he normally wouldn't have known about."

I silently agreed with Georgina's comment, remembering how Dylan never mentioned his Irish cottage and family. Some secrets, I have found, live parallel and undiscovered lives. I switched off the car's ignition and asked, "Do you want to come in? There's still some of your brown loaf left."

"I think I'll go straight home. I have a few design pieces sitting in my living room that I want to make sketches of. But I'll ring early in the morning."

Georgina exited from the passenger side of the Renault, unlocked her car door, and sat inside. I stood, watching her drive down Cottage Road until the car's red reflector lights faded away. Outside the cottage, I placed the key into the back door lock and glanced up at Marcella and Lorcan's place located on a rise above French Hill. The cottage once served as the McHale's visitor lodge on Lorcan's hundred-acre estate until Dylan's grandparents purchased the compact residence from the McHale family. I hoped I'd hear from Lorcan soon.

THE FINAL EMBERS OF THE TURF FIRE I'D LIT IN THE LIVING ROOM hearth ebbed slowly. I reread the notes in my Mead composition book and underlined Todd's name. I expected Charlotte Evans could fill in more of the blanks about him. But the motivation for Alex's murder wasn't clear, especially

Georgina's theory regarding tax evasion. Still, the issue required research. Perhaps skilled, artisan creations were more lucrative than I knew. No. I scratched out the words *tax evasion*. I was willing to bet the motive was much more nefarious.

I also made a note to call O'Shea in the morning. I hoped he had more to tell me that might point the way to a suspect. When I got ready for bed and pulled my cell phone from my pants, where it was clipped, my fingers hovered over Lorcan's phone number. But then, I stashed the phone under my pillow and went to bed. Sleep didn't come easy.

CHAPTER 14

After a night of tossing and turning, I slipped out of bed before sunrise, pulled on a pair of sneakers, a sweatshirt, and capris, and headed outside to power walk along Cottage Road. When I returned to the cottage, an hour passed while I processed emails related to Consulting Detective business. Finally finished, I dressed quickly, picked up my knapsack, and left for Letterbrack.

Very little traffic lined the road from Castlebar to my destination, but when I arrived in the tourist town, the streets and parking lots were already packed with buses and cars, which wasn't unusual for Saturday, a typical non-workday. I found a place to park not far from where Georgina and I had deposited the Renault the night before. Then, I walked to Charlotte Evans Pub. Any signs of the crowd from the night before were swept away, debris had been picked up, and chairs were turned over and rested atop the tables.

The pub door was locked, but I rang the doorbell, and a voice shouted, "Just a second." When the door opened, Charlotte appeared.

In contrast to how she'd been attired last night, she wore no makeup, and an elastic band held her hair in a ponytail.

Running shoes, yoga pants, and a zip-up jacket completed her ensemble.

"Good, you're on time," she said in greeting. "I'm about to take my morning jaunt. Walk with me. Our conversation will be more private."

I fell into step beside her as she walked briskly toward the abbey. "So, Julia hired you?"

"No, a friend of hers, Thomas O'Shea, asked me to get involved."

"Hmm, O'Shea. I know him. He's been coming around Julia for years. You'd think the two of them would have been a couple." Charlotte stopped and bent down to retie one of her sneaker laces. "But Julia was too cute for that. She had her sights on one of the richest men in the area. Nothing less would work for her."

"You sound like you don't like Julia. What are you angry about?"

"She stole Alex from me. Years ago, we were sweethearts. But then, she showed up at the abbey, acting like the poor little orphan and looking for pity from everyone. She captured Alex's attention, and he never looked at me again."

"I'm sorry. First love is sweet love, I know. But whatever chemistry you and Quinn had must have been years ago. Did you ever try to mend the relationship and be friends?"

Charlotte slowed her pace. "Of course I did. I'm not a lovesick adolescent anymore. He made his choice, and I respected him for it. But Julia lost interest in him."

"What makes you believe that?"

"I've heard the two of them in the pub, arguing, and that O'Shea character started coming around more often. Oh, he and Julia didn't think anyone noticed them. But I often saw Julia sneaking off into the woods when Alex was in his office," Charlotte said, raising one side of her mouth in a smirk.

"Oh, what do you mean by often?" I asked, thinking this was an important data point.

"Just about every week, always on a Wednesday. You'd think Julia and her friend would have been more discreet."

"You saw her every Wednesday. At any particular time?" I asked.

"She closed up her shop each week at half one, and then she'd run over to the café before walking toward the woods."

"What about last Wednesday? The day Alex was murdered."

"I've already told the garda. I saw Julia heading into the woods that day."

"What time was that? I asked, trying to pin her down."

"Oh, it must have been half one, just like usual."

"So, she closed the shop at half one and headed to the abbey's restaurant. That's your statement, correct?"

"I didn't see her go to the café. She closed the shop and went directly to the woods."

"Was she alone? Was she carrying anything when you saw her?" I asked, thinking of the tote bag Julia said she'd filled with sandwiches. "No, I didn't see anyone, nor was she carrying anything."

"What time does the pub open? I imagine you'd be busy at lunchtime," I said, wondering how Charlotte could have seen Julia when the pub would have been in full swing, as most pubs are at lunchtime.

"I'm not changing my statement if that's what you're getting at by your question. I usually take a break around the lunch hour and check out how many tourists are milling around town. Helps me plan the inventory."

"What were Alex and Julia arguing about in the pub?"

"Poor Alex, he was sitting at one of the tables, just trying to have a quiet evening with the locals, when Julia barged in and began riffing with him over their assets."

"Right there? In front of everyone in the pub? I can't believe Julia would behave in such a manner."

"She was pretty steamed up, especially when Alex turned his back on her and commiserated with his pals."

"Still. I'm a good judge of character. I can't imagine Julia choosing a public place to discuss marital affairs."

"You'd be surprised what gets talked about in the pub. We live in a fishbowl. Everyone knows everyone's business in this village. No one escapes scrutiny."

"I'll remember your advice when I'm asking questions around town. By the way, what about Todd? He appeared pretty drunk and seemed to have a vendetta with Julia. What was his relationship with Alex and Julia?"

"What a nightmare that was for Alex." Charlotte picked up the pace again as she explained. "When Todd was fired suddenly by the abbey management board, Alex offered to represent him. You see, Alex thought something had gone on between Todd and one of the other managers and that Todd was being treated unfairly."

"Sounds like Alex was a good guy."

"He was. He hired a private firm to assist with negotiating a settlement between Todd and the management team." Charlotte twisted her upper body to look at me before continuing. "That's when everything blew up."

By this time, we'd turned onto a tree-lined lane that rose in a slight incline. Wet moss and stones bordered the road that ended in front of a small church. Charlotte stopped and began doing stretches, using the trees for support.

"What happened?" I asked.

"Todd wasn't released because of a squabble between him and another manager. He'd been embezzling money, stealing right out of the safe in the abbey's restaurant. Seemingly, Sister Meghan caught him red-handed. When the truth came out,

Alex dropped Todd as a client. He told Todd he'd be lucky not to spend any time in prison."

I'd already put Todd on my interview list, but hearing Charlotte's revelation, speaking to him became my top priority. Finding out the person you'd thought would represent you and potentially keep you out of prison was dropping you as a client was clearly a motivation for murder.

"Todd must have been terrified," I stated in an effort to determine just how motivated Todd would have been.

"He was and has been. He's been drinking heavily ever since and getting into skirmishes with villagers over nothing."

"I'm surprised the police haven't been involved."

"We've been protecting Todd. He's one of ours. I guess we figured he'd eventually calm down when he realized management wasn't going to press charges."

"No charges?" I asked, not sure I'd heard correctly.

"That's what I've been hearing. I guess losing his job is punishment enough."

"What else can you tell me about Alex?" I asked.

"Arrah, he was a kind soul. Very much into nature. He enjoyed the solitude." Charlotte sighed.

"Not someone who'd be a likely candidate for murder?"

"No, but you don't have to look too far, Miss O'Brien. I saw Julia the day Alex's body was found. She locked her shop up early and headed into the woods. I know what I saw."

"You just said Julia locked up her shop early, and a few minutes ago, you said it was one thirty p.m. Which is it?" I asked.

Charlotte made a U-turn and strode in the direction of the pub. "Early or late doesn't matter, Miss O'Brien. In that argument Alex and Julia had in the pub, I heard her say she wouldn't let him ruin her life. I guess she made good on her threat."

By this time, we'd arrived back at the pub. Charlotte turned to me abruptly. "Mark my words, Julia killed Alex. If you're as good as I've heard through the grapevine, well, then you may not be as useful to Julia as she thinks. So be careful, Miss O'Brien. Especially when you're exploring the countryside—you never know who or what you'll run into." With that, Charlotte pushed open the pub door and slammed it behind her.

I headed to a coffee shop across the street and sat at a window-side table. A strong cup of herbal tea and my Mead notebook occupied my attention while I also kept an eye on the passersby. What did I know thus far? I asked myself as I drew a mind map with Alex's name in the center. The spokes coming off the center listed potential suspects and motivations. The local news and O'Shea's report confirmed the murder. I considered adding Charlotte Evans as one of the suspects. Obviously, she was jealous of Julia. But would she murder someone over a relationship that happened over twenty years ago? She definitely wanted to implicate Julia. I peered through the glass window, trying to get a glimpse of the walking trails from my vantage point. Charlotte had said she saw Julia head off in that direction the day of the murder.

The number one priority, I noted to myself, was to pinpoint Julia's timeline. I'd need to speak with Nigel about what he saw or didn't see that day from his apartment above Julia's shop. Then, I dropped Todd into the diagram. Interestingly, Julia described Alex as close-mouthed regarding his cases, but Charlotte seemed to know much more than she should have. I wondered what Sister Meghan would say about Todd. I had to speak with her, which gave me the perfect reason to call at the abbey again—without an appointment. I finished my tea, stowed my notebook in my knapsack, and headed in that direction.

Unlike the last time I'd visited, the massive teak door opened before I had an opportunity to knock.

"Miss O'Brien, what are you doing here?"

The raspy, demanding voice emanating from the woman who stood in the open doorway surprised me. Maeve Baldwin wore her usual black slacks, black fishnet sweater, and pearls. I didn't respond immediately. Instead, my brain rifled through all the instances I'd spoken with Maeve, from when she'd introduced herself as Mrs. Maeve Baldwin at a historical society meeting in Cong during the Ashford Castle case to the invitation she'd sent me to have tea with her at the castle, and the time Lorcan and I had visited her cottage in Cong. When I was working on the Turlough Museum case, I had Phillie complete background research on Maeve. She'd moved around quite a lot, living in New York, London, and Cong, but we hadn't found an official role related to her historical research or a *Mr.* to go with her *Mrs.* title. For some reason, the woman had taken a dislike to me and didn't hide the fact. Even Lorcan had agreed that she seemed overly hostile toward me.

"I should ask you the same thing, Maeve."

"Oh, I'm leading a Kentmore Abbey Historical Society meeting with Sister Meghan. We're planning an event in the Neo-Gothic church to celebrate the abbey's original owners, Martin and Mary Walsh. They're buried at the site of the church, side by side. But I know you're not interested in history, my dear. Indeed, I'd be willing to bet that if you're here, there's trouble."

I silently counted to ten and said, "Why, yes, Detective O'Shea has asked me to investigate Alex Quinn's death. I've heard some rumors about an employee dispute with the abbey's management board. Seemingly, Sister Meghan is at the center of everything *abbey*." At some point, I planned to confront Maeve Baldwin's antagonism, but this wasn't the place to do so if I wanted to get into the building she was just exiting.

"Oh, that. Why bother getting your nose into mundane

employer-employee issues? Don't you have a business in the U.S. needing your attention?"

"I suppose you're right, Maeve, but I have personal reasons for being here as well."

Maeve's eyes narrowed as she looked me over from head to toe. "Oh, yeah, the outrageously wild idea you'll find your mother after all these years. You have better odds of winning the lotto, my dear. I have another engagement I need to get to. I'll see you."

I turned away and walked to one of the casement windows to catch my breath. Maeve Baldwin belonged in the box where I'd put the police long ago. I'd never give up believing my mother had not abandoned me. The beautiful landscape and water unfolded into the vista below me. I focused on that and the job I had to do. I returned to the door and rang the bell.

"Oh, Miss O'Brien, I'm sorry. If you've come to see Sister Meghan, she's in a meeting." The young novitiate who'd spoken to me the previous time I'd tried to gain entry looked pained that she had to turn me away again.

"I think she's going to want to talk to me, especially when it could mean bad press related to a former employee of the abbey." I had no intention of going to the press, but I'd seen enough of Sister Meghan to know that she wanted to protect the abbey's reputation at all costs—maybe even if it allowed a murderer to go unpunished.

"Please, wait here."

I moved to step through the doorway after her, but the young woman turned and gently put up her hand. "No, you cannot come any further. Please, remain where you are," she said and then pushed the door shut.

When the door opened again, Sister Meghan appeared and moved out into the entry foyer like a steam engine.

"Were you trying to avoid me, or is it a coincidence your meeting has ended, Sister?"

"Follow me," she ordered.

I fell into step beside her, and we went through a side door that opened onto a walkway near the church where Charlotte and I had ended our walk earlier. Sister stopped near a wrought iron fence surrounding a small family burial ground.

"I love this bit of a resting place. Private conversations can be held here without prying eyes and ears. You want to discuss Todd."

"Yes, but first, I'm curious. I bumped into Maeve Baldwin earlier. She said she'd been meeting with you."

Sister Meghan's eyes seemed to roll in her head. "Maeve and I are old schoolmates. Whenever she's back in the country, she stops by for a visit, and we reminisce about our secondary school days. She also volunteers her expertise with our historical projects." Meghan paused. "Enough about Maeve. You intimated that you could embarrass the abbey over Todd. What do you want to know?"

"I've learned from a reliable source that Alex had dropped Todd's case against the abbey management team."

Sister Meghan stepped from one foot to another with a sign of impatience. "Too much gossip around this place."

"Maybe, but I've seen Todd. He's angry, and if the rumor is true, then he has a motive for murder."

Sister nodded. "When Alex learned Todd had been embezzling funds from the foundation, Alex went crazy angry and immediately dropped Todd's case."

"So, Alex didn't drop the case on your behalf?" I'd surmised that perhaps Alex had been asked not to represent Todd by the abbey board.

"Nonsense. Why would I do that? Todd very clearly was into illegal money-making schemes. We separated him from the business—we couldn't afford to have him or the disgrace he would bring to the community. That's the reason for the separation."

"Todd made a disruptive appearance last evening at Charlotte's Pub. He seems very focused on Julia. Any thoughts as to why?"

"Only the Lord knows the answer to that, Miss O'Brien." Sister Meghan instinctively fingered the rosary beads at her waist. "I'd be careful if I were you. Todd is deceitful—he seems innocent enough, but underneath, he's a troubled mind."

"Troubled or not, I must speak to him about Alex and his issues with Julia." I paused and then continued, "One more question, Sister. The woman I saw the other day"—I pointed in the direction of where I'd seen her—"I'd like to know her name and speak with her."

Sister Meghan's hand rose to straighten the veil that covered her hair. "I don't know who you're referring to, Miss O'Brien. At any one time, various people may be at the abbey on a respite or prayer retreat. You must respect our community and the work we do."

With that, Sister turned and entered the small church. I followed behind, but she'd locked it shut before I got there.

Frustrated, I knew I had to enlist help in getting Sister Meghan to cooperate with me. I decided to call at Georgina's cottage on the way home. She knew Sister Meghan and Maeve Baldwin. I also hoped Lady Marcella was no longer angry with me and could add some insight into dealing with Sister Meghan. Sister, Maeve, and Marcella had all known each other since their boarding school days.

I stopped at Julia's shop, but the shades were drawn, and the door was locked. I decided to call her later in the evening after I'd met with Georgina.

When I returned to the cottage, I phoned Phillie.

"Hi, boss, what's up?"

"I want you to delve into Maeve Baldwin again. Your last search didn't turn up much other than she often relocated to places like London and New York. She's a local historian with a horrible attitude toward me. I want to know more about her. Maybe I'll figure out why she's so bent on getting me out of Ireland."

"Hold on; I'll run a few queries while we're on the phone. Where did she go to university?"

"I don't know. I'm assuming because she's Irish, she probably graduated from Trinity College in Dublin. Check there."

"Nope. Nothing. I can't find a Maeve Baldwin historian anywhere. Is Baldwin a married name?" Phillie asked.

"She used the title Mrs. when I first met her, but a husband seems to be non-existent. What about publications?"

"No evidence of publication or symposium presentations, either."

"Oh, no, here I go again," I groaned, remembering when I'd scoured the Consulting Detective databases but hadn't turned up any information about Evelyn until Phillie found a reference to a research article Evelyn had authored under her maiden name, O'Malley. "Okay, keep looking and email me if and when you find anything more regarding Maeve."

We ended the call, and then I dialed Evelyn on her cell phone.

"Hi, Star."

"How's London?"

"Good, but I'll be here for a few more days. Are you okay? You sound rushed."

"More like angry and frustrated. I'm trying to get a handle on why Maeve Baldwin is so nasty toward me. For someone who's supposed to be a noted historian, her resume seems to be nonexistent. Are you familiar with her credentials?" I asked.

"I've seen her around Cong from time to time. She attended

some of the meetings that Paul held with the Cong Historical Society. But beyond seeing her at those meetings, I haven't had any reason to socialize with her."

"Hmm, I wonder if anyone in the historical society can tell me more about her?"

"Probably not. Paul was the glue that encouraged interest in Cong's history. With him gone and the shuttering of the historical bookshop.... Well, you know how these things go. The few remaining members haven't had the heart to continue."

"I suppose you're right," I said, closing my eyes and seeing Paul's smiling face. "I guess I'm back to square one regarding Maeve."

"You might try Dr. O'Dowd. She's probably in a better position to know about Maeve's research activities."

"Will O'Dowd help me? She was pretty circumspect when I was trying to find you."

"Of course, she'll answer your questions." Evelyn chuckled. "Remember, we're family. She's not going to do anything to offend her protege."

"If you say so," I replied. "Let me know when you're back in Cong."

We ended the call, and then I dialed Dr. O'Dowd, the head of the National Museum of Ireland's Archeology Branch.

"Dr. O'Dowd, this is Star O'Brien, Evelyn Cosgrove's half-sister," I said when O'Dowd answered.

"Yes, Evelyn has apprised me of the situation. I remember you, my dear. You're in search of the Holy Grail or might as well be in this life-long quest to find your mother. Well, you have family in the person of Evelyn. What could you possibly want from me?"

I smiled to myself. O'Dowd hadn't changed a bit from the first time I met her in Dublin during the Ashford Castle case. "I'm actually trying to locate a historian, Maeve Baldwin.

Evelyn thought you might know more about Maeve and her work."

"I haven't heard that name in quite some time. Maeve seems to flit in and out of Dublin occasionally—supposedly working on a book. Some esoteric historical study of Irish symbols like the shamrock." O'Dowd chuckled. "She doesn't work for me; that's for sure. What do *you* want with her?"

"I'm tracking down people who may have lived in Achill when my mother was a child. I met Maeve at a historical society event last year. I seem to remember she mentioned Achill and her childhood memories." Of course, I lied about Achill, but I didn't think a small white lie in search of the truth about Maeve was unwarranted.

"I can't help you, my dear. It seems to me your best options are with Evelyn. I admire your persistence, though. Good luck," O'Dowd said and ended the call.

Impatient for action, I began dialing Marcella's landline number but stopped before I pressed the *send* button. I didn't know how she'd react to answering questions about Maeve, and even worse, Lorcan might answer the phone. I had no idea what I'd do if he wouldn't speak to me. What was I thinking? He was out of the country. I threw on my sneakers and dashed out the door for an invigorating walk before I talked myself into a tizzy over Lorcan McHale.

CHAPTER 15

Aunt Georgina lived in a two-hundred-year-old thatched cottage in Turlough Village, a few miles outside Castlebar. Clusters of ivy hung like ringlets bordering the traditionally painted green front door. When I lifted the knocker, the door burst open, and Georgina ushered me inside.

"You're just in time. I've been cooking up a pot of potato soup. You must be famished."

During the four trips I'd made to Ireland beginning a year ago, Georgina has nurtured me with food. I loved her brown bread loaves, which she kept in endless supply. My usual meal consisted of yogurt and herbal tea, especially peppermint. But I'd grown to love the Irish mugs of strong tea served in every coffee shop and restaurant throughout County Mayo.

"Honestly, I haven't thought of food all day. I spent most of my time trying to get a line on the top suspects. A bowl of soup sounds wonderful, Aunt Georgina."

While Georgina ladled the soup into the blue heart-shaped Irish pottery bowl with a Celtic spiral design at the dish's bottom, I extracted my Mead composition notebook from my knapsack and placed the notebook on the table next to my cell phone.

"Move the book from the table, Star. Eat first, then we'll talk."

I didn't argue, swiftly placing my repository of hand-written notes and occasional mind maps upon the kitchen countertop. I slid onto a kitchen chair.

"Yum, this is delicious," I said in between slathering pieces of brown bread with Kerrygold butter. "I didn't realize how hungry I was. Thank you, Georgina."

"The world won't end in the next few minutes. The brain needs fuel to work."

Minutes later, with the table cleared, we sat looking over my notes and the list of suspects.

"What do you think?" I asked after bringing Georgina up to date with the day's conversations.

"My schedule in the shop is full, but I can move some appointments around if that's what you want. I know Meghan Brennan. Who do you want me to start with?"

"I'll continue my discussions with Julia, but I could really use some help with Sister Meghan. And, oh, that nasty woman, Maeve Baldwin, was just coming out of the abbey when I arrived. I don't know why she keeps turning up wherever I go."

"Marcella and I will pin her down about the poisonous attitude toward you." Georgina refilled our tea mugs and shook her head. "She comes and goes for long periods of time. But I've noticed she's much more visible in Marcella's life lately."

"Does she ever talk about her travels or research?"

"No." Georgina tilted her head. "Come to think of it, she *was* around quite a bit when you were working the Turlough Museum case."

"I agree. Something else... she accused me of chasing a wild idea, but she pronounced wild like *wile*. That accent keeps nagging at me."

Georgina nodded. "Aye, Maeve's origins are seeping

through. I believe she's originally from Donegal, where natives say wile instead of wild."

"Interesting. Do you think Marcella will help us? She's angry about Lorcan," I said, reaching for my phone.

"She's more hurt for her son than anything, and for you. Marcella and I want happiness for both of you. For my part, I want you to be happy. You're family." Georgina reached to touch my hand. "Marcella won't be angry for long. She's never interfered in Lorcan's life. I expect she'll allow him to do or feel as he wants to."

"Great," I said, exhaling the breath I'd been holding. "See if you can learn more about Todd from Sister Meghan. Also, ask why she's adamant about keeping me out of the abbey. I'm suspicious of that. In the meantime, I'm going to visit the Conservation Foundation. Alex was on the board."

"Right. I have an early morning appointment at the Golden Thread. But right after, I'll meet you at French Hill Cottage. I know exactly where to catch up with Sister Meghan."

"Oh, something I should know?"

"Don't worry, Star. Marcella and I will get to her. You go gather whatever other information you need. But, Star... be careful. Meghan is a serious person. If she warned you about Todd, then you need to take precautions. Have you spoken with Detective O'Shea?"

"Not yet. I'll call him as soon as I get home. I promise."

BEFORE CALLING O'SHEA, I PHONED THE CONSULTING Detective.

"You sound much better," I said when Ellie answered. "How are things at home?"

"My cortisol levels have come down. Ralph has had an offer with a firm in Jersey City, which means the daily commute will be less exhausting. I expect our evenings together will be so much more enjoyable."

"I'm happy for you, Ellie. You and Ralph deserve more time together."

"Phillie completed the research into Julia Quinns's business operation. She wants to speak with you."

"Hi, Phillie, I'm ready to listen," I said when Ellie transferred the call to Phillie's desk.

"Okay, here we go. The business is privately held by Julia and Alex Quinn."

"Wait. Stop there. Her deceased husband's name is listed as co-owner?" If so, then Julia did have a motive for murder. In a divorce settlement, the assets would be divided, or perhaps he would get all of them.

"Yes, his name is on the business ownership license as co-owner."

"Okay, when we complete this call, track down Irish law. I want to know how much Julia stood to lose in the divorce settlement."

"Will do. There's additional interesting information. The abbey owns the building where the shop is located."

I didn't respond immediately, as Phillie's statement surprised me even more than the fact that Alex was listed as a partner in the business. Like a major U.S. corporation, the abbey loomed large in the village. "What about the shop's revenues? What does the profit and loss sheet look like?"

"I searched Ireland's company registration office database, and luckily, the information is public. I grabbed the numbers for the last three years. I'll email the document to you shortly, but based on my initial perusal, the shop is solvent... in fact, highly successful."

Strong profit margins indicated another motive for Alex's murder if Julia didn't want to share. "Thanks, Phillie; I'll read through the report tonight and let you know if I need more."

"Okay, boss. Good luck."

The call ended, and I immediately dialed O'Shea's cell phone. He picked up on the first ring.

"Were you expecting my call?"

"No, I'm a bloody detective. It's force of habit to answer as soon as possible. How are you progressing with gathering information?"

"Have you gotten yourself assigned as a consultant to the case yet?" I asked.

"No, but the superintendent has been reading me in on his reports." O'Shea sighed.

"Has the murder weapon been found?"

"No, and that doesn't bode well for Julia. She's the only suspect the garda has. Finding the murder weapon might lead to other suspects."

I silently agreed with O'Shea's verdict. "Julia's shop is full of pointy implements," I said, thinking of the knitting needles, crochet hooks, and other sewing-like instruments I'd seen in her shop.

"I know." O'Shea's voice faltered. "I may not be able to save Julia from an arrest."

"Hey, that shop is full of villagers and tourists every day. Anyone could have put their hands on or purchased the murder weapon." I didn't share with O'Shea that I'd found needles thrown into the garbage at Julia's shop. She'd wiped them off and put them back on the shelves. Instead, I changed the topic. "What do you know about Todd?"

"Not much. I've heard he has a bit of an alcohol problem. Why?"

"He may have a drinking problem, but an even bigger issue is the animosity he's directed at Alex in the past and at Julia. He was embroiled in litigation with the abbey's management team, but Alex dropped him when Todd's criminal acts with the foundation came to light. He has motive. I need to talk to him."

"I wish I could be in the field, but I'm on desk duty for the time being," O'Shea replied.

"I'll return to Letterbrack in the morning. I'll speak with Julia more about Todd's behavior and track him down. Maybe he's sober in the earlier part of the day."

"Miss O'Brien, please be careful."

"Oh, are you worried about me, O'Shea?"

"Yes and no. I've seen how relentless you are when you're tracking down information. Just let the garda handle the bad guys. Focus on finding the facts that exonerate Julia. All I'm saying is not to take this case lightly. I saw Alex. Whoever did this is nasty. Besides, I don't want to have to explain myself to Lorcan if anything happened to you."

A sharp pang shot through my heart at the mention of Lorcan's name. "Have you spoken to him?" I asked.

"No, I've been too engrossed in my own issues. But I plan on stopping by his place tomorrow."

"Let me know how that goes." I don't know why I didn't tell O'Shea Lorcan had left the country. Deep down, I didn't want to verbalize that he wasn't in Ireland because then I might have to admit my fear he wasn't coming back.

We ended the call with a commitment to meet the following day. I kicked off my flats, laced up my sneakers, and headed out onto Cottage Road for a long walk.

WHEN I RETURNED, I FOUND PHILLIE'S EMAIL WITH THE attached financial pages. I printed the full report and began reading. Phillie's original assessment was correct. Cash flows and liquidity were stable. The business was profitable. Everything in the report indicated a healthy company. As I'd said to Charlotte Evans, I didn't believe Julia would hide assets from her husband. She'd already said she and Alex had an agreement not to go after what mattered most to each of them. But wanting to protect your business assets from a spouse in a divorce settlement was often a motive for murder. If Julia's timeline for the day of Alex's death placed her in the meadow, the police wouldn't look any further, arresting Julia instead.

I jotted a few notes from the report into my notebook. Next, I developed a list of questions for Julia. She hadn't wanted to discuss much when we'd been in the pub, but the clock was ticking. If I couldn't find any discrepancies in what people were saying about her, then I couldn't help O'Shea. Julia would be arrested and charged with her husband's murder. Speaking with Todd remained a high priority. I resolved to pin him down about his animosity toward Julia. Then I Googled the Conservation Foundation website for the contact phone number and a list of the board members. I called the office and left a message requesting a meeting.

I closed my notebook, set the alarm on my cell phone, and turned in for the night.

THE NEXT MORNING, MY CALL TO GEORGINA WENT RIGHT TO VOICE mail. For a moment, fear washed over me. She usually answered my calls no matter the time of day or night. But I needn't have worried because a few minutes later, she breezed into the kitchen.

"I just called you."

"Buried in my handbag. I heard the ring but couldn't put my hands on the phone. Are you ready?"

"I haven't eaten yet. Did you bring any scones or brown bread with you?" I asked, glancing around my empty kitchen.

"No, we'll eat when we get to Letterbrack. The Golden Thread is in Beth's reliable hands. Sunday's the shop doesn't open until after 1:00 p.m., Beth will take care of appointments and orders. Besides, if I'm going to approach Meghan, I want to catch her early in the day—sort of a surprise visit." Georgina smiled. "Oh, and I'll drive for a change."

I didn't argue. Instead, I grabbed my knapsack, holstered my phone to my jeans, and followed Georgina out the door. As we approached her Toyota Corolla, which was parked to the side of the barn, I saw Lady Marcella leaning against the stone wall that divided my garden from the barn's gravel driveway.

Georgina laughed when she saw the shock on my face. "She's coming with us."

"But I thought...."

"We love you, Star O'Brien. Let's go." Georgina pointed at the car.

Marcella hopped into the back seat, and the three of us pulled away from French Hill.

~

DURING THE DRIVE TO LETTERBRACK, I SUMMARIZED WHAT I knew so far, including my conversation with O'Shea.

"What I don't understand is why Meghan is being so inflexible," Marcella stated. "She used to be more open to visitors. But I suppose a murder and a threatened lawsuit are tremendous burdens to the Franciscan ministry. The sisters do so much good for the community. They don't deserve what's happening."

"Who exactly is the recipient of the ministry? My research indicates the order no longer provides respite or shelter to women and children. Although Meghan says the abbey provides support occasionally," I stated, thinking of the mystery woman I'd glimpsed near the garden wall. "From the number of tourist buses I've seen in the visitor lot and the crowds lining up to buy tickets into the garden, the place must be financially solvent. Sister Meghan is hiding something or someone." I stopped speaking when Georgina leaned on the horn and propelled the vehicle into the opposing lane in an effort to pass a truck.

"Georgina." I reached for the passenger grab handle just above me, but pulling at the bar did nothing to slow the car.

"I'm not lagging behind a truck moving along at 25 kilometers per hour. Hang on until I pass."

"Star, who do you plan to speak with first, Julia or the foundation director?" Marcella asked as if Georgina's driving behavior was nothing out of the ordinary.

"Julia. I want to see her reaction to the news regarding the murder weapon. Innocent or not, the timeline for her actions and whereabouts must be verified. Charlotte, Todd, and a man named Brendan claim they saw Julia heading into the trailhead just before Alex was murdered. I'm surprised the police haven't arrested her yet based upon witness statements."

"I know the foundation's former director. If whoever is in the office doesn't accommodate you, let me know. I'll make a call," Marcella said.

Like the other days when I visited the village, tourists swarmed the sidewalks, and buses filled the parking lot. Georgina circled the lot a few times before landing in a parking spot. We agreed to meet back at Cream, a place Georgina recommended because of their homemade scones, at 2:00 p.m.

CHAPTER 16

I found Julia in the middle of checking knitting supplies against an inventory sheet on a clipboard. Her eyes widened when she turned and saw me enter the shop.

"I wasn't expecting you back again so soon."

"Why not?"

"The garda haven't arrested me. I thought maybe they'd found the killer."

"No, Julia. In fact, the murder weapon turned out to be a thin, narrow, sharp instrument like a needle. If the garda hasn't already connected your merchandise to the potential murder weapon, I believe they will shortly. So, you and I must have a serious conversation."

"Oh." Julia dropped the clipboard to the floor and grabbed for the edge of the design table.

"Are you okay?" I reached forward to steady her trembling body.

"Not really. Look around you. Potential weapons line the walls!"

"Your timeline for the day Alex died is critical. Charlotte, Todd, and Brendan put you on the way to the woods during the time window in which Alex was murdered."

"That may be so, but it doesn't make me a murderer. Besides, did they really see me? I know Todd is angry with me, and Charlotte has an ax to grind over Alex."

"Then we must prove the so-called witnesses are liars. Witness testimony is powerful, especially when supplied by more than one person. I also have to understand more about Alex. He angered someone enough to commit murder. So, I suggest you close the shop while we have a detailed conversation."

"But... my customers, the guild members...."

"Julia, this is urgent."

Julia sighed, walked to the shop door, and flipped the *Open* sign to *Closed*. "Would you like a cup of tea or coffee? I'm afraid I'm feeling quite chilled."

"No, but you go ahead."

Julia disappeared behind the screen at the back of the shop, and I walked over to the wall display that held myriad knitting and crocheting tools. I discounted the large gauge knitting needles. According to O'Shea, the medical examiner had identified an implement that was sharp and extremely narrow. A narrow gauge, pointy, circular item piqued my interest. I took one from the display, placed it on the design table, and took a seat.

"That is used for working with fine threads like lace," Julia explained when she reemerged from behind the screen with a large mug in her hand. Her body sagged into the chair opposite mine. "What's that for?" she asked when her eyes fell on my notebook.

"My notes," I said and then continued with my questions. "I'm curious. Who has access to the beverage station there behind the screen?" I asked.

"The members of the guild. We're like family. I don't limit the members' movements in the shop."

I nodded, opened my notebook, and turned to a page with

Nigel's, Anne's, and Rita's names. "Are all the guild members listed correctly?"

Julia leaned forward and perused the list. "Yes. Why?"

"Remember the needle we found earlier in the week?" I said, pointing toward where I'd found the needle in the trash.

Julia's face paled. "I remember, but I washed it off and put it back in one of the displays." Her eyes swept the wall. "That particular needle could have been sold."

"I believe the murderer disposed of the evidence here in the trash to implicate you, Julia. That someone may be one of the guild members."

"No." Julia shook her head vehemently. "The guild members are a tight group. I won't accept that theory. Someone else, someone from outside the community, must have had a grudge against Alex."

"The tourist theory doesn't ring true, and I don't think the police will accept that notion either. Especially when they review your business data."

Julia moved her cup away and bolted upright in her chair. "What do you mean by that? Have you been investigating me? You're supposed to be helping me, not digging up details that might implicate me."

"I told you an investigation and this discussion would not be easy. You want to be prepared for whatever the police throw at you. Was Alex threatening to take his half of the business from you in the divorce settlement?"

"The shop was his bargaining chip. He wanted to keep our home. If I agreed, then he would allow me to keep the business. We'd discussed this several times, and I accepted his terms." As Julia looked around the room, tears glistened in her eyes. "My work, the guild, this is my life. I couldn't part with the shop, even if it meant giving up my home."

"But with Alex dead, you have the shop and the house." I held up my hand when Julia squirmed in her chair. "Don't argue with me. The police will see this as a strong motivation for murder. So, your timeline for the day Alex was murdered... let's go over your entire day right up to the time when Alex was killed." I pulled a pencil from my knapsack and turned to a blank page in the notebook. "Try just talking through the day. I'll take notes. Then we'll review them together."

Julia nodded and began speaking.

After a few minutes, I flipped the notebook around, pointed to the page, and said, "Is this correct?"

"Yes, I got to the shop late that morning. I'm usually here by nine so I can straighten up shelves and papers and such. I open at half nine every day of the week. That morning, I didn't arrive until nine forty-five."

"What delayed you?"

"Alex and I had an argument—over nothing really. He was in a nasty mood and told me he couldn't wait to be rid of me. I shouted back that I felt the same way." Julia pursed her lips. "I'm not a vain person, but I had to spend a bit more time on my makeup. I didn't want people to see I'd been crying."

"So, you opened the shop late that day?" I asked as a prompt to continue.

"Yes, but the shop was already open."

"What do you mean?"

"Nigel had opened up and was talking to clients about their projects when I arrived."

"Nigel has a key?"

"All the guild members have one, and more importantly, they know where I keep the spare key." Julia shook her head. "I know this sounds careless on my part, but I never expected I'd be facing murder charges. We're all one big, happy family."

"Where's the spare key?"

Julia rose, opened the front door, and lifted the edge of a huge flowerpot, which sat on the cement right outside the shop.

"It's here," she said, holding the key up so I could see it.

"That's good. Don't put it back."

Julia nodded and pocketed the key.

"Let's continue with the timeline. What happened when you arrived?"

"A normal day. As I said, Nigel was here, and at about half ten, the other guild members came in. We were supposed to discuss upcoming projects—like a design chat session."

"The other guild members aren't specific enough, Julia. Who was here?"

"Everyone on your list. Nigel, Anne, and Rita."

"So, the guild members can be your alibi."

"No," Julia shook her head. "They left the shop after our meeting—well before I went to meet with Tom."

"What time did you leave to meet up with O'Shea?"

"I don't remember exactly. I think I locked up the shop sometime after 1:00 p.m. and posted a sign on the door stating I was out to lunch. Then, I ran over to the abbey café and picked up a salad for me and a sandwich for Tom. It must have been about half one when I started on the trailhead. Maybe about thirty minutes later, I saw Alex. I panicked. I ran from the meadow and called O'Shea when I was back on the trail."

"Where did you go after you called O'Shea?"

"I returned here, threw the food into the garbage receptacle, and went home."

"You should have phoned the police and remained with Alex."

"I was frightened, and I did phone the garda. I phoned O'Shea." Tears ran down Julia's cheeks. "I'll never forget how Alex looked."

"Were any of the guild members here when you returned?"

"No, I left the *Closed* sign on the door. But I did see Todd. He was standing outside on the sidewalk when I got back."

"Was he alone?"

"Yes, I'd forgotten. He said he wanted to talk to me, but I

told him I didn't have time. Maybe that's why he was so angry the other night in the pub."

"Have you spoken to him?" I asked.

"No," Julia said.

"So, he never followed up with you after that day."

"No. Do you think he knows something about the murder?'

"I intend to find out. So, to summarize, you went into the trailhead at about half one and arrived back here to the shop at what time?"

"About three p.m. I remember because the abbey chimes were ringing the hour."

"You said it took about thirty minutes to get from here to the meadow. Why did it take longer to get back here?"

"I don't know. I called Tom. Then, I got turned around on the trail for a few minutes. I think I was in shock."

I nodded. Alex had died sometime between 11:00 a.m. and 2:00 p.m., just as O'Shea had reported. "Listen, Julia, I know this has been a tough discussion, but it's best to get all the nasty stuff out between us before the police question you."

Julia's pale skin looked paler than usual.

"Why don't we take a break?" I said, closing up my notebook. "There's a coffee shop across the street, The Place to Be, I think the sign said. If we sit at one of the outside tables, we can continue our discussion without worrying about eavesdroppers."

"I'd like that. Let me grab my tote bag, and I'll lock up."

WITH TWO LARGE HOT LATTÉS ON THE TABLE IN FRONT OF US, I focused my next set of questions on Alex. "What was Alex's role at the foundation?"

"Oh, he was general counsel. He provided advice regarding

contracts, property management, complaints, that sort of thing."

"What kind of complaints does the foundation deal with?"

"Preserving the pristine landscape in this region is a primary objective of the foundation and the local residents. Complaints ranged from concerns about gold diggers to the poaching issues plaguing the area."

"Julia, why is the shop closed?" Nigel said, approaching the table.

"Good morning, Nigel. Star and I are in the middle of a conversation. I'll catch up with you later."

Nigel's smile disappeared, and I detected a slight "poutiness" in his voice when he replied, "I suppose so."

"He has a definite crush on you," I stated when he had vanished from view.

"He'll realize at some point that he's in love with my art and not who I am as a person," Julia responded. "If you don't have any more questions, though, I'd like to get back to the shop."

"Be careful, Julia. Someone you know is working to implicate you in Alex's murder."

Julia nodded, and we parted ways.

Fifteen minutes later, I entered the Conservation Foundation offices and sat patiently, waiting to meet with the director, Susan Drew. I'd Googled her bio and saw that she'd only served at the Conservation Foundation for six months since the beginning of 2009. According to her resume, she was in her mid-thirties and had an impressive background in non-profit management.

Within a few minutes, a female with an angular but athletic build greeted me. "Miss O'Brien, I'm Susan Drew. Please, come into my office." She towered over my five-six frame by about three inches. Jet-black hair streaked with gray hung to her waist. A red athletic-type shirt topped black slacks and a pair of running sneakers. "May I offer you a refreshment?"

"No, thank you," I replied, placing my business card on her desk. "I won't take too much of your time. I appreciate you seeing me on short notice."

"Not at all. We pride ourselves on our transparency and responsiveness to the environment and the local residents. I understand you want to know more about Alex's role on the board."

"Yes, Julia tells me he was devoted to nature and preservation. But his role was more of an administrative one rather than nature policy. Is that correct?"

"True, he was our general counsel. We relied on him for advice and to perform the administrative duties associated with counsel to a nonprofit. But his role did intersect with his love of nature. He took addressing the poaching complaint reports as an important aspect of his duties."

"Oh, I thought the fishery farms were well protected from theft."

"I'm not talking about the salmon operations, Miss O'Brien. Songbird poaching. He was obsessed with the songbird poaching in Ireland—in the entire world, actually. Poor fellow. He became extremely agitated whenever an organization like the Audubon or National Geographic issued the poaching statistics."

The image of the bird I'd found near the scene of Alex's murder flashed through my mind. What if his murder and the bird were connected?

A loud knock resounded from the office door, and then Brendan poked his head into the room. "The board meeting is ready to begin. Everyone's here," he said and then focused his gaze on me. "What's she doing here?" he asked.

"I'll be right along in a moment, Brendan." Susan turned

back to me. "I hope this has been helpful, Miss O'Brien. Please don't hesitate to call if you have further questions," she said and then rose and escorted me out into the hallway. As we walked toward the exit and past a meeting room, I glimpsed Sister Meghan, Brendan, Todd, and a few others sitting around a conference table.

The director remained at the exit door until I'd crossed the threshold onto the driveway. I heard the door swing shut while I wondered what Todd was doing at the foundation's board meeting and whether Georgina and Marcella had met with Sister Meghan.

~

WHEN I ARRIVED AT CREAM, I SPOTTED GEORGINA AND Marcella sitting inside near the window. A large teapot took up the center of the table. Two plates with the remains of whipped cream and a few bits of buttery scone sat before each of them.

"I see you're enjoying yourselves," I said, sitting on the empty chair.

"We've been waiting for you a good while, so we decided to put our time to good use," Marcella said and pointed at the dessert plates.

"I'll be right back." Georgina rose and went to the counter, where I could see her ordering more tea and a sandwich plate. "Here," she said when she returned. "We'll give our report while you eat."

"I'm ready," I said, biting into the overstuffed roasted chicken, tomato, cheese, and lettuce sandwich on soft buttered white bread. "Is that peppermint tea?" I asked in between bites.

"Barry's Irish Breakfast," Georgina replied before glancing at Marcella and saying, "Meghan hasn't changed one bit since we were children. She was always the bossy one."

Marcella nodded. "She tried to pull the same stunt with us,

but we weren't having any of her pretense that she's better than us just because she's a woman of the cloth."

"She was at the foundation building for a board meeting. Seemingly, she's involved in almost every organization that has something to do with Letterbrack and the abbey," I stated.

"That's understandable. The garden renovation was funded by the government, and tourism brings revenue to the region. But her being so off-putting to you, Star, is not acceptable," Marcella said.

"Did she reveal why?" I asked.

"Only that she doesn't want bad press. She's reacting to Alex's murder and doesn't want the situation to warrant more attention than it's already receiving. But I think she's worried and scared about something. She danced around on her feet like she used to when we were hiding secrets from each other in the old days," Georgina responded, throwing the end of her multi-colored long scarf over her shoulder.

"More like she's hiding *someone*," I replied. "Did you ask her about the mysterious woman?"

"Yes, but she claims you're making something out of nothing," Georgina replied, glancing at Marcella. "Although the abbey is no longer officially in the respite business, the sisters still provide a place of refuge when needed. Sister lectured us that you can't confront people you don't know just because you think you recognize them."

"So, what did she say about Alex's murder?" I asked, moving the discussion back to supporting Julia.

"Meghan claims she has nothing more to add to what the garda have already discovered," Georgina replied.

I shook my head. "She's into everything around here. I don't believe her. Did she see Julia on the day of the murder?"

"Meghan is totally mum on the entire day," Marcella replied. "She stated we should let the garda do their work, and heavenly guidance will do the rest."

I'd begun to ask what Marcella and Georgina had learned about Todd when Marcella's cell phone rang. From where I was sitting, I made out Lorcan's name on the display. Her eyes flicked up from the phone display to glance at me before she stepped away from the table, but not far enough away that her side of the conversation couldn't be heard.

"How are you, and how is the project?" Marcella's eyes narrowed as she leaned into the phone as if she couldn't hear what Lorcan was saying. "This connection is poor. Are you okay?" She leaned in farther as she listened to whatever Lorcan was saying. When she spoke again, she said, "I'm in Letterbrack with Star and Georgina. Yes, I'll tell her. But, Son, don't stay away too long."

When she returned to the table, Marcella said, "That lad didn't sound like his usual self."

"How long does he expect to be in Wyoming?" Georgina asked.

"He didn't say. The project is having some technical difficulties. Anyway"—Marcella turned and looked me directly in the eye—"Lorcan asked me to tell you that he's spoken to Detective O'Shea, and he's relieved that you're involved."

My hand reached for the cell phone tethered to my jeans, but I resisted the urge to call Lorcan. Instead, I savored his acknowledgment of my support of Julia and turned the conversation back to Todd and asked, "What about Todd? Did Sister Meghan reveal anything more about his dismissal from the abbey?"

"Oh, she blustered her way through that part of the conversation. Told us we'd be better served minding our own souls, not some poor, unfortunate, lost soul like Todd," Georgina replied, pushing her teacup away.

Marcella smiled at Georgina, rolled her eyes, and said, "Meghan seems to have become a paragon of virtue since my school days with her."

"Apparently, her memories must be a bit cloudy," Georgina smiled back.

"Thank you both for trying," I said, and then suggested we return home.

Georgina and Marcella agreed, and we left Letterbrack.

CHAPTER 17

Georgina, Marcella, and I sat in French Hill's living room. The coals in the turf fire Aunt Georgina had lit cast a warm glow into the room. I read the notes I'd made as a result of our collective discussion and recollection of the day's meetings.

"Julia's in danger on two fronts, and I'm at an impasse as to how to protect her," I said. "I think...."

The pounding on the cottage's teak front door shattered the cozy atmosphere. When I opened the door, O'Shea thrust himself into the room.

"Detective O'Shea, we were just discussing Julia's situation," I said.

"I'm sorry for the intrusion, but my superintendent reinstated me to the case as a consultant to Séamus Riley's Galway team. I'm heading there shortly, but first, I want to know what you've learned."

"Let me get you a mug of tea. You look quite ragged." Georgina beelined to the kitchen, where I could hear the clatter of spoons and mugs. O'Shea accepted the steaming hot liquid when she returned.

"Has the coroner identified Alex's time of death?" I asked O'Shea while he took a few sips of tea.

"Yes, he pinpointed it to be sometime between one thirty p.m. and the time Julia found him," O'Shea replied impatiently.

"So, she or you could have crossed paths with the killer," I said and then asked, "What about motive? What theory have the police developed?"

"I'll get a readout from Séamus, but the team continues to focus on Julia. I hope you've been able to find strong evidence that supports her innocence."

"You know the time of death puts her in the vicinity of Alex, don't you? The only way out of this for her is to find witnesses truthful about whether or not they saw her. But thus far, Charlotte and Todd claim they saw her walking onto the trailhead." I looked down at my notes. "Todd is the one person who seems to have the most motive."

"I'm sorry, Miss O'Brien, but I have to do what I think is best for Julia and for justice to be served." O'Shea plunked his tea mug onto an end table. "At this juncture, I think it is best for you to leave the investigating to the garda."

Marcella and Georgina gasped, moved to the edges of their seats, and turned their eyes on me.

"What happened, O'Shea? Why do you suddenly want me to stop? You asked for my involvement, and suddenly, I'm worthless to you? There's no way I'm giving up. I'm sure you know well that Julia is in danger. I'm in on this until the end. *Whether you want me or not.*"

O'Shea rose, nodded at Georgina and Marcella, and said, "I cannot stop you, Miss O'Brien, but please don't interfere with the investigation." Then he walked out the door.

Marcella jumped up and began pacing the floor. "The gall of that man. After all you've done. Lorcan went all out for him as well."

"I didn't expect much more from O'Shea. We've never

seen eye to eye. He's desperate and asked for help and even went to Lorcan. But why this sudden change of heart regarding my involvement? This is weird behavior even for O'Shea."

"What do you want us to do, Star?" Georgina asked. "After my recent run-in with the garda and being falsely accused, I have great sympathy for Julia. But if we"—Georgina's eyes swept the room—"are under the garda's noses looking for information, we could be arrested, and O'Shea might get thrown off the case. I'm sure the Galway investigative team won't want a group of civilians involved."

"Then we won't get under their noses. They're focused on Julia. I'll focus on Todd and the guild members."

"I'm glad Lorcan isn't here to witness O'Shea's ingratitude, Star. He'd be fuming." Marcella smiled at me. "All right. I'll say good night, ladies. I'm exhausted." Marcella yawned. "I have an early morning call for an event I'm planning."

"That reminds me. Maeve Baldwin said she was assisting Sister Meghan with an event. Have you ever been at an event that Maeve chaired or co-chaired?" I asked.

Marcella laughed. "What? Maeve is never in the country long enough to attend, let alone plan an event. I wonder why she's spending so much time with Meghan, though. They used to be thick as thieves during our school days, but Maeve doesn't strike me as the meditative type. There's a reason she's popping up in Connemara. If you like, I'll give Maeve a call and see what I can glean from her."

"I'd appreciate that, thank you...." I didn't know how else to express my gratitude that Marcella hadn't locked me out of her life because of how I'd parted ways with Lorcan.

"Nonsense. No thank you necessary," she said, fixing her gaze on me before turning to Georgina. "I'll see you in the morning."

"I'm right behind you. I have to open the shop early. Several members of a bridal party will be in to look at patterns and dresses. Good night, Star."

"Please, check in when you get home, Georgina."

Both women hugged me and then exited via the front door. By the time the embers in the fireplace burned out, I had closed my notebook and then turned my thoughts to Marcella's comments about Maeve. My insight into human nature told me Maeve had a "what's in it for me" motive related to Sister Meghan. I wondered if Maeve's appearances at the abbey could be connected to the woman who'd disappeared through the garden door or with me, for that matter. I opened my notebook again and listed what I knew about Maeve and our interactions.

First, I jotted down Maeve's numerous appearances in my life since my first arrival in County Mayo. In every encounter, she'd made it a point to insult and urge me to leave the country, disparaging the search for my mother. At one point, Maeve even said I was "nothing but trouble" to my face.

I also recalled how she had sent me on a wild goose chase to the Castlebar Library, telling me I'd find archives with old records like marriage or birth certificates that might be useful in my search. That had turned out to be a red herring—as I'd been informed by the library director—because the National Archives in Dublin was the place for the records I sought.

According to Lady Marcella, Maeve had revitalized their friendship after many years. What if the friendship revival was only a ruse on Maeve's part to insinuate herself into what I was doing? I remembered how upset she'd been when she heard I'd visited Achill Island to speak with a woman named Margaret Hanlon, who owned Achill Island Pottery Shop, about a female child orphaned in a fire that killed her entire family.

During that visit, Margaret had told me that sometime in the 1990s, a woman wearing pearls and speaking with a Donegal accent had visited her shop, asking about a young girl whose entire family had died in a house fire.

I sat back in my chair and read my notes. I might need to reassess my observations at some point, but at that moment, I knew I had to return to Achill and speak with Margaret if only to confirm my hunch that Maeve had been the woman Hanlon spoke about.

"I'll go with you," Aunt Georgina said later in the evening when she called, and I verbalized what I suspected.

"No, I plan to drive to Letterbrack from Achill. I'll call Mrs. Hanlon's shop before I leave so I don't waste time if she isn't there."

"Okay, Star. I can't imagine why Maeve dislikes you, but I trust your instincts. If you're doubtful of Maeve's intentions, then you should be careful."

"I'm not backing down," I said, clenching the phone to my ear. "I'll phone you when I get to Letterbrack tomorrow."

BY 9:00 A.M. ON MONDAY MORNING, I WAS AWAKE, DRESSED, AND ready for the drive to Achill Island. Shortly before I left, I called the pottery shop and confirmed Mrs. Hanlon would meet me there. The trip along the wild Atlantic Way from Castlebar through Newport and on to Achill took about an hour, plenty of time to review what Georgina and I had learned from Mrs. Hanlon previously.

I'd gotten a call from Bridget Sumner, whose brother had been murdered in the Clare Island case. Bridget, knowing about the search for my mother, had heard the unusual story from Mrs. Hanlon about a house fire and an orphaned female named Margarite O'Malley. I was already on my way back to the States, so Georgina had followed up with Mrs. Hanlon. The story turned out to be true.

Mrs. Hanlon had lived on the island her entire life and was a teenager at the time of the fire. Hanlon had told Georgina that a local family, the O'Malleys, raised the orphaned child until she became a teenager. Then, she just disappeared. Hanlon thought the teen might have gone to America. But Hanlon didn't recall ever hearing anything about the girl after, and the family who took her in were long gone. Georgina had asked around, but no one she'd spoken to knew anything more.

When I'd visited Mrs. Hanlon, she'd verified the account of events she'd relayed to Georgina with one additional bit of information. After Georgina's visit, Mrs. Hanlon remembered someone who came to Achill looking for a woman named Maggie O'Malley. As I drove, I replayed the conversation in my mind.

I'd shown Mrs. Hanlon the snapshot of my mother that I kept in my wallet, asking, *"Could it have been a younger version of this woman?"*

"No, I'm certain it wasn't the person in your snapshot there. The one who came was sort of bossy. You know, snappy with her questions. She said she was looking for a long-lost cousin. I didn't like her. Not that I had much to tell. I told her I was busy in the shop and couldn't answer her questions."

"What was her name?" I asked, feeling my heart crash against my ribs in anticipation, like the ocean waves crashing against the shore.

"I don't remember. It started with an M, I think. One thing was for sure; she didn't fit in around the area."

"Oh, why?"

"Well, her attitude, for one, like I said. But surely it was how she dressed—all in black and wearing pearls to boot."

"Did she sound like an American?" I asked.

"No. She was Irish. That much, I'm sure of."

"How did you know that?"

"Why, by the way she spoke when she said it was a wild, windy day."

I raised an eyebrow.

Hanlon continued, "When she said the word wild, it sounded like wile. That's a Donegal accent."

~

MARGARET HANLON REMEMBERED ME FROM MY LAST VISIT. I didn't take too much of her time, asking questions about the stranger she had described the last time we spoke. Margaret still couldn't remember the visitor's name other than it began with the initial M, and the M character spoke with a Donegal accent.

"You said that the last time I spoke with you. Can you tell me more about what you mean by a Donegal accent?" I asked.

"Why, yes. When she asked me about the fire and the child, the woman used the word 'rare' instead of strange and 'wane' instead of child. She said, 'I've heard of a rare story concerning an orphaned wane.'" Mrs. Hanlon paused as if searching for more examples. "Oh, and we were having a terrible downpour when she visited, and she said something like 'What cat weather.' The people in Donegal use the word cat instead of awful when describing the weather. I'm sorry, but I can't think of anything more at the present," Mrs. Hanlon said.

"That's more than enough information, Mrs. Hanlon. Thank you for meeting with me," I replied.

"Have you found your mother, Miss O'Brien?"

"Not yet, but I'm hopeful for the future," I said.

When I walked out of Margaret Hanlon's pottery shop, I was confident I'd confirmed my hunch that Maeve had been the person asking about the orphaned child.

On the drive from Achill to Letterbrack, I reviewed everything I knew about Maeve again. Her interest in and sour behavior toward me. Her repeated suggestions that I leave the country. What or who was in Ireland that she didn't want me to see? She kept turning up whenever I was involved in a case.

First during the unfortunate incidents near Ashford Castle and then when Georgina disappeared, and I'd focused my attention on the Turlough Museum. According to Phillie's research, Maeve's resume and publications as a historian were non-existent. Why had she appeared just as I became involved with helping Julia? Maeve's interest in a child born in Achill, who'd basically been orphaned when her entire family died in a house fire, was so specific it couldn't be a coincidence. I couldn't help myself. I had only one conclusion regarding Maeve. She knew something about my mother.

∽

When I arrived in Letterbrack, I gave Georgina a quick call.

"Did you confirm your intuition?" Georgina asked.

"Yes," I said, slinging my knapsack over my shoulder.

"Marcella rang earlier and reported that she'd tried calling Maeve several times with no success. Marcella was surprised there was no voice mailbox set up on Maeve's phone."

"I'm not," I replied, slamming the car door shut. I'll bring you up to date later, Georgina. I want to catch up with Todd and the other guild members."

Nigel, Anne, and Rita were huddled together in Julia's shop. When I entered, a sudden hush fell over the room.

"Where's Julia this morning?" I asked.

"She phoned to say she's meeting Todd for coffee. Something about facing his demons," Nigel replied. "I warned her that he's toxic, but she wouldn't listen. We were just discussing how to make an intervention with Todd."

"Which coffee shop?" I asked, thinking of the proliferation of places on Main Street as well as some of the narrow arteries flowing across Main Street.

"Try Lord's," Anne said. "She loves their lattes. It's two blocks away on the corner of Main and Lucan Street."

"One other thing. You never had a chance to tell me last night where people get the thin wire needed for needlepoint designs."

Anne's eyes widened, and she turned to Nigel, who nodded encouragement.

"I order my supplies by mail. I don't know about anyone else," Anne replied.

"Thanks," I said and left them standing there, looking at each other. As I ran along Main Street, I heard a commotion before I even saw Lord's Café, and then when the shop came into view, I witnessed Todd pounding a table with his hand, his face a bright red blotch.

"Julia," I said, slowing my pace and pretending surprise. "I didn't expect to see you. I've been exploring the town. May I join you?"

Julia's face was as pale as the milk pitcher she held in her trembling hands. She nodded and said quietly, "I'd like that."

"You're that American snoop, aren't you? Have you found Alex's killer yet?" Todd asked, turning his attention to me.

"I'd love to know what you think, Todd," I replied.

"Maybe the answer is right under your nose if you weren't so enamored of the great Miss Julia Quinn."

Obviously, the man was a powder keg ready to explode, which I attempted to ignite. "Julia is under investigation by the police. So, I don't think she's getting away with murder. That is if she committed the crime." I paused and then said, "I have a question for you. Didn't Alex drop your case?"

Todd sat back in his chair, the color in his face washed away. "Aye, he did."

"So, I'm assuming you're happy he's dead."

"Exactly the opposite, Miss Snoop. Alex was my last chance

to get recompense from the abbey. Without him, my case is dead." Todd heaved a sigh. "I might as well be dead."

"So, why the anger directed at Julia?"

"I've asked her to let me see Alex's notes. I met with him several times in his home. I want my case file."

Julia leaned in closer to Todd. "I've explained several times, Todd. The garda instructed me to secure Alex's office. Once this horrible mess is cleared up, I'll give you the file. But until then, I'm at a loss as to how to help you."

"I will get those notes even if I have to steal them. The garda has no say over my life." Todd stood up, knocking his coffee to the ground, where the ceramic cup splintered. He kicked the shattered pieces away from him. "You don't understand. You never did," he shouted at Julia and then charged out of the shop and down the street.

CHAPTER 18

I tossed my knapsack to the ground and raced after Todd. He darted down a narrow alley between two Main Street shops. I skirted several tourists and burst into the slender opening in time to see him reaching the end of the walkway. Wishing I'd worn my sneakers instead of my Rocket Dogs, I sped up, but he gained momentum. When I emerged from the alley, I glimpsed him nearing the Neo-Gothic church, where he paused to look behind him. I pressed on, closing the gap between us. Main Street's din faded, and the cement footpath gave way to the wet, mossy lichen covering the ground along the rise to the church.

"Todd, wait," I shouted, raising my hand in the stop signal as I continued running, but then my wet shoes hydroplaned on the wet lichen. I fell flat on my face, and my chest expelled what breath I had. The pain in my knee and face struck like a lightning bolt. Stunned, I lifted my head from the ground and peered toward the church. Todd was gone, but I glimpsed the back of a linen dress as the church door closed. I ignored the damage to my body, springing up and sprinting to the church, where I opened the door.

"What are you doing here?" Maeve Baldwin blocked the entrance on the other side.

"The woman. A woman just walked into the building." My eyes took in the room behind Maeve. "Where is she?"

"You're not authorized to be in this section of the abbey grounds." Maeve's typically raspy voice sounded more like a hiss.

I exploded. "I've been patient long enough with your snappy taunts. I want you to admit why you're so bent on running me out of Ireland."

"Ladies, this is a place of worship. Please, lower your voices." I hadn't heard Sister Meghan quietly enter the nave behind me.

"Where is Todd, Sister? I saw him run into the building." I turned to face the Franciscan nun. "Instead, I find this woman," I said, pointing at Maeve. "What is she doing here? Especially since she's masquerading as a historian."

Meghan's face blanched, making her wimple look like it had color. "What are you saying, Miss O'Brien?" She marched farther into the church and stood next to Maeve.

"I told you not to allow her to involve herself in this Quinn issue." Maeve moved closer to me. "She's trouble, and she's full of wild ideas."

When I heard Maeve's words, I felt my body relax. She didn't realize that she'd just confirmed again my conclusion that she'd been the woman asking Margaret Hanlon questions.

"You have no idea how involved I am. Also, lady, you have no authority over 'this Quinn issue,' so move aside before I heft you," I snarled, sidestepping her and pushing farther into the church. "Where does that lead?" I asked, running toward the door at the altar side of the church. I pulled the handle before either of the women could stop me. A trampled grass path led from the church toward the Serenity Garden's wall. I whirled around and faced Sister Meghan.

"What are you hiding? Who are you protecting? Is it Todd?"

"Miss O'Brien, I must ask you to leave." Sister Meghan's face had turned from pale to beet red. "You have no rights in Ireland. You have no right to be disruptive in this sanctuary. Women and children who are under the abbey's care must be protected from everyone, and that includes you, Miss O'Brien. You must leave."

The explosion rocked the ground beneath us. Sister Meghan gathered up her habit and raced along the grass path. I followed. As we drew closer to the wall, the outline of a door became evident by the light seeping through around the edges. Meghan pushed against the barrier. I dogged her heels. She didn't stop me. I turned on my heel, intending to shut Maeve out, but she'd vanished.

I refocused on Sister Meghan, who was shepherding tourists out of the garden. Several employees from the abbey's café stood at the official garden entrance, waving people toward the parking lot. One end of the gardener's cottage was in shambles. I moved closer. The remains of several fertilizer bags lay strewn around the perimeter of the rubble pile. A damaged Garden Manager's Office sign lay on the ground. I ran after the crowd, looking for the woman in the linen dress I'd spotted earlier, but she'd disappeared. I hadn't seen Todd since he got away from me at the church. I didn't bother looking for Maeve, but I had no doubt we'd meet again.

When the fire engines and panda cars began streaming into the parking lot, I didn't hang around, figuring the responders would question anyone who'd seen what had happened.

I found Julia in her shop, tidying up bits and pieces of fabric.

"Did you speak with Todd?"

"No, he ran when I tried to confront him, and then there was an explosion in the garden."

"I heard the sound and wondered. Sister Meghan will be beside herself. I hope no one was hurt."

"Looked like some carelessness with bags of fertilizer, but the fire department will figure that out." I turned the conversation back to Todd. "What about the papers Todd mentioned? He was a client of Alex's. I believe Todd has a right to them."

"Maybe he does. I've just been so overwhelmed. I haven't been able to bring myself to open Alex's home office."

"Wait a minute, Julia. You told Todd that the garda said you had to preserve Alex's files. You need to tell me the truth so I can help you."

"I was just trying to get Todd off my back," Julia replied. "I guess I just want this all to be over."

"Going through a deceased person's belongings is not an easy task." I thought of the father I'd never known and his lifelong mementos in a storage facility. "I've got a hunch that Todd's instability and fear when Alex dropped him as a client drove Todd to murder." I considered my next move and suggested, "We don't have to remove the information from Alex's office, but I want to see the files. There may be something there that points more directly to Todd as Alex's murderer."

Julia covered her mouth with her hand. "I can't bear to think of Todd or another villager killing Alex. I suppose I can let you look at his office. Since the explosion cleared the visitors out of town, I'm closing up the shop early and running some errands. Do you want to meet me at my house in thirty minutes?"

"Sure," I replied.

Julia drew a quick map and wrote some street names on a slip of paper, handed it to me, and then we locked up the shop. "Wait," she said, "let me jot my cell phone number in case you get lost." I handed the paper back to her.

"I'll meet you there," I said when she handed the note back to me.

Main Street had emptied, and I didn't think it would take long for me to get to Julia's. As I walked along, once again, my thoughts returned to my conversation with Meghan and Maeve. I didn't think Meghan was in on whatever Maeve was up to, but I had to pin them both down. My cell phone rang just as I opened the door to my car.

"Star, I hope you're still in Letterbrack?" Georgina's voice sounded rushed.

"I'm just about to leave for Julia's house, and then I'll head home to French Hill. Is everything all right?"

"Marcella rang. She broke down along Sky Road, coming out of Clifden. The garage is closed. She can't get any help until the morning. Can you look for her and drive her home?"

"Where is Sky Road?" I asked.

"West of where you are. The road runs along the Atlantic and is full of panoramic views, but I wouldn't want to be stranded alone out there at night with a car that didn't work."

"Wouldn't she have an automobile club membership with a number for twenty-four-hour service?"

"I don't know, agra. We can sort that out in the morning. Meanwhile, there's a yellow level alert for a wind and rain system forecast for that area. Marcella thinks she's about halfway between Clifden and the village of Recess. I'm uneasy, and I'd go myself, but you're closer to her."

"Georgina, I'll go. No worries. I'll call you when I have Marcella."

We ended the call. I glanced at the time on my cell phone. I dialed Julia's number, but the phone went to voice mail.

"Julia, this is Star. Listen, a friend of Georgina's, Marcella McHale, broke down with her car, and she's stranded on some dark, dangerous stretch of a road. I'm on my way to pick her up, but I'll be back early in the morning to look through Alex's paperwork with you."

I pressed the *end call* button.

Soon after beginning the drive west from Letterbrack toward Moyard and Clifden along the winding, narrow roads flanked by water and dense forest, the rain fell in buckets, and the wind whipped against the passenger side of the car. I gripped the steering wheel and peered through the rapidly fogging-up window. The car didn't have air conditioning, but I reversed the recycle lever and opened one of the rear windows. Water and wind pelted the back seat, but seeing through the windshield became manageable.

When I finally reached Sky Road, I found Marcella's car pulled over onto a grass verge about the width of a pencil. I left the ignition key switched on, jumped out of the Renault, and fell on my butt as my shoes slid on the slippery grass, which was when I vowed to make better shoe choices in the future. While I worked on picking myself up from the ground, Marcella bounded out of her car and gave me a hand, saying, "Thank goodness you came along. I didn't know what I'd do, and even if some kind-hearted stranger had stopped, I wouldn't have known whether to trust the person."

After Marcella was ensconced in the Renault with the heater on full blast, I reached behind the driver's seat, grabbed a few rags, and then fought with the wind to tie the cloth to the driver's side mirror of Marcella's car as a signal that the car wasn't abandoned.

"I hope no one plows into your car," I said when I returned to the Renault.

"I think the car is pulled in far enough on the verge, so I suppose it'll be okay. Besides, we're probably the only people out in these conditions," Marcella replied, squeezing excess water out of her tunic top. "I'm drenched, and so are you, Star."

I nodded and ran a hand through my short, ebony hair. "I'm

sure the cowlicks are celebrating. Give Aunt Georgina a call. She was worried," I said.

While Marcella assured Georgina that we were okay, I kept my eyes glued on the road ahead, all the while creeping along the wild Atlantic Way. Panoramic views or not, the sooner we left Sky Road behind, the better.

After a few moments of driving in silence, I asked, "What do you think is wrong with the car?"

"I don't know. I heard a loud, crunching noise, and steering the car became really hard. I'm lucky I was able to get it off the road. I'll call the garage in the morning. They'll have to come and fix it or tow it back to Castlebar."

"I imagine that will be quite a tow. Were you in Clifden planning an event?"

Marcella sighed. "Nothing so happy, I'm afraid. My beloved parents are buried in Ardbear Cemetery."

"Oh," I said, thinking of the old Turlough Cemetery, where Georgina tended her family graves, and then I wondered where my father was buried. I made a mental note to ask Evelyn.

"Georgina told me about your father. I hope you find some peace in knowing who he was," Marcella said as if she had read my thoughts.

I appreciated her sentiments, but I didn't want to go there. Instead, I asked, "Do you think Maeve could be involved in Alex's murder?"

Marcella's hand shot out and grasped the dashboard as she turned to look at me. "What?"

"She's turned up in every investigation I've been involved with. Ashford Castle, Turlough Museum, and the abbey."

"What would her motive be?" Marcella asked.

"Me. She's been on the perimeter of my life since I returned to Mayo to find Evelyn Cosgrove." I shook my head. "I was in Letterbrack this afternoon, where I had a confrontation with

Maeve and Sister Meghan. A few minutes later, there was an explosion in the Walled Serenity Garden."

"An explosion? That's unusual. Was anyone hurt?"

"No, thank goodness. The event was attributed to a mishap with fertilizer. Sister Meghan was upset, and the tourists I saw leaving the garden looked worried."

"No wonder. There's no telling how something like that will be described on some of the tourist information sites," Marcella said. "Okay, back to Maeve. I've wondered about her interest in rekindling her relationship with me after all these years. Yeah, sure, I've bumped into her at various fundraising events, but lately…."

"The timing of these events coincides with my trips to Mayo, don't they?"

Marcella sat back in the passenger seat and answered, "I see what you're saying, but I don't believe Maeve is a suspect." When Marcella spoke again, she said, "But Meghan danced around the questions Georgina and I shot at her, which is unusual."

"I have a theory about Maeve," I said, and then told her my conclusion that Maeve knew something about my mother's disappearance.

"Your hunch is entirely plausible, but you need more proof. If Maeve is somehow mysteriously involved, then she'll have a solid backstory to fit her narrative to keep her secrets."

"I have enough information to support my conclusion."

"But if you're wrong… If Maeve is just someone who happens to dislike you, incorrectly accusing her of having something to do with your mother will place your reputation in jeopardy."

"I'm sure I'm right."

Marcella reached across the seat and touched my shoulder. "I hope so, Star. For your sake."

"Thank you," I replied, and we drove for another few

minutes before Marcella said, "Oh, look, the welcome to Castlebar sign. I'll be happy to plant my feet in front of the fire tonight."

I smiled, thinking of Marcella's kitchen with the massive oak table and monstrous open hearth, and then my heart pinged when I thought of Lorcan.

Later that evening, after I'd dropped off Marcella and checked in with Ellie and Phillie, I tried calling Julia, but her phone went straight to voice mail.

O'Shea didn't answer his phone either.

CHAPTER 19

The heavy rain and gusting wind rattling the cottage's front door woke me at 3:00 a.m. I tossed and turned for another thirty minutes before I wrapped a wool throw around my shoulders, marched into the kitchen, and made a mug of steaming peppermint tea. I found kindling that Aunt Georgina had left, relit the fire in the living room, and then sat making new notes and rereading the information I'd gathered thus far regarding Alex's murder.

I moved Todd to the top of my suspect list based on his outburst in the pub, the antagonism directed at Julia, and his downright refusal to speak to me. Furthermore, his obvious anger fit the profile of the violent way in which Alex had been murdered. Finally, Todd had been running in the direction of the garden before the explosion. Could he have caused the explosion as a diversion? His prior work in the garden meant he would have known where the fertilizer was kept. Had the police interviewed Todd with a view of Todd's motivation to murder Alex? I made a note to follow up with O'Shea in the morning.

Julia and O'Shea remained on the list, but I didn't believe either one of them had committed murder. Having spoken to Charlotte, Brendan, and Todd, I questioned their motives for placing Julia at the entry to the trailhead so specifically. Certainly, the trio seemed to have animosity toward Julia. I closed the notebook.

While I watched the embers burn down to dusty cold ash, I reviewed my earlier conversation with Maeve and then with Marcella. I was sure Maeve had a personal connection to me with a negative intent. Perhaps the glimpses I'd gotten of the mysterious woman had nothing to do with me other than my wishful thinking, but Maeve's behavior was suspicious. I couldn't imagine a connection between Maeve and my Consulting Detective clients in the U.S. No, she was threatened by me being in Ireland and the search for my mother. I had to be correct. Maeve must know what had happened to my mother. I closed my eyes for a few minutes, and then when I opened them, the sun was rising on the horizon. I sprang up from the sofa, donned my sneakers and running clothes, and went for a long walk along the cottage road. By the time I returned and stepped into the shower, I'd exorcized all my doubts. I looked forward to confronting Maeve.

The sun hung low on the horizon as I drove toward Letterbrack, but the weather had cleared. I assumed 8:00 a.m. was too early to phone Julia, so I parked near Main Street and walked the length of the town. The sidewalks were empty. Most shops wouldn't open until 9:30 a.m. Fortunately, the tea, coffee, and pastry places catered to tourists by opening early. I entered Cream, where Marcella, Georgina, and I had met up earlier in the week, and sat down at a seat near the window so I could watch the town come alive.

"Our cook hasn't shown up yet, but I can get you a hot tea, and we have lovely fresh-baked raisin scones," the server suggested when she came to the table with a menu.

When I turned my gaze from the window, I thought the server looked familiar. "We've met before, haven't we?"

"Yes, on the road. Remember the backup. You were on your way to the village for the first time."

"Yes. Don't you work at the abbey restaurant?"

The server laughed. "I do, but I'm here a few mornings a week. My cousin owns this venue. I help him out whenever I can."

"You must know many of the local residents."

The server's hand hovered above the order pad. "You're the American everyone is talking about—the one who's trying to clear Julia's name."

"I am. What do you think happened to Alex?" I asked, interested in her opinion or what she might have heard from the locals.

"I don't know. He was well known around the village for his devotion to environmental issues, and he was relentless when he saw an issue that might devastate our beautiful landscape...."

The bell over the door jingled, interrupting her. She turned toward the incoming customer, narrowed her eyes, and closed her pad. "I'll be back with your order."

I glanced over my shoulder to see who or what had caused her reaction. Todd didn't see me as he strode toward the counter. I stood, positioned my body in front of the door, and then waited. Behind the counter, I could see the server's eyes widening, but she didn't utter a word. Instead, she poured coffee from an urn into a to-go cup, which she handed to him. When he turned to leave, the hand holding the cup dropped to his side, causing hot coffee to splatter all over the floor. I braced myself for the explosion I expected. Instead, he marched toward me and said, "Let's get this interview over with."

"This mess needs cleaning up first," I replied, walking to the counter. The server gave me a grateful smile and said, "I'll take care of it." She picked up a mop and whispered, "Thank you," as she walked past me to the coffee puddle.

I reversed course and indicated the table where I'd been sitting to Todd. He took a seat. I wondered about the change in his attitude: one minute raging, angry, and defiant, and the next subdued and cooperative.

"Why the sudden interest in speaking with me?" I asked.

Todd smiled, but his hooded eyes perused the table. "The scales of justice are in motion."

"Oh, that's an interesting comment coming from someone who's been fired from his job. What's your version of justice?"

"You think you're smart, don't you? But you have no idea what goes on around this village. But musha, how could you? You're just some Yank who pokes her nose into other people's business." He raised his voice to the server and said, "Hey, can you bring me a cup of coffee?"

When the server brought another cup, he gulped the coffee in a way that I imagined he took his liquor.

"I know you were angry at Alex. But what's the deal with Julia?"

"The two of them, thinking they're better than everyone. Alex should have stayed on my case, but no, he suddenly had a conscience." Todd shrugged. "Sure, I took a bit of money from the till, but I didn't murder anyone."

"Where were you the day Alex was murdered?"

"I don't need to answer your questions, Miss O'Brien. In fact, my day is looking more optimistic with each passing moment."

"Oh? What's turned everything around for you?"

"You aren't up on the local news, are you? The murderer is about to be revealed."

"And that would be?"

"I may be wrong, but panda cars passed me on the road, lights flashing like a beacon in a foggy ocean—straight down the path to Julia Quinn's place. Methinks the lady's about to get arrested."

I jumped up from my seat, grabbed my knapsack, and blasted through the shop door. Once I was in my car, I used the directions Julia had written down for me to find the narrow byroad to her house, driving as fast as I could on the narrow, rutted lane.

Todd may have sounded delirious, but he was correct about one thing: when the sign with the words *Quinn Homestead* and the driveway came into view, I saw several police cars lining both sides of the avenue. Two uniformed police officers blocked the entrance. I slammed on the brakes and nosed my car into one of the gaps between police vehicles.

As I ran toward the officers, I heard Julia Quinn's name over the garda radios. One of the officers stepped forward, blocking further movement.

"I'm sorry, but this is a crime scene. The public is not allowed in."

"I'm not the public," I said, pulling away from his arm. "I'm a friend of Julia's. I have an appointment with her. Let me through."

"I see. Well, the detectives will want to talk with you then. Please wait." The officer moved me away from the driveway to one of the panda cars.

I wrapped my arms around myself while my brain spun in an endless loop—*No, not Julia. Not Julia. It can't be Julia.*

"Here come the detectives." The officer pointed toward several men striding toward us along the driveway.

"O'Shea," I gasped. "What are you doing here?"

Two men in navy blue suits flanked O'Shea, and four more uniformed police came up behind them. As they drew closer, I noticed the guys in the suits each had a grasp on O'Shea.

He stumbled when he heard my voice. I ran toward him. One of the detectives held up his free hand to me. "I don't know who you are, but please stand back. This is an active crime scene."

"I can see that," I replied to the detective and remained where I was. "I want to know what happened."

The four policemen behind the detectives surged forward, creating a barrier between me and O'Shea. One of them said, "You're okay, miss, but you have to move aside."

I complied and followed the detectives as they and O'Shea walked toward one of the panda cars. I wasn't close enough to hear what they were saying, but I could see O'Shea doing most of the talking. Apparently, some part of the discussion was about me because one of the men motioned me over to the car.

"What's going on? Is Julia okay?" I demanded.

O'Shea opened his mouth to speak, but nothing came out. Instead, his shoulders slumped, and he stared at the ground.

The taller of the two detectives introduced himself as the person in charge. "I'm Detective Riley, Miss O'Brien. Unfortunately, Julia Quinn is deceased. Detective O'Shea found her body and alerted us."

"Dead? But that can't be. I was working with her. I left a message yesterday saying I'd drop by in the morning." The words poured out of me like water. I didn't know what to say or do. "Let me see her. I want to know what happened."

Riley placed his hand on my arm. "We can't let you do that, and besides, you don't want to...."

"I want to know how she died," I interrupted, not wanting to leave that to my imagination. If she'd been killed by the person who murdered Alex, I didn't want to imagine her friendly, kind face marred in the way she'd described what had happened to him.

"I'm sorry, but we cannot share that information with...."

"Tell her," O'Shea interrupted. "I've worked with this woman in the past. In fact, I asked her to look into Alex Quinn's murder."

Riley's face froze, and his eyes narrowed to slits before he commanded, "I'm in charge, O'Shea. I want both of you to move to the side while I speak to my men."

"But...."

"You heard me, O'Shea."

O'Shea's scar blanched white with anger like a fire iron. His hands balled into fists. I touched his shoulders. "Let's do what the detective ordered. You can brief me."

O'Shea nodded, and we moved out of earshot from the police.

"What happened?" I didn't know what else to say. My stomach roiled in fear and anger.

O'Shea took a breath, straightened his shoulders, and stared toward Julia's home. "I called her last night, but the phone went to voice mail." He stopped as if searching for words.

"What time was that? I called around six p.m., and she didn't answer either."

"Late. Maybe ten p.m. I wanted her to know I was on the investigative team, and we planned to interview her this morning."

Could Julia already have been dead when I phoned? What if I'd chosen meeting with her as planned instead of rescuing Marcella? Would I have prevented whoever murdered Julia from getting to her?

"When...?"

"The medical examiner thought last evening sometime. She's in full rigor, so it could be twenty hours or less from my discovery of her," O'Shea said, not waiting for me to finish.

"Was it the same as...?"

"No, not like Alex. We have to wait for the official reports, but I'd guess she was poisoned. She'd vomited, and her salad plate was on the floor next to her." O'Shea shuddered. "I can't do this." He walked away and banged his head and fists on one of the lot's oak trees.

In the meantime, the group surrounding Riley dispersed, and then he marched over to where O'Shea stood. O'Shea nodded, straightened his tie, and followed the detective back to me.

"I've instructed Detective O'Shea to return to Castlebar. He's no longer a consultant to the investigating team. You, Miss O'Brien, are no longer needed." He turned on his heel and walked away.

"But I may have insight into who might have wanted Julia dead...."

Riley didn't answer.

"I must get on to my Superintendent. Can you meet me in the village? In, say, thirty minutes?" O'Shea said to me.

"Yes. I'll be in a place called Cream. It's on Main Street across from the Bank of Ireland branch," I replied, and then I zombie-walked to my car and sat there stunned for a few minutes before driving away.

I chose a seat on the café's sidewalk. The idea of being surrounded by four walls made me want to scream. People meandered by, but I didn't notice whether they were tourists or Julia's friends. I clenched my phone in an effort to stem the flow of tears that threatened to erupt. Instead, I focused on my anger —anger at myself for not stopping Julia's murder. Anger at the good Franciscans for not cooperating in Alex's investigation, and that was when Maeve Baldwin approached the table.

"Miss O'Brien. I've heard the news about Julia Quinn. I hope you're proud of yourself. Tinkering around, asking questions, acting like you belong in Ireland. Well, I'm sure Julia must wish she'd chosen someone else to be her advocate."

"Your taunts and innuendos are nothing but a smokescreen. I believe you know something about my missing mother. When I get to the truth, you'll wish you'd never set your foot on Achill Island."

"I don't know what you're insinuating, but I won't stand for any of it." Maeve's hand went to the string of pearls dangling from her neck.

I jumped up and grabbed the pearls, pulling her closer to me. "You know something about my mother."

"Oh, Lord. Get ahold of yourself, woman. You've gone over the edge with your wild fantasies."

"There it is. You say *wile* instead of *wild,* which means you're from Donegal. I have a witness—someone who identified you and the visit you made to Achill Island, where I understand you were looking into the history of a woman named Maggie O'Malley."

"What's going on?" O'Shea asked, glancing from my face to Maeve's.

"I'm happy to see a garda, Detective O'Shea. Apparently, Julia Quinn's death has been a terrible shock to Miss O'Brien. You may want to escort her to a doctor's office."

"You're a liar," I said.

O'Shea put his hand on my shoulder. "Star, we need to talk. Can you finish whatever is going on with Miss Baldwin later?"

I leaned away, letting the pearls fall from my hand. O'Shea was right; I needed to focus on Julia's murderer.

Maeve smiled and sauntered away.

I sat down, and O'Shea took the opposite seat. Minutes passed before he spoke again. "I need to know you'll continue to work with me."

"So, now you want my assistance?" I said, clenching the cell phone tethered to my pants. "Yesterday, you fired me." O'Shea put out a hand toward me, but I moved back. "I'm angry, O'Shea. Julia was my friend, and she's dead. I'm not some yo-yo you can wind up anytime you feel like it. What do you want from me?"

"Look, I'm sorry. I was all caught up in my ego. I'd been appointed to the investigative team as a consultant, and I didn't want to muddy the waters by saying you were working with me." O'Shea ran a hand through his hair. "I was wrong, and I'll understand if you don't want to continue," O'Shea said, rising from the seat.

"Stop," I said. "Sit down." The anger I'd been feeling dissipated as I admitted to myself that most of it resulted from my interaction with Maeve. I wasn't going to let her get away with whatever hand she'd had in my mother's disappearance. I yearned to get into the abbey and speak to the mysterious woman—but I'd promised O'Shea and Julia that I'd assist in finding Alex's killer. I had failed Julia. I wouldn't fail her again.

"Yes, O'Shea. You, no, *Julia* can count on me—I'll be her voice."

CHAPTER 20

"Did you speak to your supervisor?" I asked.

"Aye, and I'm officially off the case," he replied, pounding the table with his fist. "How could I have been so stupid? I should have made sure Julia was protected."

"O'Shea, I'm sorry about Julia." What do you say to someone when a loved one's death has crushed their heart and soul?

"My grief must wait, Miss O'Brien." O'Shea's eyes filled with tears, which he wiped away with the back of his hand. "I'm continuing to hunt down this killer. I don't care what my superintendent says. Given the circumstances, Séamus won't share information with me, but I'll try him. I'm sure he wants to solve this case as much as I do."

"Okay, we'll conduct parallel lines of investigation and brief each other as we go along."

O'Shea nodded. "I never thought I'd say this, but I'm pleased you're working with me."

"What did you learn at the crime scene?"

"Julia was poisoned. The medical examiner identified Datura Stramonium mixed into her salad greens. There was a to-go box on the kitchen counter."

"This Datura thing? What is it?"

"It's commonly called jimsonweed. It looks like a salad green but is deadly toxic to humans." O'Shea sighed. "She'd have gastro and neuro symptoms, maybe even hallucinations, depending upon how much was in the food. The medical examiner will determine that when he performs the post-mortem."

"Would it have been painful?" I asked.

"Yes." O'Shea's face crumpled as he fought back the tears.

"How did that end up in her salad? Wouldn't she have noticed it?"

"No, you wouldn't notice anything odd since it looks just like any other mixed green." O'Shea paused and then continued, "There have been jimsonweed cases in the country. Sometimes the greens growing near other crops like peas gets mixed in during harvesting."

"Do you know where the to-go box came from?"

"No identifiable markings."

"Okay,"—I nodded—"I need to know how the poison got into Julia's take-out salad. What do you plan to do next?"

"I'm heading over to the abbey café to look at the work schedules and interview the staff. Someone might have seen or remember a to-go salad order, especially if it were for Julia."

"When I last saw Julia, she planned to head home, and I was supposed to join her shortly thereafter. She never said anything to me about picking up an order at the abbey. But then I got a call from Georgina. Marcella's car had broken down, and she needed a ride home. Won't the investigative team interview the café staff?"

"They're still at the scene—dusting for fingerprints and the like."

"You're making a huge assumption, O'Shea, about where the salad came from. There are other food venues in the village."

"I've got to start somewhere."

"I'm betting Todd killed Julia. He was delirious with glee when I spoke with him before driving to Alex and Julia's house." I stood up and said, "I'm going over to Julia's shop to speak with the guild members. I'll check in with you later, O'Shea."

O'Shea nodded. "Thank you. I don't think I can face Julia's friends. My superintendent wants me in his office. After I speak with the abbey café workers, I'll head back to Castlebar."

O'Shea walked away, and I strode to Julia's shop, where I glimpsed Rita and Anne huddled around Nigel through the glass window. Anne's sobs greeted me when I opened the door.

"Is it true?" Rita Barrett asked.

I pursed my lips, refusing to break down in the face of the group's heartache. "Yes," I replied.

"What, what can we do?" Anne asked in between heaving sobs.

"Get tough. We have a killer to catch, and what you may have seen or heard could be the clue that brings this person to justice. I know you want to cry, but my advice is to get angry instead."

"But we're not detectives. I can't do this." Anne rushed from the shop, knocking over a display rack of tote bags.

Nigel's face crumpled as he picked up the monogrammed bags, several of which had Julia's initials on the front.

I looked at Nigel and Rita and said, "Right, Todd is at the top of my suspect list."

Rita grabbed her bag from the floor and jostled past the group. "Anne is right. I don't want to be a part of this chaos. My husband warned me about getting involved. I'm leaving."

"I'll help, Miss O'Brien. I loved Julia."

My heart softened at Nigel's words. I knew how difficult losing your love was, and in Nigel's case, the love hadn't been reciprocated, not in the way he'd wanted. The only assistance I could give him was to focus on finding who killed Julia.

"Nigel, you said you have a bird's eye view of the town from your studio. Did you see Todd yesterday?"

"Several times."

"Where?"

"The first time was when I went to the café to pick up a salad at about one p.m. Todd was getting a sandwich and a salad as well."

"Oh, I thought he wasn't welcome at the café."

"He knows one of the servers. She slips food to him when she can. He's not working, and well, we look out for him. Julia asked us to be extra kind to him."

"Why do you think she did that?"

Nigel smiled. "Julia was one of the most generous people I know. I think it was because she was orphaned. Whenever I lost faith in my creativity, she'd tell me to have courage and strength. I guess that's why I loved her. She believed in me."

"Did you see where Todd went when he left the café?"

"He started walking toward the Conservation Foundation building, stopping on his way to speak with Sister Meghan."

Once again, Sister Meghan seemed to be in the midst of everything in Letterbrack. "Did you notice anyone else speaking with him? Did he make any other stops?"

"Charlotte called out to him when he was with Sister. He waved but kept on going after Sister left him." Nigel shuffled his feet, knocking over his tote bag. A sheaf of artist pages fell out.

I reached down to pick up some of the papers. My heart lurched when my eyes focused on one of the drawings. "Where did you get this?" I asked, pulling the paper from the pile.

Nigel's face expressed surprise. "I move around the village, the abbey, and the garden grounds, looking for subjects. I've seen that woman in the garden several times. I made a quick sketch."

"Did you speak to her?" I asked. I couldn't take my eyes from the image.

"No. I try to be inconspicuous when I'm sketching a subject. I think she's staying in the abbey. I've seen Sister Meghan talking to her."

"Anyone else?"

"Another stranger. An older woman. Dresses all in black and wears pearls."

Maeve Baldwin again. I was sure of it. What did she have to do with the woman in Nigel's portrait? My right hand reached to touch the locket I wore. I already suspected Maeve knew something about my mother. If my suspicions were true, then Sister Meghan might be complicit.

I handed the sketch back, stuffed my notebook into my knapsack, and instructed Nigel to stay close to home before I exited. When I looked back, he held his face in his hands, and the sound of his sobs was heartbreaking.

When I arrived at the foundation building, I strode past the reception desk and climbed the stairs toward the room where I'd seen the foundation board members assembled for a meeting when I'd spoken to the director two days earlier. As I approached the room, shouting and phrases like "No" and "What will the tourists think?" reverberated along the hallway. When I heard Sister Meghan say, "We must do what is necessary to protect the abbey," I didn't wait; I barged into the room.

"Does that include harboring a murderer?" The room quieted, the occupants' eyes on me.

Susan Drew stood and opened her mouth to speak, but Sister Meghan put her hand up in protest and said, "I'll handle this," then she bustled out of the room, catching me by the elbow and pulling me with her. "I advise you to control yourself, Miss O'Brien."

"Is that what you call permitting cold-blooded murder to occur, Sister?"

"I already told you, neither I nor the abbey have anything to do with Alex's death. Why can't you understand that?"

"Julia would have a different opinion, Sister."

"What about Julia?"

"What? You haven't heard the news, Sister. You're the one losing control. I thought you knew everything about everyone in Letterbrack. Julia is dead, Sister." I paused to let my words sink in. "Poisoned. Probably with some deadly herb from the garden, Sister. You know the secret, off-limits section."

Sister Meghan gasped, and her hand moved to the rosary beads encircling her waist. "You cannot frighten me with your theatrics, Miss O'Brien."

"But you should be worried, Sister. How will the God you care so much about respond when it's revealed you've been harboring a murderer?"

By this time, some of the meeting members had assembled at the conference room door. I could hear murmurs and whispers. I turned to face them and said, "Yes, you heard correctly. Julia Quinn is dead at the hands of a murderer who's sitting in the room with you."

Susan covered her mouth with her hand and then walked over to a phone on the wall.

Brendan folded his arms, shook his head, and said to no one in particular, "I'm just glad I stayed out of this investigation and away from the Yank right from the beginning." He pushed past the group and walked down the corridor toward the exit before turning back and shouting to Meghan, "Stop talking, Sister, and call a lawyer."

I charged into the room where Todd sat, doodling with a pen on a pad of paper. "There's your killer," I said, pointing at Todd and turning to face Meghan, who'd returned to the room.

Todd pushed the pad away and dropped the pen from his hand but didn't say a word.

"You've been protecting him, haven't you, Sister?" I asked.

"Miss O'Brien, calm yourself, sit down, and we'll discuss your allegations sanely," Meghan said.

"You look like the one who needs to sit, Sister. Feeling uneasy about refusing to answer my questions? I've wondered why you wouldn't tell me about the mystery woman and prevented me from entering the abbey. What are you hiding?"

"Nothing, child. Please, sit down, and we'll discuss." Meghan's face blushed red as a beet.

"I won't accept your excuses any longer. I saw Todd at the church yesterday at about the same time I saw the mystery woman that you're so intent on sheltering. When I attempted to follow her, the explosion near the gardener's cottage occurred."

"That has nothing to do with Todd or the woman you're so intent on meeting."

"The issue in the garden. Was it a diversion? Some way to keep me from focusing on Todd?"

"Oh, my Lord." Meghan threw her hands up in the air. "Todd couldn't have killed anyone this morning. He was with me."

"Where was he yesterday evening, Sister? Did you have him under your nose then? Because according to the medical examiner, Julia was killed yesterday."

Sister Meghan's face paled, and she grasped the rosary beads in her hands.

Susan placed the phone back on its hook without having made a call and took a seat at the table. "Sister, what is going on?"

"Todd has admitted his past mistakes. He's been visiting with me in the chapel for guidance each day. We've prayed together."

"Thank you, Sister, but I don't owe this woman anything."

Todd's voice rang out in the room, startling the remaining board members. "I know I've been a burden to many in the village because of my drinking and my behavior. But I'm working on being a better person."

"Sister, I need a better explanation for what's going on. The foundation's reputation, our funding, and our government grants are at stake. I"—Susan waved her hand around the room, taking in the board members, who squirmed in their seats—"we cannot condone this behavior."

"I remind you, I chair this board. I know how this looks, but no ill will come to us. We are a protected organization. In the end, good wins." Sister's hands moved over the rosary beads as she spoke. "Let's continue with our meeting. The poaching issue must be addressed."

Susan's shoulders slumped, and then she said, "Very well."

I moved farther into the room. "What's wrong with you?" I asked the group seated around the table. "Two of Letterbrack's residents have been murdered, and you just sit around worrying about grant money and poaching."

"I'm afraid I'll have to ask you to leave, Miss O'Brien," Susan said, walking over to the phone on the wall again.

Footsteps echoing through the hallway became louder. Detective Riley and his partner marched into the room. "Good afternoon," Riley said, turning to Sister Meghan. "Sister, you need to come with me." He motioned to two police officers who stood at the entrance to the room.

"I'm in the middle of chairing this meeting, Detective. I'll speak with you later."

"I'm afraid this matter cannot wait. The abbey's restaurant has been closed while we are investigating Julia Quinn's death."

Meghan sprang from her seat. "You have no right to barge into abbey business."

"Sister, this is not a request," Riley stated. "You're to

accompany me to the abbey kitchen while we question the staff."

Sister Meghan's skirt billowed when she stormed out of the room. Riley and his men followed her toward the building's exit.

"Mr. O'Toole, in light of the matter at hand, I must request your resignation from the board. Please, leave immediately," Susan said to Todd and then spoke a few words into the phone. After she hung up, she looked directly at Todd and said, "I've alerted security, but I hope their assistance won't be necessary."

Todd pushed back from the table and sauntered toward me and the exit door behind me. I raised my hand in an attempt to stop him. "Be careful, Miss O'Brien; there are witnesses in the room. I may have to sue you."

Instead of stepping back, I moved within inches of his body. "Trust me. I'll get to the truth," I warned just as Charlotte burst into the room.

"Todd, come with me," she demanded, elbowing her way past me and pulling him by the arm.

Todd moved past me, all the while smirking in triumph.

My teeth were gnashing so hard that I bit the inside of my cheek. I backed away from the conference room, moving toward the door Charlotte and Todd had disappeared through. When I didn't see them, I forced myself to put one foot in front of the other until I reached my car. I opened the passenger door, threw my knapsack onto the seat, and then leaned against the car for support, allowing the tears to course down my face. Passersby glanced at me and then just as quickly looked away. When the initial rush of tears staunched, I crossed to the driver's side of the car and got in.

"Georgina." My voice cracked when she answered the phone. But then I managed to get the words out. "Julia is dead."

"No, that can't be." Georgina's voice sounded as rattled as mine. "Where are you?"

"I'm on my way home. Can you meet me at French Hill?"

"Of course. Are you all right to drive? I can come pick you up."

"Don't do that." I wiped my cheeks dry and turned the key in the ignition. "I'll need my car. I'll see you later."

"Be careful, agra."

We ended the call, and I ignored the sobs that threatened to erupt from my chest. Instead, I texted Phillie and instructed her to find every restaurant menu in Letterbrack that served a kale salad and send it to me.

As I drove out of Letterbrack, I could see a group of tourists waiting to enter Julia's shop. Life would go on, but not with Julia. As for me, I continued with the long, lonely journey over the Connemara roads back to French Hill.

CHAPTER 21

When I pulled onto the grass verge alongside the barn at French Hill, I was relieved to see Georgina's and Marcella's cars. I jolted out of mine and ran toward the cottage. The front door opened. Georgina rushed out and pulled me in. Marcella, standing in the middle of the living room, nodded when she saw me. The sick feeling I'd had during the drive back to Castlebar lessened at the sight of them.

"Sit." Georgina pointed at the loveseat. "Tell us everything."

"I missed something," I said when I'd finished recounting the day's events.

"Nonsense." Marcella spoke for the first time since I'd entered the room.

"Julia must have had information regarding whoever murdered Alex," Georgina added.

"Like what?" I said, punching the cushion next to me. "Sister Meghan keeps covering for Todd. What have I overlooked?"

"You didn't miss anything. If anyone bears responsibility for what happened, it's the garda," Marcella said. "They haven't solved Alex's murder, have they? You're being too hard on yourself," she added.

I shook my head. "No, I'm not...." My iPhone, which I'd thrown onto the coffee table when I came through the door, rang. Lorcan's name flashed on the display. I picked up the phone and pressed *accept*.

"Lorcan." I barely breathed his name, not believing it was him on the other end of the phone.

"Star, are you okay? Are you home? Are Georgina and my mother with you?" Lorcan's ordinarily quiet and modulated voice spat out the questions.

"You heard?"

"About Julia? Yes, my mother rang as soon as Georgina told her. Are they with you? Are you home?"

"We're in French Hill," I replied when I really wanted to say how much I missed him, how sorry I was, and how much I needed him at the moment.

"Good. Star, I'm sorry for not answering your calls. I was being pigheaded."

"I wish you were here." I pressed the phone against my ear as if I could wish him into the room with me.

"I do, too. But I can't return to Ireland until I've resolved the issue I'm working on. Meanwhile, I've asked my mother to give you all the support you need."

I glanced at Marcella and Georgina, who'd moved to the other side of the room. I guessed they wanted to give us some privacy.

I nodded. "Yeah, they've been great."

"I rang O'Shea and spoke with him. The poor mite is broken up. I hope you continue to work with him, Star. He needs a strong-minded person at his side."

"Yes, I saw him this morning. I'm sorry he has to go through this. When do you think the Wyoming project issues will be resolved?"

"I don't know." Lorcan's voice sounded muted. "I have to go.

The team is asking me to look at the new set of blueprints we've designed. Promise me you'll remain careful."

"I will."

We ended the call. I placed my cell phone back on the table.

"That was Lorcan."

Marcella nodded. "I called him, Star. I wanted him to know about O'Shea's loss. But I know how much my son loves you, too."

I jumped up from the sofa, ran toward Marcella, and threw my arms around her. "Thank you," I said, wiping the wet tears on my cheeks.

Marcella held me at arm's length and said, "You are welcome. But remember, he's my lad, and if you ever break his heart, I will come for you, Star O'Brien." Then, she embraced me.

"The best thing to do is to get a good night's sleep," Georgina interrupted. "You can start fresh in the morning," she continued, taking my hand and pointing me toward the bedroom.

Within minutes, Georgina had seen me tucked into bed with a warm water bottle at my feet. I heard murmurs in the living room and then, after a bit, silence. I fell asleep with Lorcan's voice and words lessening the horrible pain I felt each time I thought of Julia.

In the morning, I forced myself out for a run along Cottage Road. The crisp, cool air against my skin was soothing. The sky was a clear blue palette with puffy, cotton-ball clouds hanging over Nephin Mountain in the distance. MidWest Radio had reported a dusting of snow on Nephin over the nighttime hours, which was weird because it was summer in Ireland. The wind rustling through the pine trees that bordered the field reminded me of Lorcan and his wind project. Farther along the road, a scattering of sheep stared at me in surprise when I stopped to take in the green landscape and the quiet solitude.

When I finally returned to the cottage, I felt more determined than ever and was happy to see Aunt Georgina's car parked near the barn.

"I've cooked a full Irish breakfast, Star," she said when I walked through the back kitchen door. "Get yourself into that chair and eat up, girleen. You have work to do."

I obeyed, reaching across the table for a thick slab of Georgina's homemade brown bread. After slathering the slice with butter, I heard my stomach growl in anticipation. "I didn't realize how hungry I was," I said. "I hope you're planning to join me," I commented when Georgina placed two dinner-sized plates brimming over with eggs, bacon, sausage, black pudding, beans, and sliced tomato on the table.

Georgina nodded, took off the colorful, textured linen apron she wore, and seated herself in front of one of the plates.

In between bites of the runny-yolked eggs, I studied Georgina. I noticed she wasn't wearing one of her signature scarf ensembles. Instead, a pale green linen blouse tucked into belted black pants complemented her tiny yet sturdy frame.

"You're not wearing a scarf."

"I wasn't feeling buoyant, but I'm celebrating Julia's creative gifts." Georgina pointed at the textured apron. "That piece is one of her designs. She gave it to me last year when we worked on a wedding ensemble together."

I reached across the table and touched Georgina's hand. "I'm sorry about your friend," I said, realizing that Georgina must feel as devastated as I did over Julia's death—perhaps even more.

Georgina turned my hand over in hers. "We've had some losses recently, haven't we? Maybe too many. I'm beginning to understand why you protect yourself from loving too much."

I didn't respond, but Georgina's words touched my soul in a way I'd never experienced before. I thought of Lorcan and his anger and hurt. He'd lost a friend when he'd lost Dylan.

Georgina had lost a beloved nephew. They might not know my pain, but they were unflinchingly willing to share in it with me. At that moment, I felt selfish for not seeing how much other people loved me or how my obstinance might hurt them.

"So, Star O'Brien, what's your plan?" Georgina released my hand, picked up her teacup, and leveled her dark brown eyes at me.

I rose from the table, cleared the dishes, and went to the living room for my notebook. When I returned, I opened the notebook to the suspect list.

"We review the case and what we know so far, and then we look for earlier clues I or the police missed."

"Why the question mark after Todd's name?" Georgina pointed to the name at the top of my list.

"According to Sister Meghan, he has an alibi for the morning Julia was found. But Julia died the night before, so he stays on the suspect list," I said and then asked, "Do you think Sister Meghan would lie to protect Todd?"

Georgina pursed her lips and narrowed her eyes. "No. She wouldn't do anything to endanger the work the Franciscans do for the community. If she said he was with her in the morning, I believe her. She wouldn't be persuaded to alibi someone falsely."

I nodded. "Then we have to interview every person who pointed the finger at Julia. Someone is lying, and that someone may be the murderer." I opened the notebook to a blank page while Georgina went to plug in the electric kettle and brew another pot of tea. When she'd refilled our mugs, she glanced at the list I'd made.

"Why is Nigel at the top of the list?" she asked.

"He's not. I haven't prioritized. I've just written names and potential motives. Look." I turned the notebook so Georgina could read what I'd written.

"I don't agree with this list and some of the motives," Georgina said.

"Why not?"

"Sister Meghan, for one. I don't think she'd kill anyone."

"I disagree. She had the means. Remember, I saw a pair of yoga pants under her habit and the mud-caked shoes. Alex was representing Todd in the termination case. If Alex won, the sisters might have lost the lease on the abbey."

"What! How could that be so?"

"Civil lawsuits can be brought against religious organizations. So, no, the abbey is not protected. In this case, if a court ruled that Todd was wrongly treated, he could turn around and go after the sisters and their property."

"That may be so, but why would she kill Julia?"

"She stays on the list." I twirled my phone on the table in front of me. "What gets me is, what is the motive for killing Alex and then Julia? I mean, who commits murder over a litigation case that wasn't even going to happen since Alex dropped Todd, and where does Julia fit into that?"

"Perhaps that's your issue, Star. Are you sure this whole tragedy has something to do with Alex's cases?"

I nodded. "You're right. Without pinpointing the motive, finding Alex's killer is a futile effort. But what else?"

"What else was Alex involved in that would incite someone to kill him?" Georgina asked.

"Songbird poaching," I said without a moment's hesitation. "I don't know if the poaching is a motive for murder, but Alex was involved and dedicated to preventing this kind of crime, especially through his work at the foundation." I stopped, remembering the dead songbird I'd found at Alex's crime scene. I'd wondered at the time where the bird's nest was. Maybe there wasn't one. Perhaps Alex had surprised someone in the act of stealing the baby, and it had been dropped.

"Has anyone mentioned the poaching?" Georgina asked.

"As a matter of fact, yes, Susan Drew mentioned how Alex brought statistics information about the problem to the foundation board. Just yesterday, the board met to discuss the issue."

"Okay, that's a realistic path to explore, Star. Then what about Julia? What did she know that motivated someone to poison her?"

"Alex was involved with the foundation. In fact, according to Julia, his work with the board took up a good part of his time. I'll have to speak with the director again," I said, writing her name on the list. "But Julia had nothing to do with the foundation. So, what's the connection?" I threw my pen onto the table. "I'm hitting my head against the wall on this."

Georgina picked up the pen and handed it back to me. "Keep writing."

I quickly updated the list to include Rita, Anne, Charlotte Evans, and the foundation board members. Although O'Shea's name was on the list, I didn't believe he'd committed murder, but he had knowledge from the detectives working on the case. Therefore, he was the first person I planned to interrogate this morning.

"I can see why Lorcan enjoyed working with you," Georgina said.

"Why do you say that?"

"He's the engineer, and you're the analytical type, making lists and Venn diagrams," Georgina said, pointing to the notebook page where I'd drawn circles and arrows connecting people and jotting down potential motives. "You two have more in common than you admit, Star." Georgina stood up and began moving the dirty cups into the sink.

I leaned back in my chair but didn't say a word.

"Star, someone's just pulled up next to the barn."

I rose and glanced out the kitchen door. Tom O'Shea

walked determinedly toward the cottage. I met him at the front door.

"You saved me a call," I said, pointing to one of the Queen Anne chairs on either side of the fireplace.

O'Shea sat.

Georgina walked into the room. "Can I get you a cup of tea, Tom?" she asked.

"No, Georgina."

"He doesn't have time for refreshments. I have questions, and I want answers," I said, moving from the kitchen to the living room. I grabbed one of the kitchen chairs and plunked it down in front of the Queen Anne chair O'Shea had collapsed into.

"I'll be off then, Star. See you later," Georgina said, tipped her head to O'Shea, and walked out the front door.

O'Shea's face looked like a shaver hadn't touched his skin in a week. His red-rimmed eyes stood out over his blanched cheeks. He looked older than the thirty-seven years I assumed him to be since he'd been friends with Lorcan and Dylan when they were in school.

"You're staring. Do I look that bad?" O'Shea asked, running his right hand through his hair.

"Maybe, but I can't fix that issue. What updates do you have?"

"I've been put on administrative leave, for one. The chief thinks I'm too close to the case. I'm not even allowed desk duty."

"That's convenient."

"What do you mean?"

"Just another way the investigation can keep people like me and you from asking too many questions."

"Aye, 'tis so. But I have friends in the department."

"Like Keenan?"

"I won't say, but this isn't going to keep me from finding out the bloody truth about Julia."

"What else has your inside man told you?"

O'Shea nodded. "Julia was poisoned and died sometime between six and ten p.m. in the evening—long before I found her the next morning."

"Do the detectives have any suspects? Are they looking at Todd? What about Charlotte Evans? She ushered Todd away from the foundation meeting just before the detective squad showed up."

"I intend to talk to him. He was seen near Julia's place the evening she died."

"I'm returning to Letterbrack. Everyone who knows Julia and Alex must be reinterviewed. We shouldn't be seen together. Some of Julia's friends may feel more at ease if they talk to me instead of a member of the garda."

"I agree. Who do you plan to speak with?"

"Charlotte Evans, the guild managers, and the foundation board members. You should interview Sister Meghan. She'll probably be more willing to speak to a lawman."

"Sounds good. Right, I'll be off." O'Shea rose from the chair.

"Where do you think you're going? I'm not finished asking questions. So, sit."

"But...."

"Remember, you're not the detective. I want answers."

O'Shea sat back down. "I'm ready."

"How often do the police investigate employee crimes like theft or embezzlement?"

O'Shea shook his head. "Never. Those types of cases are difficult to prove. Usually, the corporation takes care of the issue."

"Todd's case was an employee-employer dispute, but then Alex learned Todd was stealing and dropped him. Something else was going on other than Todd's work issues." I paused and then brought up Georgina's theory. "I wonder. Georgina mentioned tax dodgers often don't answer questions from strangers. I didn't pursue that line of thought when Georgina mentioned it. But maybe that's what's missing. People often have secrets. Perhaps Alex stumbled upon something someone killed him over."

"If someone is self-employed, tax cheating is a difficult case to prove. Besides, as far as I know from Julia, Alex wasn't into that kind of lawyering," O'Shea said.

"I wonder how the guild reports earnings. Based upon the number of tourists purchasing goods in Julia's shop, I'd guess the members are earning substantial income from their creative endeavors." I stood, saying, "I'll be right back," and walked into the room with my computer. I jotted a quick email to Phillie, asking her to find any reported revenues or tax arrears issued for the businesses owned by the guild members. When I returned to the living room, I asked, "What other kinds of cases was Alex dealing with?"

"I don't know, but I can inquire through my contact about paperwork at Julia's place. Alex kept a work office in the house," O'Shea said, shifting in his seat when he mentioned Julia's name.

"That's good because I just don't think tax evasion is a strong motive for murder. Something else was going on. Something caused someone to cross a line and murder Alex *and* Julia." I paused and then said, "Georgina heard from Rita that she's been hiding income from her husband. I wonder what else she's hiding."

"But what would Julia have to do with Alex's legal clients? From what she told me, Alex was strict about keeping his clients' information sacrosanct," O'Shea said, his voice sounding desperate.

"Someone saw her as a threat. She must have known or witnessed something that put her life in jeopardy." O'Shea may not have wanted to consider Rita as a suspect. Still, short of any other leads, she'd just moved up in my mind: her and her husband's behavior toward me, as well as his swearing he'd seen Julia go into the woods around the time Alex was murdered. I paused and locked my gaze on his eyes. "You haven't told me everything, have you, O'Shea?"

O'Shea's face blanched, and he picked at his sweater before responding. "One of Julia's tote bags was at the scene with Alex's body."

I felt the breath knocked from my body. The anger coursing through my blood overcame my surprise at O'Shea's words. My brain ran through all the possible scenarios. Julia and O'Shea had lied to me. They were playing me for a fool. Julia killed Alex, and O'Shea was covering for her. "You had better tell me the truth... and all of it."

"I'm sorry. In hindsight, I should have told you." O'Shea jumped up from the chair and paced the living room. "Maybe Julia would still be alive."

"Calm down. How do you know Julia's tote bag was at the scene?"

"Because I found the blasted thing when I went to the murder scene. The bag was laid at Alex's side."

"Where is the bag?"

"I gave the bag to Julia."

"Whatever possessed you, O'Shea? I thought you were a law-and-order man."

"I am. But when I saw Julia's bag, which was empty, I immediately assumed the garda would focus on her."

"Oh, yeah, I believe that's what your type does. Take the easy route and blame the innocent."

"Julia swore she didn't kill Alex, and I took her at her word. I returned the bag to her."

"So, is the bag in the shop?" I asked, thinking of the monogrammed totes sitting in Connemara Crafters.

"I don't know. Julia left a voice mail saying she wanted to talk to me about the tote, but we never had a chance." O'Shea's voice broke, and he buried his head in his hands.

"When did she leave that message?"

"On Monday, in the afternoon. When I called back, her phone went to voice mail." O'Shea shook his head as if to clear it. "I've messed this up royally, haven't I?" O'Shea said.

"I'd say. But at least we have something to go on. If the tote bag was planted to make Julia look guilty, then the killer is someone in Letterbrack who had access to one of the monogrammed tote bags. That should be easy to track down."

"You've seen Julia's shop. That's going to be like searching for a needle in a haystack."

"Still, this verifies my gut feeling that someone's been trying to frame Julia for Alex's murder," I replied, thinking of the needles in the trash can. "Maybe Julia recognized something about the tote bag and who might have wanted to kill Alex. The tote bag might even be in her house."

O'Shea stopped pacing. "I don't know how I'm going to get into her house."

"You're not. I will," I said, closing my notebook. "You go ahead and catch up with Sister Meghan and Todd. I'll be along later."

"I'll let you know what I find out," O'Shea said before closing the front door behind him.

"You bet you will."

As I watched O'Shea walk along Cottage Road to where his car was parked, I wondered if the O'Shea I'd known before this tragedy would ever reclaim his life.

CHAPTER 22

As soon as O'Shea vanished from sight, I plunked my notebook into my knapsack and pulled on a black hoodie, sweatpants, and a pair of sneakers. I arrived in Letterbrack at noon, driving along the scenic route without confronting delays. I continued through the village Main Street until I reached Julia's house, where I slowed the car but didn't stop. The driveway was deserted.

I continued along the tree-lined road and finally parked off the road behind a wall of Hawthorn bushes. Her house was fairly isolated and well back from the road, so I didn't expect to encounter anyone. After I exited the car, I silenced my cell phone, holstered it to my sweatpants, and stealthily walked through the dense shrubbery in the direction of Julia's house.

When the greenery released me into a manicured back garden, an array of birdhouses attached to poles, trees, and shrubs assured me I'd reached Julia's place. Curious, I walked toward a medium-sized shed that occupied one corner of the garden. The door was locked, but the unfettered window allowed me to peruse the shed's contents. Birdhouses of various colors and sizes perched on most of the shelving I could see through the window.

Three surveillance cameras sat atop another of the shelves, and then my stomach sank when I noticed tote bags similar to the ones in Julia's shop sitting on the floor. Bird seed bags peeked out of several of the totes. What if it was Alex who brought Julia's tote bag to the murder scene? O'Shea's tampering with evidence may have done more to implicate Julia than to absolve her. If Alex had brought the bag to the scene, what was he doing with it? Had he taken to feeding birds in the meadows? I thought of the poor dead bird I'd found when I walked the scene. Had Alex found an abandoned nest and returned with food for the babies? I took one last look through the glass and turned my attention to the rear of Julia's house.

I walked slowly, taking my time to listen for other footsteps or a car pulling into the driveway. The house was a crime scene, so caution guided me. I didn't need to have the police, or anyone else, for that matter, see me snooping around.

As expected, the back door was locked, but one of the windows into the dining room was unlatched and partially raised. When I pushed on the sash, the window slid up easily, and I climbed through. Once inside, I remained motionless, listening for movement, but dead silence and the smell of disinfectant greeted me.

Crossing my arms to keep from touching things, I walked from the dining room into the kitchen, where I assumed Julia had fallen. The crime scene investigation unit had done a good clean-up job because any evidence of what had happened had been removed. Birding brochures and catalogs sat on one of the kitchen counters. Oddly, I didn't see a tote bag.

I moved from the kitchen through the empty rooms where I could see Julia's designing fingerprints in the furniture coverings and artwork on the walls. One hallway was lined with framed diplomas and commendations for Alex. When I peeked into the first room off the hallway, the bookshelves filled with legal texts indicated Alex's office. His desk was clean except for a legal newsletter outlining changes in tax fraud cases and more bird brochures, these about creating bird sanctuaries. I picked up the newsletter and turned it over. When I saw Alex's name on the mailing label, Aunt Georgina's tax avoidance and secrets theory came to mind.

Using the sleeve of my hoodie, I flipped through the brochures but didn't find anything to pinpoint the motive for Alex's and Julia's murders. I returned to the hallway and moved deeper into the house, looking for the bedroom. Once again, I could see Julia's hand in the textured coverlet neatly folded at the bottom of the bed. Two night tables flanked the bed. I walked over to the one with the *Birding Essentials* magazine atop it and opened the drawer. A handful of mini discs lay inside. I pulled them out and stuffed them into my hoodie pockets, willing to bet the discs were from the surveillance cameras I'd seen in the shed. Further exploring of the other nightstand didn't uncover anything else. I returned to the kitchen and continued my search there, opening drawers and cabinets. Still no tote bag, but I did find Julia's appointment book. Why hadn't the police taken the book with them when they searched the home after Alex's death or after Julia's death?

Of course, they hadn't, I said to myself, because they hadn't looked hard enough. Because they'd assumed she killed Alex, and they chalked her death up to suicide.... I didn't finish the thought because trying to get into the minds of police investigators was a waste of my time. I opened the appointment book to the last day Julia had posted an entry, which was Monday, the last day I'd seen her. Two items listed in the to-do column stood out. One was to call Rita Barrett about receipts. The other was an entry to meet Nigel at the pub on Monday evening, the evening Julia was poisoned. I unhooked my phone from its holster and snapped a picture of the page. Other entries in the weeks leading up to her death were of the garden variety, listing things like guild meetings, replenishing shop inventory, and walks in the woods. The walks in the woods must have been the days she met up with O'Shea.

I wondered if Alex had looked at her appointment book and figured out what was going on. Was that why he was in the meadow that day? I shook my head. If so, why did he have a tote bag with him? I think he would have left the work of attempting to snap guilty pictures of his wife with a lover to someone else. I closed the appointment book, placed it back into the drawer, and stared out the kitchen window for movement. Satisfied I was alone, I moved into the dining room, lowered the window into place, and exited through the back door.

AFTER CIRCLING MAIN STREET SEVERAL TIMES, I SNAGGED A parking space outside Cream. Remembering how I'd had to chase Todd, I relegated my knapsack to the back seat, checked that the discs were secure in my hoodie pocket, and holstered my phone. When I reached the local post office, I express-mailed the discs I'd found to Phillie, enclosing a note in the padded envelope for Phillie to buy whatever equipment was needed to look through the images. Satisfied the discs would arrive at the Consulting Detective office by the next day, I headed to Julia's shop. Anne and Rita were sitting around the design table, working on crafts. My thoughts turned to how I similarly dealt with grief—throwing myself into work.

Nigel was behind the cash register, chatting up clients as they checked out knitting items as well as tote bags. What an ingenious way to get rid of evidence. Any one of the bags could be the one O'Shea removed from the scene and returned to Julia.

"Nigel, I want to speak with you," I said, breezing by the

register and standing at the back of the shop close to the stock room.

Nigel raised his eyes from the cash box to acknowledge my request. "A minute, please."

From my vantage point in the room, I noticed Anne and Rita exchange glances before they rose and headed for the door. I stepped in front of them and said, "I need to speak with you about Julia."

Rita pushed past me without saying a word. Anne shook her head and said, "I cannot help you." The tinkle of the bell over the door announced their exit.

"Yes?" Nigel sighed when the shop finally emptied of customers, and he joined me.

"When was the last time you spoke with Julia?"

Nigel shifted his artist pad from his hands onto a table. "I talked to her here in the shop on Monday morning."

"You're lying. Julia had an appointment with you on Monday evening, the night she died." I pulled my phone from its holster and indicated the photo I'd taken of Julia's appointment page. Nigel puffed his cheeks before blowing out a breath.

"I thought you wanted to help. Instead, you're hiding information that may help pinpoint Julia's murderer."

Nigel's face crumpled into a mass of lines. "Yes, we had an appointment to meet at the pub. She planned to provide feedback on my portfolio," he said, reaching into his messenger bag. He pulled out a binder, gripping it as if it were a lifeline. "But she called and blew me off. Said she didn't feel well."

"Did she describe what was wrong?" I asked.

"No, but she sounded stressed."

"What time did she call?"

"I don't know. Maybe around half five," he replied and then raised one of his hands and pounded the portfolio. "When I heard she'd ingested poison, I blamed myself." He lifted his eyes to mine. "I should have checked on her."

"Why didn't you?"

"I didn't realize she was in danger. I mean, who would think she was poisoned? Moreover, I was angry that she didn't want to meet," he admitted, ignoring the tears cascading down his face. "I went ahead to the pub and had a few ales to drown my stupid, immature nature."

I murmured something like, "That's for sure." Nigel would blame himself no matter what I said to allay his guilt. "You were at the pub. Who else was there?"

Nigel wiped his tears, putting the portfolio case back on the floor beside his chair. "The usual crowd, Anne, Todd, and Brendan."

I nodded, comparing his list to my suspect list, focusing on Anne, Rita, and Brendan. "What about Brendan's wife?" I asked, wondering whether her resistance had to do with secrets she was holding. One thing I knew for sure... I had to talk to her.

"No, she wasn't in the pub. She likes to have a few beers and talk about how well her Etsy business is doing, but Brendan said she wasn't feeling well." Nigel's eyes widened at his words. "You don't think she could have been poisoned as well?" he asked.

I shook my head.

"I can check with the kitchen staff at the abbey. They'd know if there were complaints," Nigel offered.

"If tourists fell ill due to the food, the village would be crawling with media. No, Julia was pinpointed. Someone added the poison to her food."

Nigel spent a few moments staring out the shop window. "What am I supposed to do?" he asked.

"Get accepted into design school like Julia wanted for you."

Nigel's hand reached for his portfolio case, and for the first time since we'd begun talking, he smiled. "I can do that."

"One more thing."

"Yes?" Nigel leaned forward, anxious to help.

"The sketches of the woman in the garden. I'd like one of them."

"Oh." Nigel sat back. "I don't know if I can...."

"You're not planning on presenting them as part of your portfolio, are you?" I asked.

He shook his head. "No, but...."

"Then, you won't mind giving one to me," I said, holding out my hand.

Nigel acquiesced, pulled the portfolio from the floor, and opened the case. He paged through his sketchbook until he came to the woman sitting on a bench amidst a bed of flowers. "Here," he said, carefully removing the page from the pad. "Do you want me to sign it?"

"No, this will suffice," I said. "About the woman with the pearl necklace... when was the last time you saw her?"

"I can't really say. It seems to me as if she's around a lot lately—almost always talking to her," he said, pointing to the sketch in my hand. "And then, other times, speaking with Sister Meghan."

"Why don't you lock up the shop?" I said, rising from my seat. "It will keep for a day or two." I touched his arm, moving him toward the door.

After he locked the door, we stood on the sidewalk for a few moments. "I'm so sorry," Nigel said.

"Don't keep beating yourself up. Just remember what I said. Keep your promise to Julia."

He nodded, smiled, and turned to walk along the sidewalk toward the pub. I watched as he pulled open the pub door, and then I returned to my car to place the sketch on the back seat. I didn't think Nigel had murdered Julia, and at least one piece of the puzzle had been filled in. Julia hadn't felt well when she called Nigel. I had to figure out how and when the salad had made it to her house. I drove toward Main Street and headed toward Brendan and Rita Barrett's house.

When I arrived at their cottage, I was surprised at the condition of the space surrounding the cottage. Buckets, tin cans, netting, fishing spears, and all sorts of what looked like junk littered the front yard. The day's grayness dimmed in contrast to the grimy windows and chipped exterior walls. I parked my car and picked my way to the cottage door. When I knocked, I glimpsed a curtain's movement.

The front door opened, and Rita stepped out onto the cement path.

"I've told you. I want no part of your Yank investigation." Rita's eyes glared at me through thick horn-rimmed glasses. I could see bits of bunting stuck to her apron under the oversized, stained gray sweater she wore. Her steel-gray mannish haircut hugged her head.

"Oh, I'm sorry. I interrupted your gardening," I said, pointing to her gloved hands.

"These are quilting gloves," she said, taking them off and sticking them in a sweater pocket. "That's how much you know."

"I know Julia phoned you the day she died—about receipts."

Rita rocked back on her thick-soled shoes as if shocked by my words. "How did you...?"

"I know more than you think. What did you and Julia discuss?"

"I refuse to discuss Julia with you. You should leave. I have work to do." Rita turned toward the cottage door.

"Yeah, you don't have to speak with me. But the police won't be turned away. You'll have to answer their questions."

"That may be, but as I said, I'm not discussing Julia with

you. Good day." Rita walked through her front door, slamming it behind her.

I waited a few minutes, but she didn't appear again. I stood in the messy yard and wondered about the reason for the apparently run-down home. I took a peek around the corner of the house and noticed what looked like a well-cared-for garden filled with heads of cabbage, lettuce greens, and herbs. Perhaps Rita took care of the garden, and Brendan tended the front yard. Whenever I'd seen Rita at the shop, she'd been dressed in a maxi wrap dress that wasn't showy but also didn't look like she shopped at Dunnes, and I remembered Brendan had been wearing what looked like LL Bean clothing. The truck he drove was a late model, and the two-seater Mini Cooper parked amidst the junkyard contrasted with the cottage's exterior and its surroundings.

Phillie's analysis of the shop's financial reports indicated a healthy tourist trade that I was sure the guild members profited from. Of course, if they were hiding money from the tax man, the run-down conditions made sense—but not totally. The tax department, at least in the United States, could pull your returns and put you into an audit.

No, I didn't believe delinquent or fraudulent tax reports were the motivation for Alex's and then Julia's murders. From what I'd heard about Alex, he had no problem dumping a client if he thought the person had lied. Todd was a good example. Alex was too busy with his role at the foundation and bird watching. If, through his legal work, he discovered tax fraud, he'd just drop the person and be done with it. Besides, as Julia had indicated, Alex was close-mouthed about his clients, so the ex-client wouldn't have any reason to worry.

By the time I reached the foundation building, I'd convinced myself that hiding one's assets was a non-starter for murder. Still, I didn't trust Rita. Like Maeve, she was hiding *something*. What? I didn't know yet. But I would. I just needed to figure out how to get her to divulge her secrets.

I was going to have to know more about Alex's role on the board. The preservation of Connemara's precious natural resources was his primary passion. I've found that passion is an excellent motivation for murder. Perhaps the director could shed more light on the issues or cases Alex was working on when he died. When I parked my car on the gravel driveway, I emerged facing Croagh Patrick. "I hope you have some answers for me," I said to the holy mountain and headed toward the foundation's massive oak door.

CHAPTER 23

The director opened the door before I rang the bell.

"I'm just leaving for the day," she said. "The board members have had enough excitement. We've adjourned until next month."

I would have loved to be a fly on the wall during the discussion that ended in the board's decision to be unavailable.

"I won't take too much of your time," I said, pushing over the threshold. "I have a few questions about Alex."

The director closed the door behind us and directed me down a corridor toward a small conference room. The door was locked, and after she opened it, she didn't turn on the lights or open the blinds. "We can talk here," she said, indicating the empty chairs.

I didn't think the director was in on anything nefarious; nonetheless, I didn't sit, choosing instead to stand with my back to the conference room door.

"The first time we spoke, you mentioned Alex's intense anger whenever a poaching report was received."

The director nodded. "That's correct. He became almost impossible to work with at times. In fact, he stormed out of a board meeting once when the board voted against installing trail cameras in the wooded areas."

"That's interesting. Is that kind of surveillance even possible?"

"Yes, the sensor cameras used to track songbird migration and nesting habits have been employed successfully in other countries to track poacher movements. But the board just doesn't have the funds needed."

"He must have been peeved."

"He didn't give up and pursued the idea with each board member."

"How did the board react?" I asked.

"He couldn't sell them on the idea. He was pretty bitter at board meetings after that. In fact, I considered removing him from the board, but he was too important in our legal cases."

"Did he ever bring the matter up again?" I asked.

"He muttered a few times when a new poaching activity report arrived from the Connemara National Park and Wildlife Service. Something to the effect that he'd find a way to form a surveillance team."

I pictured the electronic equipment I'd seen in Alex's shed. Had he caught someone red-handed poaching birds? If that were the case, I imagined Alex would have accosted the perpetrator immediately.

"What kind of equipment is needed to poach a bird?" I asked, thinking of the bird I'd seen in the meadow and imagining how difficult it would be to catch something so fragile in one's hands.

"Ah," the director sighed. "The villains use all kinds of cruelty, including noose traps, mist nets, and adhesives. They even lure birds with food and recordings of bird vocalizations. If a trap is used, the poacher returns to check on them."

"So, Alex's point in installing and using sensors was to track the poachers?" I asked.

"Yes." The director shifted her weight and walked toward the door. "But as I explained, we didn't have the funds. I doubt that was the reason for Alex's murder."

"What do you think happened?"

"Alex wouldn't have done anything to besmirch the foundation's reputation or tarnish the draw this region has to the tourist trade." The director shook her head. "No, it must have been tied to a legal case or his marital issues."

"That seems like an easy explanation for the residents of Letterbrack. All too easy. But it doesn't explain what happened to Julia."

"I understand the garda were closing in on her for Alex's murder."

"You can continue to believe that fairy tale, Director, in an effort to stay within your bubble. But most of the time, I've found the truth is right in front of you."

I turned and exited the room and then headed back when I thought of one more question. "I've noticed that several board members live in Letterbrack, like Todd, Sister Meghan, and Brendan. What about the two people who were at the last meeting?"

"They're from the Castlebar area. Another reason not to hold meetings that are disrupted when a board member has to drive miles to attend," she replied.

"Sure," I said and left the building.

I SAT IN MY CAR, THINKING ABOUT WHERE TO FOCUS. THE ENTIRE situation seemed hopeless. I pulled my notebook from the knapsack and read through the pages I'd written. First, there were the witnesses: Charlotte, Brendan, and Todd. Each swore Julia had headed into the woods around the same time that Alex would have been in the meadow. Then there was the tote bag, which O'Shea had removed from the scene and given to Julia. I'd given up on finding that piece of evidence. God only knew where it could be—probably in a tourist's carry-on bag winging its way to Wisconsin.

What about the meeting Julia didn't keep with Nigel the night she died? My gut told me he was telling the truth, so I'd accepted his explanation that she didn't feel well. My gut also told me that the director's dismissal of Alex's concern with poaching songbirds had more of a backstory than the director was willing to share. I circled Todd's, Charlotte's, and Brendan's names on the Venn diagram I'd drawn and placed the notebook on the seat beside me. I turned the key in the ignition and drove toward the local salmon fishery.

As I followed the signs for Atlantic Salmon Farms, the village buildings dwindled out of sight. Finally, a lone sign with an arrow indicated an unpaved, sandy trail outlined with tire tracks. I turned and drove for another two miles through a densely forested area before arriving at a series of buildings. One truck with the salmon farm's logo occupied the immense parking area. When I stepped out of my car, I could hear the hum of machinery mixed with the squawking of gulls. Pine forest and seaside odors scented the breeze.

"Hello," I called out before moving away from my car, noting the absence of cameras or security guards. When my call went unanswered, I walked over to the truck and peeked inside the back storage area, which held pails, plastic storage containers, netting, hooks, and brushes. Assuming this was the same truck I'd seen Brendan drive away in during my first visit to Letterbrack, I bet he was at work.

"Anyone here?" I said, following the cement path to the front of the building. In contrast to the macadamed parking lot, the building's frontage faced an amazing vista with a sweeping view of the craggy shoreline, which formed a boundary between the forest and the aquamarine Atlantic Ocean. This side of the Atlantic was nothing like the New Jersey side of the immense body of water. Large net cages floated in the coastal waters. "Brendan?" I shouted his name this time so I'd be heard over the sound of the equipment.

"You're on private property," a male voice stated from behind me.

Turning toward the sound, I stepped back when I saw Brendan holding a spear gun.

"Whoa," I said, holding up my hand.

"You," he replied, obviously recognizing me, but he didn't drop the spear gun.

"I have questions concerning Julia, Alex, and the board. I understand you serve on the board."

"I'm working," he said, using the spear gun to indicate the work platform. "I don't answer questions and don't have time for some Yank snoop."

"Can you drop the spear? I'm unarmed."

He propped the gun against a nearby workbench, stalking away onto a platform anchored between the floating sea cages.

"Hey, I wanted to speak with you because you're a witness against Julia Quinn, and she's dead," I said, following him out onto the narrow walkway. "In my opinion, that shoots a hole in your theory that Julia killed Alex."

Brendan stopped walking and grabbed the railing to steady himself from the sudden rocking motion caused by the fast-flowing coastal waters. I stood my ground.

"Haven't you heard about love triangle murders? What about that garda detective Julia has been seeing? Yeah, I've seen them together. They probably hatched the plan to kill Alex. I heard the detective is on administrative leave," Brendan said, using air quotes to emphasize his last two words. "He probably killed Julia. Isn't that how all love triangles end?" Brendan bent down, pulled a piece of equipment from the water, and examined it before dropping it back into the water.

"You might be correct, but I don't think Julia killed Alex. He'd agreed not to look for his share of her business assets."

"If not Julia, then who? Everyone in the village revered Alex. You know. The whole kid from a rich family who grew up here thing."

I studied the clear sky before posing my next question. "What about Alex's role on the board? According to the director, Alex had gotten distracted with poaching activities."

"Oh, geez. Alex and his poaching crusade. Look around you. Do you think anyone would venture out here to poach salmon? I'm on duty every day of the week, and I've never seen or had to report a poaching issue." Brendan walked back toward me. "No, my money is on the love triangle issue." When he got within a few inches of me, he stopped and put his hands on his hips. "I've answered your questions. I've said I saw Julia going into the woods the day Alex was killed. That's all you need to know. Please remove yourself from the area. I've work to do."

I nodded, returned to my car, and drove toward Letterbrack. Maybe I'd have more luck with Charlotte and Todd.

CHARLOTTE WAS SETTING UP GLASSES BETWEEN WIPING THE equipment for the evening trade.

"What are you doing here?" she asked when I walked through the door.

"Are you okay?" I asked, observing her red-rimmed eyes.

"Let's just say I'm having a day," she replied.

"You heard about Julia?"

"Yes." Charlotte nodded and threw the bar rag into the sink behind her. "You know, I used to wish she were dead. Instead, I'm crying for her and Alex. I don't get it. Do you?"

Her words brought to mind the O'Briens, Dylan, and my

mother, and then I envisioned Lorcan, whom I hoped I hadn't lost through my stubborn-minded behavior. But, unlike Charlotte, I kept my tears in check. I learned long ago that crying was a losing game.

"I think we just never know how our emotions will react to tragedy," I said. "Sometimes, we hold hurts inside that don't serve us well anymore. Just like the one you nursed against Julia."

While Charlotte moved down to the other end of the bar top, I watched the door for patrons. I hoped to get her talking about Julia's timeline on the day Alex died before any customers captured her attention.

"You look like you could use a refreshment," she said, handing a bottle of Perrier water to me and opening one for herself. "I guess you're right. I've harbored resentments all my life, and look what it's gotten me," she said, waving her water bottle around the pub.

"You sound regretful. Isn't this one of the most popular pubs in the region?"

"Yes, that it is. But it's all I have. If I'd opened my heart up years ago, I might have had a hand to hold in my later years. Instead...." She hoisted the bottle in a toast.

I sipped the sparkling water, enjoying its cool, crisp feel. I glanced at my iPhone. The day was slipping away into evening, and before long, the locals would surge through the door.

"Charlotte, are you sure you saw Julia heading into the woods the day Alex was killed?" I asked.

"Not really," she said. "I mean, I've seen her heading into the woods many times. But that day, I can't swear to it."

"Then why did you?"

"I've already explained: jealousy, anger, resentment. All the vices, if I think about it."

"Do you believe Julia killed Alex?"

"No, and I don't believe Todd murdered him either."

"That's interesting," I said. "What do you think happened?"

Charlotte placed her hands on the bar as if laying out her cards. "Alex was here the night before he died, meeting with a group of local farmers."

"Was that a regular occurrence?" I asked.

"Yes, a weekly kind of thing. They talked about government subsidies and the price of hay bales." Charlotte cleared her throat before continuing. "I didn't mean to eavesdrop, but they were sitting close to the bar. I heard Alex say that he was onto something nefarious. One of the farmers laughed, saying he hoped it had nothing to do with tax avoidance."

"But you heard Alex deny the tax issue, right?" I asked.

Charlotte nodded. "Yeah, I mean, Alex was a human resources kind of attorney, and he'd never do anything illegal, or at least I never heard that. Just look at Todd. Alex dropped him as soon as Alex discovered Todd lied about the reason for his termination." Charlotte sighed. "I'm sure it had something to do with Julia. That's why I lied about seeing her, but with her dead, I'm not so certain."

"Take your time. Tell me what you heard Alex say."

"Something like, 'I know who's at the heart of it, and I'll prove it.'"

"What do you think he meant?" I asked.

"What else could it have been but something to do with Julia? Alex and Julia were in the middle of the divorce. They fought constantly, often in the pub. So, when Alex was killed the next day, I assumed he'd been talking about finding something to hold over Julia's head in the divorce agreement." Charlotte's chest heaved as if she'd unloaded a heavy burden. Her hands picked up a cloth, and she wiped the counter.

"Did you ever hear Alex talk about his work at the foundation?"

"Often. Especially with the locals. Everyone in the village is adamant about protecting the environment. Because of his work on the board, Alex shared information about good practices and what was being done in other countries to stop the horrific treatment of songbirds."

"Did he ever say he'd take legal action against anyone?" I asked, wondering if Alex's comments in the pub might have been referring to the poaching issues he'd been so angry about at the board meeting.

Charlotte shook her head and twisted her lips into a grimace. "What, in Letterbrack? No, no way. As far as I know, Alex only ever shared information. He never took action." The pub door opened, and a group of tourists sat at a table. "I've got to get to work," she said, grabbing menus.

"Thanks, Charlotte. This has been helpful," I said. "And, hopefully, for you also."

Charlotte moved from behind the counter, walked me to the door, and said, "I loved Alex, but I realize I was clinging to a fantasy. I should have moved on years ago."

When I got into my car, I sat for a moment, thinking about Charlotte's obsession with Alex and her admission about Julia. I, too, hoped Charlotte would move on. I started the car and headed toward French Hill, hoping O'Shea had better luck with Todd and Sister Meghan.

CHAPTER 24

When I got back to French Hill, O'Shea was sitting in his car. I still felt angry that he and Julia hadn't told me about the tote bag, but I put my feelings on the back burner. Finding Alex and Julia's killer and bringing that person or persons to justice was my primary goal. Then, I planned to blow the doors off the abbey and identify the woman from the garden.

"Where have you been? I was getting worried," O'Shea said when he stepped out of his car and followed me through the cottage's kitchen door.

"I keep having to remind you that you're not the detective in charge, O'Shea. Take a seat," I said, indicating one of the Queen Anne chairs in the living room. "I'll put the kettle on, and we'll compare notes."

O'Shea sank into the chair like a deflated balloon. I quickly boiled water and plunked tea bags into a couple of mugs. I didn't ask if he wanted the milk and sugar I added to his. I figured the sugar would perk up his energy.

"Did you learn anything from your discussions with Sister Meghan and Todd?" I asked, putting the tea mug on the table next to him. I sat in the opposite chair and took a sip of my tea. The warmth felt good.

O'Shea shuffled his feet and ran a hand through his hair. "Todd is a royal pain in the butt. For someone who claims innocence, he acts like a criminal with a guilty conscience. I had to chase him down one of the side streets into the abbey's garden."

The phrase *been there, done that* came to mind. "But did you catch up with him?"

"Yes. He's not sure he saw Julia walk into the woods on the day Alex was murdered. Todd claims he corroborated Charlotte's story just to get along. He actually said, 'You know, go along to get along.' The man seems to be a bit erratic."

"He's recanting what he told the police about Julia the day of the murder?"

"Yes." O'Shea's shoulders heaved. "He doesn't add any value to the case other than promising to tell the guards he lied about Julia."

"I have to agree with you, O'Shea. Focusing on Todd is a distraction at this point. Charlotte Evans has also had a sudden change of heart, or should I say a sudden shift in her understanding of time." I glanced down at the notebook, which I'd grabbed from my knapsack. "Julia had two appointments in her appointment book on the day she died," I said.

"How do you know that?"

"You don't need to know the details, O'Shea. Trust me on this one."

"I hadn't heard about her appointment book or scheduled meetings," O'Shea said.

"I'll bet the crime scene investigation team missed it, which is a good thing because she noted her meetings with you, although not by name. But I'm wondering if Alex had figured out what was going on and planned to confront both of you that day."

O'Shea passed his hands over his eyes and then looked up at me. "I don't know what to do. I've never been entangled in a case before, and I'm afraid it's getting worse."

"I can't lessen your anxiety, O'Shea, but I can bring justice for Alex and Julia. That will have to suffice."

He nodded silently.

"So, Julia had an appointment with Nigel and a note to call Rita Barrett about receipts. Nigel claims Julia called and canceled the night she died. He said she wasn't feeling well. He thinks that was about five thirty p.m. Any thoughts?"

"She must have eaten the salad before then. You said she closed the shop early, correct?"

"Yes, and I think that means someone got to her between the time she arrived home and the call to Nigel," I said. "When I first met Julia, she commented about an abbey salad with ingredients like kale and pears that she loved."

"Yes," O'Shea agreed. "She always had that when we met in the meadow, and I recall there were bits of what looked like dried-up pear in the carton at her place."

"I've had my assistant, Phillie, download all the menus from restaurants in the area, but the only one that serves a salad with pears is the abbey's Garden Café, which might be helpful in pinpointing who picked up a kale and pear salad in a to-go order," I said, looking at my suspect list. "One more thing, did you ever hear from your contact in the poaching unit?"

"I did. Nothing worth following there, either. He checked, and there are no open cases in the Connemara region."

"Any complaints that didn't go anywhere?" I asked.

"Zilch."

"The foundation director described Alex as frustrated and angry about songbird poaching activity in the area."

"Well, I pray to God Julia and Alex weren't killed over a flock of birds." O'Shea slammed his mug on the table.

"I don't agree, O'Shea. I got a peek into Alex's work shed.

The entire building was dedicated to bird paraphernalia. According to Charlotte, Alex kept the entire village abreast of recent bird poaching activities. Maybe your detective friend wasn't paying attention to the complaints. I've had experience with law enforcement types who ignore private citizens."

O'Shea huffed out a breath and nodded. "Maybe. I'll check with him again. But it's a long shot."

"I'll take whatever I can get. What about Sister Meghan? Were you able to get into the abbey?"

"Yes. She's pretty upset about Julia's death. Sister blamed herself and said she should have made sure the café was inspected."

"That's interesting. What did she mean by that?"

"She recently hired a new head gardener. Sister said she needed to ensure the new employee could recognize poisonous greens."

"What?" I almost spat out the sip of tea I'd taken. "Does the abbey actually grow poisonous plants that might accidentally get mixed in? That just sounds weird and irresponsible for a public-facing tourist attraction."

"Maybe. Sister kept fingering the beads hanging from her waist. Her lips were moving—I assumed in prayer." O'Shea leaned forward and placed his head in his hands. He contemplated the floor before he said, "No. Julia's death is not the result of tainted food. Think about it. If the food served at the abbey were tainted, then more people would have reported sick. No. Someone put the poison into Julia's salad."

"But you aren't any closer to pinpointing the killer?"

"No, I'm not, and neither is Riley," O'Shea replied. "What about you? Any theories of the case?"

"I have one, but as the police typically do, you've dismissed the idea."

O'Shea shifted in the chair. "I don't blame you for your attitude. I'm ready to listen."

"I believe Alex happened upon a poaching scheme and was prepared to take the evidence to the authorities."

O'Shea's eyes widened.

"Don't look so surprised. Let's review what we know thus far."

"Go ahead." O'Shea leaned back in the chair and closed his eyes.

"Good news, two of the three Julia timeline witnesses have fessed up that they didn't see her going into the woods the day Alex was killed."

O'Shea opened his eyes. "Who's the third witness?"

"Brendan. He runs the salmon fishery, and he's on the conservation board."

"You spoke to him."

"Barely. He's antagonistic. I spoke with his wife, and he's told her not to cooperate with any questions from a Yank," I said, using air quotes to emphasize the word Yank.

"Being suspicious of outsiders is not a crime. In fact, his reaction is more the norm." O'Shea shrugged. "But go ahead, lay out your reasons for your poaching theory."

"As I said, Alex was obsessed with protecting the environment and the wildlife, especially the songbirds. I found a dead bird the first day I visited the meadow where you found Alex's body. I assumed the tiny baby had fallen from a nest. But what if the bird was killed at the same time Alex was murdered? What if Alex caught someone in the act of stealing the bird from a nest?"

I heard O'Shea sigh from across the room. "Far-fetched."

"Come on, O'Shea. The police have a specialized unit that focuses on poaching activities. Once again, you're refusing to accept the unusual." I stood up and paced the floor. "If you can't wrap your head around what I'm saying, then someone is going to get away with murder. Is that what you want?"

I scanned the living room, wishing Lorcan would walk

through the door and knock some sense into O'Shea. Impatient and frustrated, I reached for the cell phone tethered to my waist.

"I'm sorry," O'Shea said. "I'll follow up with my contact again. Also, I'll talk to this Brendan fellow. Perhaps he'll be more open to speaking with a member of the garda."

"Good luck with that. He knows you've been suspended."

"So, I'll have Keenan do the asking. He's been chomping at the bit to give me an assist."

I nodded. I'd forgotten about O'Shea's partner, Keenan. "What's he doing while you're on administrative leave?"

"He's been assigned as lead detective on a car smuggling case, but he's upset. The boys he's teamed up with haven't exactly embraced him with open arms." O'Shea shook his head. "I've managed to put a spanner into Keenan's life as well as my own."

"Yeah, interfering with a murder case when you're a police detective doesn't do much for your reputation, does it?"

O'Shea shrugged. "He'll get over it. Okay, I'll go back to my contact about the poaching. Keenan will talk to Brendan. Anything else I should be thinking about?"

My eyebrows shot up at O'Shea's question. Maybe he was beginning to understand civilians had brains. "I need to speak with Rita again. She's a member of the guild. She may be able to verify Julia's timeline the day Alex was murdered." I stopped pacing and looked at O'Shea. "I admit chasing Rita could be another dead end like Todd, but you've got to travel down all roads to find the truth. Oh, and the abbey."

O'Shea frowned. "What about the abbey? I've already covered Sister Meghan."

"You said a new lead gardener is working for the management board. We should speak with that person." I picked up my mug and took another sip. "I'll track the person down." I didn't mention to O'Shea my ulterior motive, which was to get back into the garden and abbey.

"Right." O'Shea stood and walked into the kitchen, rinsed out his mug, and set it on the drying rack. "I'll be off. I'll ring you when I've spoken to Keenan." O'Shea's eyes sought mine. "Be careful. If what you're saying about poaching is spot on, then we're dealing with dangerous criminals who are probably involved in more than poaching songbirds. Lorcan would never forgive me if something happened to you." O'Shea straightened his shoulders and exited through the front door.

I sat in the living room and reread my notes. When twilight had fallen, and I couldn't see the paper in front of me anymore, I switched on the cottage lights, made another cup of herbal tea, and picked up the landline phone in the kitchen. While I listened to the ring tones, I watched a pair of cardinals frolicking from one to another of the pine trees that form a natural barrier against the wind in the cottage's back field.

"I need your knowledge," I said when Aunt Georgina answered.

"What can I do for you?" she said. "Not making any progress?"

"I have a theory, but I need an objective viewpoint and a person the locals feel comfortable with. I'm not that person."

Georgina laughed. "Don't be so hard on yourself. You've begun to develop a reputation as someone who can ferret out more information than the garda."

"Oh, great. I love the ferret analogy. You're probably right about my notoriety, but I've hit a wall with Sister Meghan and Brendan's wife, Rita. Do you think you can take some time from the Golden Thread?"

"I have a wedding dress design appointment in the late afternoon. But I can ask my assistant, Beth, to open and mind the shop in the morning. What time do you want to leave for Letterbrack?"

"The earlier, the better. How about I pick you up for a change instead of you coming to Turlough? I'll be by at seven am."

"Perfect. We'll have just enough time for a cuppa in the hand. Is everything else okay?"

"No, but I'll explain in the car on the way. I'll see you in the morning."

We ended the call. I tidied up the kitchen and checked the door locks. Then, I went to bed. I wondered if Lorcan would be as worried as O'Shea had noted. But then again, I had more pressing things to think about. I fell asleep meditating on how Georgina and I would uncover the truth about Alex, Julia, and the mysterious woman in the abbey.

CHAPTER 25

Georgina and I discussed the case during the ride to Letterbrack. I brought her up to speed on O'Shea's intent to ask his former partner, Keenan, to take a go at Brendan while O'Shea followed up on my poaching angle theory.

"What you've described makes sense. But I'm not sure the villagers would stand by silently if they knew poaching was happening," Georgina said. "You'd have heard something from someone—maybe among the guild members."

"I'm not that certain. The town, the gardens, the abbey, the guild, you name it—everything is a tourist attraction. I think the foundation and the abbey management team might turn a blind eye to what was happening if addressing the issue meant tarnishing the tourist trade."

Georgina shook her head. "No, Sister Meghan wouldn't allow for murder. She might want to keep the investigation under wraps, but she'd want to know what was happening and bring the perpetrators to justice."

"Well, we'll put your belief in Sister to the test shortly," I said.

A clear blue sky and bright sunshine heralded our early

arrival in the village. The garden wouldn't open until 9:30 a.m. Very few people strolled along Main Street. We pulled into the abbey parking lot and exited the car.

When we passed through the massive double doors into the abbey lobby, the silent peacefulness belied the situation. I wished I was arriving on a retreat instead of confronting Sister Meghan.

Georgina inhaled the crisp air and tossed the ends of her signature scarf over her shoulder. "Let me handle this," she said, lifting the door knocker to the abbey door. With her hand still on the knocker, the door opened inward, pulling Georgina forward and into Maeve.

"What are you doing here?" Georgina asked after she'd regained her balance.

"Perhaps you should be asking yourself the same question, Georgina. Why do you continue to associate with this incompetent Yank who believes she's some kind of an investigator?"

Georgina's eyes widened. She pushed forward, causing Maeve to step backward. "You won't bully me or anyone else for that matter." Georgina shifted her weight forward again.

"You conveniently disappeared the other day when there was an explosion in the garden," I said, narrowing my eyes. "Did you cause the storage facility fire in Bohola?" I asked, planting my body between Georgina and Maeve.

Maeve laughed. "Of course not, but you'll grasp for any straw, won't you?"

"Why are you here? What kind of scam are you running?" I leaned in even closer, clenching the phone holstered to my capris.

Maeve's lips tilted upward. "You don't know anything about running an operation. You're just a lightweight." Maeve grinned. "Have you figured out what's going on in Letterbrack?

Right under your nose. Do yourself a favor, Star O'Brien, go back to the States where you belong."

"You don't scare me. Rest assured. I'll catch up with you."

"What's going on?" Sister Meghan's voice reverberated throughout the lobby. "Maeve, I won't have this kind of behavior in the abbey. I want you to leave immediately."

Maeve fingered her pearl necklace in the same manner in which I'd seen Sister Meghan finger the rosary beads encircling her waist. "Remember our agreement, Meghan," Maeve said.

"The only agreements I have are with the Lord. I won't condone the way I've heard you speak to Miss O'Brien. I'll deal with you later, Maeve," Meghan said, ushering us into a small sitting room just on the other side of the doorway.

"Please, sit down," Meghan said. The young nun I'd met several days earlier arrived with a tea tray. Sister Meghan indicated the mahogany coffee table, where the sister placed the tray and silently left the room.

"I must apologize for Maeve," Sister said, pouring tea into the three cups. "I've known her since we were schoolgirls, and I know what she can be like. But I hadn't witnessed her behavior firsthand for quite some time. Go ahead. Help yourself," Meghan said, pointing to the sugar and creamer bowls.

"As you said, we've known each other for a long time, Meghan," Georgina began, stirring a lump of sugar into her teacup. "I appreciate your concern regarding Maeve's toxic attitude, but Star and I want to speak with you about another matter."

Sister nodded. "Julia, I expect. I've already spoken to the guards and the other man, O'Shea." She placed her teacup on the table and continued, "Forgive me if I sound like Maeve, but what do you think you can do that the guards aren't doing?"

"Meghan, Star may not be an official law enforcement representative, but Julia did ask her to look into what happened to Alex. You can at least answer our questions—for Julia's sake."

"Very well. Appearances are often deceiving. I'll give you that." Sister Meghan leaned forward in her chair. "Go ahead, Miss O'Brien. But make it quick. I have an organization to manage."

I ignored her snarky remark and got to the point. "What do you know about the poaching ring in the area?"

Meghan's mouth twisted into a grimace. "What do you mean?"

"Don't feign ignorance. I've spoken to Susan Drew, and I overheard you speaking to the board about the issue the other day. Alex cared deeply about potential songbird poaching in the heart of Connemara. The board ignored his requests. You chair the board, Sister. Therefore, you ignored his requests."

"Alex's passion for justice became an obsession. His demands were turning into harassment of the board members. At first, I tried talking to him, but that didn't work. Finally, I thought if we ignored him, he'd temper his vigilante stance."

"But he didn't. He initiated his own investigation."

"No, I'd have known," Sister said.

"Would you? I found surveillance equipment on his property. In fact, he was on the verge of identifying who was running the ring."

"That's nonsense. I never heard Alex say that."

"But he did. In the pub. A public place for everyone to hear."

"I didn't know." Sister's voice sounded like it was coming from far away.

"Alex was murdered by whoever is running the poaching operation," I said, presenting my theory as fact. "Any ideas, Sister?"

"I had no idea things had gone that far in Alex's mind. But no. I cannot fathom anyone in the village or surrounding community involved in killing defenseless birds." Meghan started to rise to her feet.

"Sit down. I'm not finished with my questions."

Georgina reached over and patted Meghan on the shoulder. "Please, just listen to Star. Her instincts are usually correct."

Meghan sighed and nodded.

"I think Julia figured out what was going on. I'm sure the police told you that she was poisoned...."

"The abbey had nothing to do with that," Meghan interrupted.

"I agree, but I've heard the garden contains poisonous plants. Someone could have used a deadly plant to kill Julia."

"No, no, no." When Sister shook her head, her wimple shook with her. "No plant or herb in the garden is capable of causing death. Maybe a bit of a stomach upset if the digestive system doesn't tolerate certain herbs." She paused and then continued, "I've known Julia since we took her into the abbey. She never exhibited or complained about eating greens or herbs out of the garden. No, whatever the poison was, it didn't come from the abbey garden."

"Detective O'Shea says you've hired a new lead gardener. Who is that person?" I asked, wondering if the mystery woman was the new gardener.

"The new hire is a recent graduate of horticulture school. There's no way he wouldn't know the difference between benign and toxic ingredients."

"What about the woman I've seen with you and Maeve?" I asked.

"You certainly are relentless, aren't you, Miss O'Brien?" Sister folded her hands in her lap. "I will tell you this. The abbey provides refuge to women and children from time to time. Julia is a good example of what we do at the abbey. When a female refugee enters our protection, she works in the garden as a way to heal until other arrangements can be made."

"I want to interview the person I've seen. You said she works in the garden. She may have seen something suspicious."

"No, Miss O'Brien. I cannot allow you to speak to anyone under our protection unless the person grants permission." Sister rose and walked toward the door through which we'd entered. "I believe I've answered your questions, Miss O'Brien. Georgina, please give my regards to Marcella."

A small door on the other side of the room opened. The young nun appeared and guided us toward the exit. Sister Meghan disappeared from the room.

"I'M FAMISHED. DO YOU HAVE TIME FOR LUNCH AND A CUPPA?" Georgina asked when we reached Main Street.

"Sure, I'd like your feedback about our conversation with Sister. Let's go to Lord's. I think it's only two cross streets from here."

I plunked my phone and knapsack onto a sidewalk table while Georgina went inside to order. When she returned, I had my Mead composition book in front of me.

"I ordered an herbal tea and a brown scone for you," Georgina said.

"Let me help you with that," I said, standing and taking the laden tray from her.

Once we'd organized our cups and plates, I nodded at my notebook and said, "I've jotted down a few thoughts but would like to hear from you first."

"Maeve Baldwin is up to something, but I don't think it's connected to Julia's death," Georgina said while she spread raspberry jam on one of the scones.

"I agree. The only time I've seen her is at the abbey, and with the pearls and her manner of dressing, I doubt she's ever been on a walking trail, let alone in the woods." I twirled the tea mug that Georgina had placed in front of me. "As much as I want to ferret out, as you say, what she's up to, I have an obligation to follow Julia's case to the end. But then...."

"Funny, though. Both she and Meghan dismiss you on appearance's sake," Georgina said. "I guess part of it is the fact that you're an outsider."

"Yeah, at first blush, people, especially the police, dismiss me, but I've learned to be relentless when I'm after the truth. Sometimes, appearances are deliberately misleading." I spun my notebook around so Georgina could read my notes. "Case in point. Rita and Brendan's house. Everything looks decrepit and uncared for. But Rita has a business going with the guild. Brendan works for the salmon fishery. What are they hiding?"

"They just might be too busy or sloppy homeowners," Georgina replied.

"I don't believe that. This town is awash in secrets and lies. Just consider Julia and O'Shea with their secret meetups in the woods. Charlotte at the pub wanted revenge. Sister Meghan just wants to hide behind her status as a person of the cloth to avoid answering questions. In my opinion, Alex was hiding the fact that he was spying on his neighbors in the hopes of finding a poacher."

"You may be right, Star, but I don't think there's much more we can do. As you said, you're an outsider, and my influence with Meghan didn't get us any closer to identifying the killer."

"I won't accept defeat. Keenan and O'Shea may have a breakthrough," I replied, tearing off a corner of my scone and popping it into my mouth before I pushed the plate away. "Come on. Let's go talk to Rita Barrett."

Georgina gathered our belongings while I carried the tray back into the shop.

"We'll try the guild shop first. Perhaps Rita is there," I said when I returned to the sidewalk.

The shop doors were open, and a group of tourists milled

throughout the store. I spotted Anne and Nigel, who rushed from behind the cash register to greet us.

"Any word about Julia?" he asked.

I shook my head.

"The shop looks so busy. What's going to happen to it?" Georgina asked.

Nigel rolled his eyes. "I've been trying to speak with Sister Meghan about the lease. The guild members would like to take over Julia's portion. But I haven't been able to get Sister to give me the time of day."

"I'd hate to see Julia's creations and entrepreneurial spirit die with her," Georgina replied, digging into her purse for a business card, which she handed to Nigel. "Give me a call. Julia and I collaborated on several designs. Perhaps I can do something to help you and the guild keep this going."

"How are the rest of the guild members holding up after Julia's death?" I asked.

"We're devastated, but we agreed to honor Julia by doing our best. So, here we are," Nigel said. Anne touched his arm but didn't speak.

"I'm happy to hear that. Will you be offering the same goods and services?" I asked.

"Pretty much. Everyone's committed." Nigel's face beamed as he glanced around the shop. "Except for Rita. She hasn't been feeling well lately, which reminds me I need to call her later."

"Oh, stomach upset?" I asked, thinking of Julia.

"I don't think so. She just gets quiet once in a while and takes a few days at home. I think she's just a homebody." The bell over the shop door rang, and Nigel hurried toward the newcomers. "I've got to get back to work. Thanks for stopping, and thanks for the card, Georgina."

"Isn't that Detective Keenan?" Georgina asked, pointing at a dark blue sedan that sped by when we stepped back outside onto the sidewalk.

"O'Shea must have convinced him to venture out of his assigned jurisdiction," I said, watching the car drive along Main Street toward the salmon fishery. "I wonder if O'Shea spoke with the National Park and Wildlife Service contact in Connemara."

"If he said he would, then he will. I've known Tom since he was a wee lad kicking the football around with Lorcan and Dylan during the summer evenings. Detective O'Shea will follow through."

Georgina's mention of Lorcan sent a quiver of loneliness through my heart, but I focused my thoughts on the task at hand.

"Come on. Let's find Rita while Keenan pays a visit to her husband."

CHAPTER 26

Rita and Brendan's cottage cast off the same desolate and abandoned condition I'd witnessed on my earlier visit. If anything, the number of buckets, netting, and fishing spears had increased exponentially. I also noticed a few shovels tossed onto a plot of newly dug-up ground.

"Be careful you don't trip or cut yourself," I cautioned Georgina when we emerged from my car. "Some of that equipment is rusty."

"Did you notice the dirt mound?" Georgina asked as she stepped out of the car.

"I did."

Like the last time, I stood on the cement walk in front of the cottage and glimpsed a hand pulling a curtain away from one of the front windows.

"Let's wait. I'm sure Rita will appear momentarily."

Georgina threw one end of her scarf behind her. "How in the mother of God does the woman exist in this mess?"

"As I said, appearances are sometimes intended to deceive."

The front door opened, and Rita stepped outside.

"Georgina Hill, I'm surprised to see you. Since when do you appear unannounced at another woman's home?" Rita's eyes ricocheted between Georgina and me. I didn't think she'd changed her clothes since the last time I'd seen her.

"We've just come from meeting with Nigel and Anne," Georgina replied. "I'm planning on lending a hand. I want to see Julia's efforts continue."

Rita removed her glasses and wiped them with the edge of her sweater. "I appreciate your concern, but I'm not interested."

"Are you willing to let your work with the guild go to waste? How are you feeling?" Georgina moved closer to Rita. "I know everyone is devastated over Julia, but the members are doing their best to move forward."

"I don't like the company you keep," Rita replied, placing the horn-rimmed spectacles back on. "I told your companion I'm not part of her investigation."

"I can see you're upset. Star's my niece. She can help." Georgina's voice remained steady as if she were trying to calm a baby.

Rita's mouth formed a smirk. "You think you're so smart," she said as she looked at me.

"The first time I saw you in the village, I noticed your husband turned you away from Julia's shop after he'd spoken to me. What was that all about?" I asked.

"That was nothing. Brendan forgot his employee badge at home. He asked me to drive it out to the fishery for him while he went and picked up his lunch at the abbey. The staff knows his schedule and always has his order ready for him—like clockwork."

"Does the abbey even begin serving lunch that early in the morning?" I asked, remembering it was between 9:30 a.m. and 10:00 a.m. when I'd seen Brendan outside Julia's shop.

"I don't pay too much attention to time, Miss O'Brien," she replied.

Frustrated by her answer, I asked, "Why have you refused to talk about the last time you spoke to Julia? Why aren't you going to the shop? What are you avoiding?" I moved closer to her.

"Rita, someone killed Julia. Don't you care?" Georgina reached forward to touch Rita's hand. "If Star knows you spoke to Julia, then whoever killed Julia knows also."

"That's right. Julia's appointment book was right out there on one of her kitchen counters. What are you afraid of? I can't think you want to hide out here indefinitely," I said, indicating her house.

Rita pursed her lips and drew her hand away from Georgina. "I don't want Brendan to know about...."

"What are you hiding?" I asked, stepping back in an effort not to crowd her.

"If truth be told, I've been withholding my income from him...," Rita gushed, tears streaming down her face. "I've never been truthful about what I make from my quilt business."

"Why in the world would you do that?" Georgina asked, searching through her purse for a tissue, which she handed to Rita.

"Brendan's always been condescending about my work. He's made little of me and the effort I put into each piece. So"—Rita dabbed her face dry and stuffed the tissue into the pocket of her sweater before continuing—"I decided he didn't deserve the fruits of my labor."

"But why wouldn't you talk to me about Julia and the receipts?" I asked.

"Because I don't want the tax man in on my income either. Julia knew I wasn't reporting my sales. She called me to say she couldn't keep my secret anymore." Rita's tears restarted, and she looked Georgina in the eye. "Maybe I was the reason why Julia was killed."

"Do you have the receipts Julia called you about?"

"No, I burned them in the fireplace," Rita replied, wiping her tears away and folding her arms as if in defiance.

"At some point, you need to tell him and settle up with the tax man, Rita," Georgina said.

"I don't know if you're telling me the truth, but I'll find out." I touched Georgina's arm. "Let's go."

Rita turned and walked away.

Georgina and I sat in the car for a few moments before I started the engine.

"The poor girleen," Georgina said, "living amidst all this wreckage to hide a few euros from her husband and the tax man—hardly secrets worth killing over."

"Appearances are masks, hiding our true emotions and misdeeds. When you look closely, you can see where the demons hide, even under the rubble," I replied and backed out of the driveway.

AS SOON AS WE CROSSED INTO CASTLEBAR'S TOWN LIMITS, Georgina asked if we could stop at the Golden Thread before returning to her cottage.

"I'll be right out. I want to check in with Beth."

While I waited, I called O'Shea's cell phone, which went directly to his voicemailbox. "Geez," I said to myself when the voice attendant informed me the box was full.

Georgina waltzed out of her shop door with a huge smile on her face.

"What's going on?" I asked.

"Everything went smoothly. Beth is a wonderful assistant."

"Have you ever thought of retiring or selling the business?" I asked, realizing I'd never delved into Georgina's future plans or what she devoted time to other than helping me whenever I was in Ireland.

"Retirement is just a dream, agra. Dylan's grandparents, his mother, me—we all grew up in the Castlebar area, and here is where I plan to be."

"But do you ever think of traveling? I'd love it if you visited the U.S."

"My roots are in County Mayo, Star. I hope one day you'll feel the same way."

I thought of Evelyn, the father I'd never meet and the mother I hoped to find one day. At least I knew more about myself and my family than when I arrived in Ireland a year ago—more than I ever expected. I sent a quiet thank you to Dylan in my heart.

"I'm happy I had this time in my life getting to know you, Georgina," was all I could say.

"Don't look so sad. Tell me. Have you considered opening a Consulting Detective branch in Ireland?"

I laughed. "You never give up, do you?"

"I've told you before, you have friends and family here. Don't forget that when you're mulling over what I've suggested."

"I won't," I replied, busying myself with clicking in my seatbelt so Georgina wouldn't see the tears forming in my eyes.

"Good. Let's get me home. I'll whip up something in the kitchen, and we can eat together before you go back to French Hill."

THE SOUNDS OF THE TABLE BEING SET CARRIED INTO GEORGINA'S sitting room, where I jotted notes from the day's events into my Mead composition book. I paged back to the Venn diagram I'd drawn and circled Brendan and Rita Barrett's names. When my cell phone rang, I picked up on the first tone.

"How did your meetings in Letterbrack go?" O'Shea asked.

"The more I speak with the residents, the more frustrated I

become. Sister Meghan denies knowledge of poaching activities. She doesn't believe Alex would take vigilante actions even if there were a problem."

O'Shea grunted in reply. "If my poaching contact were here, he'd agree with Sister Meghan. He did reveal, however, a number of cases pertaining to the illegal hunting of wild deer. But he promised to keep the songbird theory in mind and call me if he comes across anything unusual."

"What about salmon poaching?" I asked.

"Aye, there have been cases of illegal netting of salmon. Salmon angling is critical to the rural communities like Connemara. But I doubt if anyone local would get involved in something that threatens conservation efforts or carries hefty fines."

I thought about how Brendan armed himself with a spear gun when I visited. Was he aware of the poaching activities? Did he know who was behind them?

"Did Keenan speak with Brendan?"

"He did, and the bloke threatened him. Brendan also refused to say much. He commented that he'd already spoken with the officials. What about Brendan's wife, Rita? Any headway there?"

"Yes and no. She's been hiding her real income from her husband and the tax man."

"So, we're back to tax fraud as the motive for Alex's murder?" I could hear the question in O'Shea's voice. "I just keep thinking Julia stumbled across something that led the murderer to eliminate her, something more dangerous than tax fraud," he said and then asked, "What else did Rita say?"

"She confirmed Julia called her the day she died. Julia told Rita she couldn't keep her actual income secret anymore," I said.

"I wonder what caused Julia to reconsider."

"I don't know, but Rita's worried about having her secrets revealed."

"I guess we're back to square one then. A tax fraud scheme that Alex somehow uncovered in the course of his usual work, and Julia was collateral damage." O'Shea's voice stilled, and then he said, "But I can't imagine the other guild members like Anne and Nigel hiding exorbitant amounts of income. But maybe someone else among Alex's clients might be."

"One more thing. The night Julia was poisoned, Todd, Brendan, Anne, and Nigel were at Charlotte's Pub. Rita was a no-show, and according to her husband, she wasn't feeling well with a stomach upset. And when I spoke to Nigel and Anne yesterday, they said Rita wasn't feeling well lately."

"Right, I'd better speak to Rita myself first thing in the morning," O'Shea said, and we ended the call.

After finishing the baked ham, tomato, and cheese sandwiches Georgina prepared and clearing the table, we sat over mugs of tea while we discussed what we'd learned from our meetings earlier in the day.

"O'Shea indicated he's reconsidering the tax fraud motive for both murders," I said. "He's planning to talk to Rita Barrett tomorrow."

"What do you think, Star?"

"I understand why O'Shea has refocused his efforts, but I'm still skeptical. Alex dropped clients if he learned they were cheating. Why kill Alex when someone could just go hire someone more amenable to the person's situation, or more importantly, a tax accountant."

"You still think the poaching is the issue?" Georgina asked.

"Yes. The surveillance equipment, his behavior at board meetings, which almost got him thrown off the board, and the meadow where he was found"—I paused and then continued — "either he was lured there, or he intentionally went there to catch someone in the act of poaching."

"But why kill Julia? If Alex was murdered by someone capable of killing baby songbirds, what would Julia have to do with that?"

"I'm fairly sure the narrow-gauge needles used to kill Alex came from her shop and found their way back there after the murder. The tote bag O'Shea found at the scene, which he returned to Julia, reinforces my belief that someone tried to frame Julia. She must have figured out who the murderer is."

"So, what's next?" Georgina asked.

"I honestly don't know," I said, rising to my feet. "Good night, Georgina. I'll call you in the morning."

CHAPTER 27

So, where do I go from here? I asked myself when I woke to a light drizzle smearing the windowpanes the next morning. Impatient for action, I threw on my sweats and braved the damp air for a power walk along Cottage Road. When I finally returned to the kitchen, my brain had filtered through the potential scenarios several times. I quickly towel-dried my hair and changed into jeans, a sweatshirt, and dry sneakers. With a steaming cup of peppermint tea in front of me, I grabbed my Mead composition book and began writing.

Several things I knew for sure: Alex had been described as a gentle soul, but illegal poaching angered him. When he didn't get the foundation's support behind him, he purchased his own surveillance equipment. Although I hadn't observed a camera where his body was found, I'd seen them in his gardening shed. He must have been conducting his own investigation. Had Alex confronted the poacher? Had the poacher lured Alex to the field? Had the poacher known Julia and O'Shea's meeting place and used that knowledge to frame Julia?

Without concrete evidence, I could only surmise the murder weapon had come from Julia's shop and had been placed back in the shop. O'Shea had removed a tote bag with her initials from the murder scene. The needles and tote bag would have been tangible evidence against Julia if the police had found them, but with no physical evidence, as well as Charlotte and Todd's recanting of explicitly seeing Julia enter the woodland the day of the murder, the police would have had a difficult time making charges stick.

I paused to read what I'd written and wrote a question mark in the center of the page and next to it, Brendan Barrett's name.

He claimed he'd seen Julia enter the woodland trail and vehemently blamed her for Alex's death. Brendan served on the foundation board. Rita had said he usually went to the café early to buy his lunch before work. How could he have seen Julia? She'd said she was late getting into the shop the morning Alex was killed.

Next, I wrote the words *tax fraud* in the middle of the page. O'Shea swore the police had little interest in tax evasion cases, which meant someone could have been committing fraud with no fear of discovery. Had Alex stumbled into a major tax evasion scheme while working with one of his clients? Had he threatened to go to the police? When Julia phoned Rita about the receipts, had the woman gone into a panic and killed Julia? Maybe Rita had lied about wanting to keep her assets hidden from her husband. Maybe Rita and Brendan were in on it together? What if he was involved in a tax fraud scheme, too, and decided to take matters into his own hands?

Finally, I wrote *access to Julia* in the center of the page. In order to murder her, someone had to have picked up her salad order and delivered it to her in person. According to Nigel, Julia had blown him off the evening she died. He'd been at the pub with Brendan and other guild members. The only missing member was Rita, who'd been sick. Was Brendan protecting her when he'd refused to answer questions? Was protecting Rita the reason why he'd stuck to his version of the time he'd seen Julia the day of Alex's murder?

Glancing at the clock, I closed the notebook and logged onto my computer to check for messages from Phillie and Ellie. My cell phone rang at the same time I saw the email with Phillie's name.

"Phillie? It's five o'clock in the morning in New Jersey. What's going on? Is everybody okay?" I asked nervously, thinking of Ellie, Jim Hipple, and Skipper.

"I've been up all night working on those discs you sent. It took a while, but I was able to find one or two with what looked like a human image. Most of the discs are filled with animal and bird wildlife. I just sent the two that looked half-readable. If you decide you need the remainder, let me know."

"Hold on," I said, clutching my phone in one hand and pressing the enter key with the other to open her email, which had two attachments. I scrolled down, opened the files, and glanced at the shadowy images. I raised the phone back up to my ear and said, "Hey, get some rest. I'll take it from here."

"Okay, boss, but if you need me, just call my cell," Phillie replied, and we ended the call.

I downloaded the images onto my hard drive and enlarged one to full screen. The photo was grainy and taken after sunset, making the trees and landscape eerily white against the night's dark inkiness. Unfortunately, most surveillance images only capture blurry shapes of people and not the actual person. But... I held my breath as I zoomed in on a patch of light adjacent to a tree in the foreground. I cropped the image down to that particular area, and after rotating several times, I concluded I was looking at a pair of shoes.

I opened the second image and looked at the same spot. This time, I thought I saw a hand reaching upward to the tree branches. I zoomed in again and tried cropping that section, but couldn't make out much more. However, I was convinced Alex had caught the poacher on his surveillance cameras. Or, and I hoped this wasn't the case, the lens had caught Alex when he was setting up the camera.

Finally, after perusing both images again, I emailed the files to Georgina for safekeeping, packed my knapsack, and called her.

"Any news from O'Shea?" Georgina asked when she heard my voice.

"No. He's planning to speak with Rita, and I'm going to drive to Letterbrack to speak with her husband."

"Oh?"

"Yeah, I just can't square his testimony about seeing Julia enter the woodland just before Alex's estimated time of death. I think he's protecting his wife."

"Didn't Rita say he buys his lunch at the abbey every morning? If that's the case, how could he have seen Julia the day of the murder?" Georgina asked.

"Right. Excellent question to which I intend to get an answer because Rita may have lied to us about hiding her assets from Brendan. He may be in on the whole thing."

"If he's protecting Rita, he won't talk to you. He's made that clear already." Georgina paused and then continued, "I'll go with you. He might be more open to one of Rita's acquaintances."

"I doubt if he'll open up to you, Georgina. He strikes me as the kind who is paranoid about speaking with anyone." I stopped, searching for words that wouldn't hurt Georgina's feelings. "I'll call you after I speak with him and before I leave Letterbrack."

"I guess you're right, but be careful," Georgina replied hesitantly.

"And, oh, I just sent two image files to you—no need to do anything but save them to your hard drive. I'll see you later, Georgina," I said and got off the call quickly before Georgina changed her mind.

~

THE EARLIER DRIZZLE HAD ENDED, BUT THE WEATHER HAD GROWN blustery by the time I arrived at the Salmon Fishery. Brendan's truck was in the parking lot where it had been the last time I visited. I walked around the building to the work platform. His back was turned to me, his hands and head hovered over a tiny cage. I shouted to catch his attention before he started throwing what looked like fish bait into the tanks.

"Mr. Barrett, I need a few minutes of your time," I shouted, thinking he hadn't heard me approach over the sound of the machinery rotating the water in the sea cages. Remembering our last encounter and his agility with a fishing spear, I kept my distance and shouted his name again several times. Finally, he turned and, glimpsing me, quickly closed the gap between us.

"You shouldn't be here." His body bulk seemed to increase, matching the anger in his voice.

"I won't take too much of your time," I said. "I see you are in the middle of feeding."

Barrett turned his head to look over his shoulder. "You better have a good reason for being on the property, Yank."

I stepped back farther, keeping an eye on his hands. Unlike last time, I didn't see a fishing spear nearby.

"I just have a few questions about Alex and the foundation. I thought since you're on the board, you might be able to fill in some of the gaps for me."

"Haven't you already spoken to the director?" Brendan's eyes narrowed as he tilted his head and glared at me. "I think you've disrupted board business quite enough with your comings and goings."

"You're right. I've spoken to the director, but she probably has a different perspective than you might have. After all, you live and work in the region, and you knew Alex outside of board business."

"If answering a few questions gets you off my back and out of the region's business, then go ahead. Fire away."

"Thank you. I appreciate this," I said, continuing to gauge the distance between us. "I'm wondering why the board didn't agree to purchase surveillance cameras when Alex suggested the poaching issues in the area?"

Brendan rolled his eyes and said, "Have you ever heard the saying talking never brought in the turf? That was his problem. He was all bluster and statistics and reports, but he didn't do anything about the issue. Yes, he was angry when the board turned him down, but he just took no for an answer and didn't pursue the matter any further."

"Are you sure he didn't purchase surveillance cameras and begin his own investigation?" I asked.

Brendan's face flushed crimson, and he stepped closer to me. "What's this all about? I don't know anything about cameras. All I know is Julia killed her husband. I've told you and the garda before. Julia was the guilty party."

"Yes, you've said you saw Julia heading into the woods the day Alex was murdered. But"—I paused and locked my eyes on his before continuing— "that just doesn't jive with what Rita told me and Georgina Hill," I said, bringing up Rita to see if she'd been telling the truth.

"Rita has nothing to do with this," Brendan sputtered the words, turning to look behind him. My eyes tracked in the same direction, but I still didn't see a fishing spear, so I continued with my questions. He turned back to me and stood firm with his hands on his hips. "I want you off this property immediately, or I'll notify the authorities that you're trespassing."

"I'll be out of your hair in a moment. But I have to discuss Rita with you. She told me you usually went to the abbey's restaurant each morning to pick up your lunch. How could you have seen Julia? In fact, Julia was late to her shop that morning. How do you explain that?"

Brendan's weight shifted as if he'd been sucker punched in the gut when he heard my words. "Get out," he said, speaking in low guttural tones.

I didn't wait for answers. Instead, I asked, "Are you protecting your wife?"

Barrett's laugh ricocheted out over the water and through the trees. "You really are off base, aren't you? I've told you and the garda that I saw Julia walking into the woodland the morning of Alex's murder. Rita has nothing to do with anything."

"Has Rita spoken with you? She confided in Georgina and me. Did you know she's been keeping secrets from you? She seemed worried about hiding assets from her quilting business."

Brendan laughed again and stepped back as if something I'd said allayed his anger. "Rita and I are perfectly fine without interference from the likes of you. I don't know what she told you, but you've nothing to worry about. I have work to do. You'll have to excuse me."

I shook my head. "No. Julia didn't kill Alex. But I'm wondering if Rita had something to do with his death or Julia's." I paused and let my words sink in. "Julia phoned Rita the day Julia died. Julia told Rita she couldn't keep information about Rita's income secret anymore. I even have Julia's entry in her appointment book about the call."

Barrett stood silently. His gaze strayed from me to the woods behind me. "An interesting theory but one that won't go anywhere coming from you. Why would Rita want to murder those two? They were doing a good enough job of destroying their lives themselves." Barrett shifted his weight and turned his eyes back to me. "I have to get back to work. You can see yourself out."

Barrett twisted his body to return to where he'd been positioned when I first arrived. At that moment, my eyes caught a flutter of color from the cage he'd been bent over when I arrived. Barrett must have seen it as well, as he planted his feet firmly in front of me.

"I'm sorry you had to see that, Miss O'Brien," he said.

I squared my body to his and peered around him to the space where I'd seen the splash of color. My gaze fell upon a small bird with a yellow breast and bright blue wings beating against the cage.

At that moment, my poaching theory, the probability that the camera had captured images of the poacher and that Brendan was the predator, grew to a crescendo in my mind. My suspicion of Rita had obscured what had been in front of me all the time. Brendan's refusal to answer questions, his cynical view of Julia and Alex, and his obvious lie about seeing Julia enter the trailhead. I'd suspected someone had planted the needles in the shop and the tote bag at the scene. Nigel, Anne, and Rita had keys to the shop, which, in light of Rita's behavior, had cast her in a suspicious light, but Brendan could have used Rita's key to plant the needles.

I knew then that I was in danger, but I couldn't stop myself and said, "You killed Alex, and then you killed Julia when the police didn't find the so-called evidence you planted to make her look guilty."

"A pity the garda won't hear your raving accusations, Miss O'Brien." Brendan raised his fist.

"The police will want to hear what I have to say as well as the evidence I have," I responded, feeling my body freeze with fear. "I'm not going anywhere. You see, I have the discs from the trail cameras Alex used to find the poacher."

"Hand them over," Brendan shouted, advancing toward me.

"Don't waste your time; I don't have the images with me.

Oh, yeah, multiple people have copies for safekeeping. You know, in case something happens to me."

"I hope you like salmon because, in short order, you will be 'swimming with the fishes' as they say in your American movies." Barrett's voice carried clearly in the increasingly windy gusts, which threatened to knock us off the platform.

"I don't think so," I replied, glancing at the surface rings of the salmon pens. "Maybe you should have paid more attention. Those were just movies. You're the one who should be worried about going for a swim." I backed away from him, my eyes searching for an escape route while my brain searched for a way to keep him talking. Remembering what O'Shea had told me about the nefarious nature of poaching schemes and their networks, I asked, "What do you think your silent business partners will do when they learn the police are on to you? I hope you can swim," I taunted.

Brendan's eyes widened. His head swiveled from left to right, taking in the expanse of water and the woodland behind us. He was afraid.

"You're lying. The garda haven't a clue."

"Are you sure? Do you think I'd approach you without a backup plan? The police are with your wife, asking questions. I expect they will arrive momentarily."

"You're a bloody liar," he shouted.

"Why don't you turn yourself in?" I prompted. "The brig will be safer."

"I... I...."

"The clock is ticking...," I interrupted, taking advantage of his hesitation.

He ran. I chased.

His arms pushed through the densely forested woodland. I could see him fighting branches as his body drove through the underbrush. The boughs grabbed at my sweatshirt. The machinery's sweeping sound faded as we plunged deeper into the woods. My foot caught in a bramble of brush. I fell. When I pushed myself up, he'd disappeared from sight. I kept going, paying attention to branches that looked pushed aside or broken by human hands. I tripped again, this time on a Wellington boot. I'd noticed Brendan was wearing Wellingtons when I arrived instead of the boat shoes I'd seen on him in previous encounters. The boot had to be one of his! Good, this might slow him down. I threw the Wellington farther into the shrub and ran.

In contrast to the time of day, the sun didn't penetrate the darkness caused by the dense coverage of the pine trees. Blood roared in my ears. I strained to catch any noise that indicated Brendan lurked nearby. When he fled from the platform, he'd grabbed a pole spear. I weighed whether he would continue running or use the weapon. I heard the crunch before I felt the rush of wind. The spear tip flew past and embedded in a tree behind me. I held my breath, waiting for a sound or stir of movement, signaling where he was. The arm that wrapped itself around my chest and pressed against my neck reeked with sweat and fish.

"Ah, my little chickadee. Did you think you'd win this race?" Brendan's voice was a whisper in my ear.

I jabbed my left arm into his chest and stomped my sneaker onto his unbooted foot. He dropped his arm and crouched, rubbing his foot. "You witch, you'll pay for this," he said through clenched teeth.

I didn't wait. I ran, all the while listening for footsteps. I figured I had a few precious moments before he caught me. My eyes swept the ground around me. I had no idea which way to go or what I would do if he laid his hands on me again. All I knew was I had to keep running and get to a footpath, hopefully happening upon tourists—or to a clearing near one of the lakes where I might find an angler.

The crashing sounds coming from in front of me didn't

make sense. He'd been behind, but perhaps I was experiencing spatial disorientation in the gloomy darkness. When the thrashing noises increased, I threw my body under a thick bramble bush and held my breath. My eyes fell upon the heels of a pair of shoes. At that moment, I truly wondered if I was imagining things. One of Brendan's feet should have been bare. Yes, I reassured myself. One of his feet *was* bare; I'd stomped on it. I took a deep breath and inched forward, raising my eyes. O'Shea! Never was I so relieved to see a cop in my life. I jumped up, and O'Shea turned with one of his arms raised in a punching position toward me.

"Miss O'Brien," he whispered, dropping his arm.

"He's nearby," I replied quietly. "I don't know—he might have a knife."

O'Shea nodded and motioned for me to lead the way. I backtracked as best I could remember from where I'd run from Brendan. It didn't take long for us to find him. The moans and agonizing screams echoing through the leaves like wind on a stormy day shattered the silence. O'Shea and I glanced at each other and broke out into a run. Within moments, we emerged into a clearing near a small lake.

"Help me; help me." Brendan lay on the grass writhing in pain, eyes squeezed shut.

O'Shea put his hand up and held me back. "Don't go any farther. This could be a trap," he said and then moved forward slowly until he stood above Brendan's face. I pulled my phone from its holster and dialed emergency services. While I was reporting the incident, I could see O'Shea's contorted features. The scar on his face was stark white in contrast to the flush of blood suffusing his face, and then I saw the gun he pulled from his pocket and shoved against Brendan's face.

"No," I shouted. A flock of birds rose out of the stand of trees behind us. "O'Shea, no." I raced forward, closing the gap between us. "Don't do this." I placed my hand on the arm holding the gun. "He's not worth it."

I looked around, hoping the police were on the way, and measured how long I had to get O'Shea to put the gun away before help arrived.

"Look, look at his foot." I pointed at the almost severed bloody mass of bone and flesh apparently caught in a gin trap. "There's no better justice than this kind of revenge."

I pulled my sweatshirt off, dropped to my knees at Brendan's waist, and began wrapping the sweatshirt around the upper part of his leg.

"O'Shea, help me hold this tight. We can't let him die. He's got to pay for what he's done and have a long time to think about it in prison."

O'Shea finally responded. Looking up at the clear blue sky, he shoved the gun into his pocket, removed his pants belt, and dropped to his knees next to me.

Once the tourniquet was secured, Brendan lay back, struggling to stay conscious from the blood loss and pain.

"How did you know to look for me?" I asked O'Shea.

"Georgina," he replied as I heard a rush of voices and running feet streaming out of the woods and into the clearing. The police had arrived.

CHAPTER 28

The invitation from Sister Meghan took me by surprise, especially since it came on the heels of Brendan's arrest. I hadn't thought she'd want to discuss *anything* related to the abbey or Letterbrack with me.

I arrived early in the morning. Sister Evangeline ushered me into the same room I'd been in when Georgina and I last met with Meghan.

"Sister will be with you momentarily, Miss O'Brien. Please, be seated and make yourself comfortable." Sister Evangeline smiled and lightly touched my arm before leaving the room.

Comfort wasn't a word to describe how I felt. From the first moment I arrived in Letterbrack, I had yearned to get into the abbey. Finally, that day was here, and a flutter of butterflies danced in my stomach. Why did Sister want to meet with me? Why the sudden change in attitude toward me, especially since Sister seemed so influenced by Maeve?

Sister Meghan entered the room and sat on a chair opposite me before she said, "Miss O'Brien. I won't waste your time with *mea culpas*. I have a story that you will undoubtedly find painful to hear. I can tell you I'm mortified." Sister closed her eyes and fingered the beads that encircled her waist. When she reopened her eyes, she continued, "Please, be patient with what I have to say because I don't have all the answers."

"Whatever you have to say, Sister, please say it," I replied and leaned forward in my chair. "If this is about Julia and Alex, I don't hold you or the Conservation Foundation accountable for what happened to them."

Sister nodded but continued to hold the beads in her hand. "Miss O'Brien, I must inform you"—Megan stopped, took a deep breath, and then continued—"the woman who has been in the abbey's care has identified herself as Maggie O'Malley."

I shook my head as if to clear it from the feeling of not being able to believe what I heard was true or real. "My mother is at the abbey," I said, clenching the cell phone holstered to my capris. "What do you mean? Where is she? I want to see her immediately."

"I'm sorry, but I promised I'd speak with you first." Sister leaned forward as if to touch my hand.

A flush of anger rushed through my body; I jerked away and strode to the far side of the room. When I turned back to Sister, it was all I could do to keep myself from grabbing her by the shoulders and shaking the daylights out of her. Instead, I asked, "How long have you known she was my mother?"

"Only since yesterday when she told me. Until then, she'd scarcely spoken to me. Most of the time, her conversations were with...."

"Maeve," I said, interrupting Sister.

She nodded and patted the seat I'd vacated. "Miss O'Brien, your mother requested I speak with you and fill in some of the gaps. Please, sit down."

"You better have good reasons for having my mother behind the walls of this place," I replied through clenched teeth, but I returned to the chair, and then Sister recounted my mother's sad history.

Sister confirmed my mother was orphaned. A house fire

killed everyone in the O'Malley family, with the exception of the youngest child, Margarite. The child was taken in and raised by a local family, also with the O'Malley surname, until she became a teenager and disappeared.

Sister's version of the story, as told to her by my mother, aligned with what Georgina had learned when she spoke to Margaret Hanlon on Achill Island. But where Margaret Hanlon's story ended, my mother had filled in the rest for Sister Meghan.

Maggie and the O'Malley's son, Michael, had been teenage lovers, and when Maggie realized she was pregnant, she ran away to New York City, where she found support in a woman's shelter until she had her baby and secured a job.

"But how did she manage to move from a shelter to an apartment?" I asked. My first memories were of our cozy apartment in the Bronx, not some women's shelter.

Sister Meghan smiled. "Apparently, your mam was good at math, and she quickly found employment as a bookkeeper in the city. The salary allowed her to support both of you."

I nodded when I heard Sister's explanation. I hadn't known where or what my mother did, but I remembered that she came home late sometimes or was on the phone in the hallway of our apartment, whispering in her soft voice.

"Sister, none of what you've said explains why my mother disappeared or where she's been all this time."

"I'm terribly sorry, Miss O'Brien, but if I'd known...."

"Known what?" I interrupted. "What do you know, Sister? This is *my* mother we're talking about. I want to know what happened. I want to see her."

I jumped up from the seat and paced the room while Sister Meghan spoke softly, almost as if she were in a trance, while she described an FBI handler's evil and deceitful appearance in my mother's life.

I wasn't surprised to learn the handler's name—Maeve Baldwin.

According to what Maggie had told Sister, Maeve had been assigned to surveil the family Maggie worked for. She'd spotted a young woman who'd answered the front door of the home. Subsequently, Maeve had arranged to bump into the young woman and, upon hearing her Irish accent, had initiated an investigation into Maggie. When Maeve learned Maggie was from Achill Island with no living family members other than a young child, Maeve presented a dilemma to Maggie—with the intention of turning her into an informant.

One day, Maeve approached Maggie with documentation indicating she was about to be arrested on suspicion of fraud and tax evasion. Maggie had denied Maeve's implication, but Maeve had persisted in frightening Maggie into believing she'd be made a scapegoat for the family's illegal activities, would go to prison, and her child placed into the foster system.

Maggie had panicked, thinking she'd lose her child, but Maeve offered a solution, telling Maggie if she were willing to work as an inside informant, Maeve would ensure Maggie's child would be kept safe should anything happen to Maggie.

With no one to turn to for advice, afraid for herself and her daughter's safety, Maggie had agreed to Maeve's proposition. Finally, Maggie had done something she hadn't done since the day she left Ireland; she'd written a letter to my father. She hadn't divulged her whereabouts or her situation, but she had revealed he had a child, a daughter named Star.

I stopped pacing and dropped into a chair while my hand clenched my phone like a life preserver. Sister Meghan rose from her seat, placed one of her hands on my shoulder, and said, "I know this is difficult, but your mother has experienced tremendous pain and anguish for the sacrifice she made and the dangerous, intimidating position Maeve put her in to go after a criminal organization. Your mother is afraid you'll hate her."

"Hate her?" I asked, and then I didn't hold back, letting the tears stream down my face. "I could never do that. I love her as much as the six-year-old Star, who never believed her mother abandoned her." Finally, I dried my tears and said, "But why is she at the abbey? More importantly, where has she been for twenty-three years?"

Sister returned to her seat and said, "I don't have all the answers. I can only tell you what Maggie related to me. I'm sure there's more to learn, but she's in a precarious state of mind. I felt it was best to listen and not delve too deeply, but you're right to question what happened when Maggie's assignment ended. I asked the same question."

"What did my mother say?" I asked. In the United States, when a person becomes a confidential informant, the person more or less says goodbye to their identity and loses their freedoms and constitutional rights. I wondered if this was what had happened to my mother. In my mind, there couldn't be any other explanation for her absence from my life.

"According to your mother, Maeve continued to use her in several more undercover projects through the years, involving drug cartels, human trafficking, and child pornography."

"Sister, you and Maeve expect me to believe my mother's been a mole in more than one criminal project? That just seems outrageous and dangerous."

"Miss O'Brien, I asked your mother why. What kind of hold did Maeve have on your mother for that length of time? Your mother told me each time a child pornography or child sex ring case surfaced, she thought of you and how she'd feel if something like that happened to you. Your mother believed she was doing the right thing."

Sister held her rosary beads in her hand as she spoke. I got to my feet, walked to the far side of the room, and banged a fist on the wall.

Sister's words struck me like a slap across the face when she said, "Your mother's mental health is fragile. Maeve was worried Maggie would crack under the pressure of another assignment. So, Maeve brought her here about a year ago to rest and keep out of sight."

"If you knew any of this for an entire year...." My eyes burned a hole in Sister Meghan's face.

"No," Sister insisted and shook her head so hard her wimple slipped, and a patch of salt and pepper hair was exposed. "We often provide shelter and rest to women and children who are victims of violence." Sister continued to finger the beads at her waist. "Maeve used me and the abbey's good intentions when she brought your mother here. We believed Maggie was another battered woman. I had no idea until your mother told me the story."

"But why didn't my mother ask to see me when she arrived in Ireland?"

"My dear child, she didn't know you were in Ireland until that day you caught sight of her. She told Maeve she wanted to see you, but Maeve convinced your mother her mind must have been playing tricks, and you were nowhere near Ireland."

I took a deep breath and demanded to see my mother immediately.

Sister Meghan tried to quiet me, saying, "When I said you needed patience, I meant with your mother, not with me. Her mental state is precarious. I've dealt with women who have been battered by their partners. Your mother is exhibiting similar trauma symptoms. She doesn't think she can face you. Please, Miss O'Brien, courage and strength are what's needed with your mother and yourself."

"Where's Maeve?" I asked.

"I don't know. I've rung several times, but her phone has been disconnected. She will not be welcomed at the abbey."

I clenched my phone and my teeth to keep from saying something I'd regret. Instead, I ran across the room. "I'll be back after I take care of some unfinished business," I said, and then I left the abbey, got into my car, and drove to Cong.

MAEVE'S MODEST-LOOKING COTTAGE SAT ON A SECLUDED, wooded road not far from Ashford Castle. Driving solo wasn't the only contrast to my prior visit. Instead of electrified candles lighting each of the front windows, darkness prevailed. Maeve's Irish bloodhound, Midwatch, didn't materialize when I opened the gate and strode up the cement walkway to the front door.

"Maeve Baldwin," I shouted, banging on the unadorned black door. Nothing but silence greeted me. I walked from window to window, trying to see signs of life. What looked like sheets covered most of the living room furniture. Finally, after unsuccessful attempts to open the front and back windows, feeling the emptiness and knowing in my soul Maeve had vanished like the ghost operative she was, I returned to my car. Once inside, I stared through the windshield, my thoughts churning through Maeve's attempts to keep me out of Ireland. I wondered if she had planned to use my mother in additional undercover assignments. In the quiet, dark interior of my car, I opened my mouth and screamed, all the while slamming my fists on the dashboard.

Taking a life was against my moral code, but I knew for certain if Maeve ever crossed my path again, she'd pay for poaching a young woman's life and child. I turned the key in the ignition and drove toward Letterbrack and Kentmore Abbey.

S<small>ISTER</small> M<small>EGHAN</small>'<small>S</small> <small>FACE</small> <small>APPEARED</small> <small>ON</small> <small>THE</small> <small>OTHER</small> <small>SIDE</small> <small>WHEN</small> I knocked on the abbey's door. "Follow me, Miss O'Brien," she said and then ushered me into a small chapel within the abbey. The chapel was empty, and Sister quietly closed the door behind us, saying, "Please, sit down."

"I really don't have time for this, Sister. I demand to see my mother," I replied, touching the locket I wore.

"Yes, I understand, my child, but I want to stress again that your mother is under tremendous strain." Sister smiled at me and continued, "I can see your mother's bone structure in your face, Miss O'Brien. I hope you have the same courage and strength running through your veins because, as much as your past was painful, the road to recovery for your mother will be long and hard."

I remained standing while Sister spoke, but my eyes fell upon the candles burning at one of the side altars. For a moment, I flashed back to the many times my mother and I attended Our Lady of Angels Church in the Bronx. She'd always lit three candles.

"Keep your eyes on the altar, Star," she scolded whenever I fidgeted.

I asked her about the three candles, and she smiled and said, "It's a light for the one who's not here."

I hadn't known what she might have meant by that at the time, but standing in the abbey's small chapel, I knew what they meant to me. "I'm here, Sister, and I'm ready to do whatever I need to."

S<small>ISTER</small> M<small>EGHAN</small>'<small>S</small> <small>VOLUMINOUS</small> <small>HABIT</small> <small>MADE</small> <small>SWISHING</small> <small>SOUNDS</small> <small>AS</small> she led me through a side door in the chapel that opened into a private garden behind the abbey. From there, I followed her along a path toward a green door set into a granite stone wall, and then I heard the door close behind me, and Sister was gone.

I stood at the edge of a luscious grass line, my eyes following the lawn's sweeping concentric lines toward the lone figure whose back was all I could see.

She sat near the formal garden area, forget-me-nots bursting from the ground. I approached quietly, thinking the flowers' symbolism was appropriate. I saw her back tense, and then she turned. My breath held still. Her face was just as I'd imagined it when I would gaze at the crinkled snapshot, which I'd carried in my wallet. Her wavy, thick black hair was peppered with gray and cut short, almost boy-like, and I realized my life-long cowlicks were something we had in common. The crinkle lines around the edges of her eyes were darker and etched deeper. I used to think the lines were from laughing and not having a care in the world, but I didn't think that was the case any longer. She wore a gardener's uniform, and her hands picked at her trousers.

"Star," she whispered and began rising from the bench, her eyes spilling tears.

"No, don't move," I cried, running toward her. Tears cascaded down my face. Everything I'd known and suffered from the foster homes to the adoption, Dylan, my anger with the police—melted away as I closed the gap between us. Finally, I arrived and knelt quietly in front of her.

"Momma." I couldn't say anymore.

Her hands gripped mine, and her eyes held my gaze. "My little Star," she said, then stopped speaking.

I got to my feet, sat beside her on the bench, and said, "You don't have to say anything. Sister explained. I know, when you're ready, you'll tell me more. I just want you to know how much I love you."

My mother nodded, reached forward, and touched my hair. "My little Star, will you forgive me?"

"There's nothing to forgive, but I do want to know everything."

Maggie seemed to freeze when she heard my statement. "I don't know how...."

"It's okay," I said.

"No"—she shook her head—"I don't know how to explain. It's been so long since I didn't have to watch my words."

Sister's advice about being patient rang in my ears. I sat back on the bench and pulled my locket from under my sweater so my mother could see it.

A brief smile flitted across her lips, and she said, "Our locket."

"Yes, our locket," I said, accepting that my questions wouldn't be answered until my mother was ready. I could wait because I wanted to be there for her. For the moment, nothing mattered, only that I had my mother back.

She rose from the bench, offered me her hand, and as we had often done when I was a child, we walked together toward the garden gate and whatever the future would bring.

EPILOGUE

Former Detective O'Shea slumped in the back corner booth at the Davitt Restaurant.

"O'Shea," I said when I slid into the seat across from him. I didn't ask how he was. His red-rimmed eyes spoke volumes.

"Miss O'Brien."

"So, Brendan Barrett spilled his guts."

O'Shea's grimace emphasized his scar and highlighted more lines in his face I hadn't noticed before. "Yeah, he confessed to the entire tragedy, which started with Alex's copping on to Brendan's criminal activities."

"I wonder why Alex didn't go to the authorities immediately. If he had, he and Julia would be alive," I said.

O'Shea shook his head. "Alex confronted Brendan but seemingly didn't do anything right away. Maybe he was working on getting more concrete evidence on his surveillance cameras. Unfortunately for him and Julia, we'll never know his reasoning."

"But Brendan wasn't satisfied with Alex's silence, was he?" I asked, prompting O'Shea.

"According to Brendan, Alex really pushed his buttons. Whenever they'd see each other at the pub, Alex would smile at Brendan and tip his hat, sending Brendan into a paranoid frenzy. He'd laid off the poaching for a while because he didn't want to be caught red-handed. But he couldn't hold off his poaching scheme partners for long. He knew he had to kill Alex whether or not the authorities had been notified."

"So, he plotted to kill Alex and implicate Julia for his murder," I said.

"One night at the pub, Brendan saw his chance when Julia and Alex had a major row," O'Shea replied.

"Yes, Charlotte Evans told me about their argument," I said, remembering our discussion. "She was convinced Julia had something to do with Alex's murder. But her prejudice against Julia was based upon jealousy. Unfortunately, when greed, jealousy, and hate are involved, people often manufacture faulty motivations to meet their own needs."

When O'Shea didn't respond, I asked, "I guess Brendan easily got his hands on what he needed to implicate Julia?"

O'Shea sighed, and his lips twisted in a smirk. "He could have simply taken them from his wife, but he devised an elaborate scheme that backfired on him." O'Shea stopped and slammed his fist on the table. "A scheme that ended in Julia's death."

"What kind of scheme?" I asked.

O'Shea got control of himself and described Brendan's unsuccessful attempt to frame Julia. "During the argument in the pub, Brendan spotted several gauge knitting needles poking out of her tote bag. He grabbed a cocktail napkin from the bar and retrieved one needle, slipping the napkin and needle into his work tools messenger bag. Later, he took one of Julia's tote bags from his own house and planted the bag at the scene."

"I've never been able to figure out how he knew where you and Julia met."

"We were sloppy. Julia and I didn't think anyone would happen upon us in the secluded meadow. We should have met in a different place each time we got together. But, well, Julia and Alex's divorce was already proceeding, so we didn't see the need to hide." O'Shea looked down at the table where his hands lay balled in fists.

"But how did he find that one meadow?" I asked again. "As you said, O'Shea, it was secluded. Did he follow you?"

"No, he had songbird nets in a section of the forestry surrounding the meadow. He was gathering his prey one day when he happened to hear us." O'Shea looked up at me. "You should have seen Brendan's face when he made that part of his confession. He looked ecstatic, and I wanted to kill him."

"But how did Alex learn of your meeting place? Do you think he captured an image on his surveillance cameras?" I asked in an effort to move O'Shea beyond his anger.

"Brendan lured Alex with an anonymous note suggesting, and I quote Brendan, 'the place and time Julia meets with her love.' Brendan provided a time earlier than when he knew Julia and I would show up. When Alex arrived and found the tote bag, he picked it up, and while he was going through it, Brendan attacked Alex with the needle, killing him immediately. Brendan destroyed the note, took the murder weapon with him to plant in Julia's shop, and left the tote as incriminating evidence."

"But being an inept criminal, his efforts to plant the so-called evidence failed," I said.

"Inept but successful in murder, Miss O'Brien," O'Shea said, turning his red-rimmed eyes to me. "When Brendan realized the investigative team hadn't found any evidence, he panicked, convincing himself that killing Julia would wrap up Alex's murder in the eyes of the guards."

"So, he poisoned her," I said.

"Yes, he simply bought a salad at the abbey restaurant, spiked the mixed greens with the toxic greens from his garden, and delivered the salad to Julia using the excuse he needed to drop off some brochures for his wife, Rita."

"But why did he think Julia's death would close Alex's case?"

"For the love of God, I don't know. Brendan seemed to think people would believe Julia was guilty and took her own life with poison." Once again, O'Shea pounded the table with his hand. "Stupid, stupid, stupid," he said.

I didn't know if he referred to Brendan or himself. "I read in the newspaper that the entire poaching ring has been rounded up."

O'Shea nodded. "Yeah, Brendan gave them up, but I have no doubt some other unsavory creature will start up the nasty business all over again. My colleague, my former colleague," O'Shea corrected himself, "tells me songbird poaching is an ongoing issue in Ireland and most of Europe."

I nodded, having gotten a briefing that morning from the National Park and Wildlife Service, who'd also met with the members of the Conservation Foundation to educate and explain the issue. The government had stepped in, providing grant money for ongoing workshops. The local community had pitched in and purchased more surveillance cameras.

O'Shea fell silent again, and I asked, "What are your plans?"

"Nothing particular. Being a detective has been my life. I don't know what else to do. I've rented a cottage in Cleggan." O'Shea's eyes filled with tears, which he quickly wiped away. "I'll probably fish and try to get on with it," he said.

My heart ached for O'Shea. I knew how deep the hurt cut and how long the sorrow lingered. "Listen, O'Shea, we've had differences, but those are behind us. If you need someone to listen, you call me."

He nodded. "I heard the news about your mam. What do you plan to do?"

O'Shea's question was one I'd been asking myself for the

last few days. I had a series of steps in mind, which I hoped would work, but I wasn't ready to put my hopes on the line yet.

When I didn't respond, O'Shea nodded. "I understand. Well, all I can say is thank you, Star O'Brien," and then he stood, touched my shoulder, and walked out of my life.

I remained seated, remembering the first time I'd had tea with Georgina and Lorcan in this booth. He'd challenged me to return to Ireland for a meeting he promised to arrange with the director of the archives in Dublin. Lorcan had known I'd rise to the bait, and for that, I'd be forever grateful.

I sensed a presence before I felt a hand graze my shoulder. Thinking O'Shea had returned, I glanced around.

"Lorcan?" My heart lurched at the sight of him.

"Star," he replied, settling into the seat next to me.

"When did you get back?" I asked calmly when what I really wanted to do was wrap my arms around him.

"Just this morning. Tom told me he was meeting with you."

I didn't answer, not trusting myself to speak. From the first moment I'd seen Lorcan, the gravitational pull was undeniable. An attraction I'd stifled, and then when he'd left for Wyoming without a word of goodbye, my guilt and shame for the way I'd acted made me realize I never wanted to part that way again. Deep in my soul, I knew I was ready for Lorcan to be more than a friend, but I wondered if he felt the same way.

"Star, I know we parted on angry terms. I'm sorry about that. I should have respected your right to make decisions that affect your life," he said, pushing his John Lennon–style glasses up the bridge of his nose.

"I should have been more sympathetic to your desire to support a childhood friend. I'm sorry, too, Lorcan," I replied.

"So, are we friends again?" Lorcan's eyes held mine.

"Most definitely," I replied, smiling up into his beautiful blue eyes.

"Most definitely agreed." Lorcan reached for my hand. "But,

Star, I want our relationship to move beyond friendship. What do you think?"

I squeezed his hand, took a deep breath, and said, "Yes, I want that too."

"So, what's next, Star O'Brien?"

I moved my hand away and settled back against the booth. "Georgina and I have been talking. I'm keeping French Hill Cottage and opening a second Consulting Detective branch in County Mayo."

Lorcan's blue eyes blazed as he smiled at me. "Does that mean you're moving to Ireland?"

"Absolutely not. I have responsibilities—Ellie, Phillie, my clients at the Consulting Detective in New Jersey, and my puppy, Skipper." I tapped the table as I listed all the reasons for returning to New Jersey, and then I said, "But I've learned I can widen my circle. I have a family in County Mayo, which includes my mom, Evelyn, when she returns from London, Aunt Georgina, your mom, and you, Lorcan."

"How do Ellie and Phillie feel about all this?" Lorcan asked.

"We're working through how the expansion affects them and our U.S. clients. But in the meantime, I'm flying both of them over for an early December launch. Ellie will bring her husband, and I've applied for Skipper's canine passport."

"What about your mam? My mother told me about what she's been through. I can't fathom how broken she must feel."

I relished hearing Lorcan's question. Above all else, I had my mother back in my life. "I'm not sure what she'll decide. I'm trying to give her space to think things through. She remains at the abbey until I've made some renovations at the cottage. After a life of subterfuge, she's enjoying the solitude, and we've enjoyed the privacy of the abbey for our visits and talks. All I can do is travel between County Mayo and Ridgewood, but I'm confident all will be well." My hand went to the tiny gold children's locket, which she'd sent to my father years ago.

Lorcan placed his hand over mine and said, "Whatever you decide, we'll take care of it together. Okay?"

I nodded.

"Right, I'm starving. I haven't eaten since I left Wyoming yesterday. Let's order some food. What would you like?" he asked, pulling the menu toward us.

"Tea, brown bread, butter, and vegetable soup," I laughed.

"Good, I see your love of brown bread hasn't changed." Lorcan smiled. "I've missed you, Star O'Brien."

"And I you, Lorcan McHale."

"Then let's not fall out with each other ever again. Do you think you can manage that?"

"Lorcan McHale. I'll...."

Lorcan's gentle kiss interrupted whatever I'd planned to say.

The END

ABOUT THE AUTHOR

MARTHA M. GEANEY, Ph.D. is the author of the highly praised non-fiction, women's leadership book, *Bring Your Spirit to Work: One Woman at a Time*.

She is also the author of the Star O'Brien Irish fiction series which is set in the west of Ireland.

Martha divides her time between Florida and County Mayo, Ireland. Sometimes, she is joined by her Schipperke puppy, Turlough.

She is currently working on her next Irish mystery series, starring Artemis Penelope Braxton.

Follow along on Martha's web site for updates regarding her writing schedule and in person events: *www.marthageaney.com*.

AND A FINAL NOTE FROM MARTHA—

Thank you for reading *Death near Kentmore Abbey* and for following along with Star as she unravels the mysteries of her life. Please leave a review on Amazon or Goodreads.

And if you have questions or feedback that you'd like to share, please contact me at *www.marthageaney.com*. I love to respond to your comments.

www.ingramcontent.com/pod-product-compliance
Lightning Source LLC
Chambersburg PA
CBHW070550120726
47909CB00007B/2300